THE GREEN EMBER

Books by S. D. Smith

Publication Order:

Best read in publication order, but in general, simply be sure to begin with The Green Ember.

THE GREEN EMBER

S. D. Smith

Illustrated by Zach Franzen

Story Warren Books

Trade Paperback edition ISBN: 978-0-9862235-0-1
Hardcover Edition ISBN: 978-0-9862235-1-8
Also available in eBook and Audiobook

Cover and interior illustrations by Zach Franzen, www.zachfranzen.com
Cover design by Paul Boekell, www.boekell.com
Map created by Will Smith

Printed in the United States of America.
20 21 22 23 24   12 13 14 15 16

Story Warren Books
www.storywarren.com

For Anne and Josiah
Quaerite primum regnum Dei

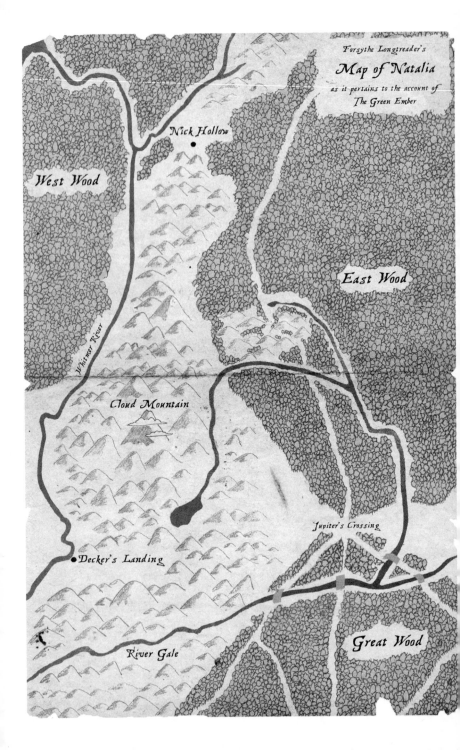

PROLOGUE

Two soaked and battered rabbits washed up on the shore of Ayman Lake. Gasping, Fleck crawled onto the stony beach, rolled over, and tried to clear his mind. Galt was already standing. "We have to go, Fleck," he said, eyes darting from the lake to the tree line.

"I'm no traitor," Fleck managed to say through ragged breaths.

"Traitor?" Galt cried. "The winning side gets to decide who the traitors were. We've lost, Fleck. It's over. Even you, Captain Blackstar, can do nothing this time. We have no chance."

"We? *We* have no chance?"

"*He* has no chance," Galt said, head down, edging toward the forest.

Fleck stood slowly, staggering. The usually grey fur of his arm was blotched with dark scarlet. One eye was swollen shut.

"He can be saved," Fleck said, reaching for his sword. His hand closed on air. His scabbard was empty.

"Nothing," Galt said. "There's nothing we can do. It's the end of the world."

"But the oath, Galt. Remember? We can still turn this. King Whitson needs us. Prince Lander needs us," he said, pointing to the burning ship. "I'll never turn traitor."

"You're only a traitor if you betray yourself," Galt said. He sprinted off, disappearing into the trees.

Fleck struggled to stay upright. Swaying, he turned from the fleeing rabbit to face the lake. Charcoal smoke corkscrewed into the sky. The blackened boat teemed with enemies. Flames snapped at the red diamond standard as the last kingsbucks grappled with the invaders on the deck. Whitson Mariner stood among them, his sword poised and his harried shouts echoing over the lake. Fleck straightened and stretched his arm. Pain flared. Unbearable agony. He bent, wincing. He opened his eyes and saw King Whitson, fighting desperately to protect Prince Lander. Fleck rose, ignoring the pain, and shouted across the water.

"My place beside you, my blood for yours! Till the Green Ember rises, or the end of the world!"

Swordless, Fleck Blackstar hobbled to the water's edge and plunged in.

from *The Black Star of Kingston*

Chapter One

HEATHER AND PICKET
CATCH A STAR

Heather had invented the game, but Picket made it magic. She remembered the day it began. She had been out in the meadow behind their elm-tree home, lying on a blanket in the sun. Heather was little then. Her long furry ears bent slightly in the wind, and the bow she invariably wore over one ear was starting to come undone. That day Mother had done a carnation bow, an intricate weave of one long ribbon made to look like a large flower, and pinned it to one ear. Picket was little more than a baby then, sleeping in his crib.

Heather had gathered several sticks and was thinking hard about them when a powerful gust of wind almost knocked her over. The gust finally loosened her bow, which came down in a tangle of scarlet ribbon, draping over the sticks she held. She was unaware that she held the ingredients for a game that would later give them endless hours of fun.

She had crossed two short sticks and made an X shape. Then she added another, giving it six points. She tied them together with the long scarlet ribbon. Heather smiled. It

11

was pretty, like a star. The end of the ribbon trailed back a few feet, and she considered wrapping all of it around the bound pointed sticks. But she stopped suddenly, and then the wind picked up again as she tied off the ribbon around the star at its center, leaving its long scarlet train to flap in the breeze. She stood, holding her small invention aloft, smiling wide. With barely a thought of why, she flung the toy as hard as she could. It sailed through the air like a shooting star, the ribbon trailing a scarlet wake. It disappeared into the tall grass. She frowned, afraid it would take forever to find it.

That's when the game came to her. When Picket woke up, she explained it to him, hoping he would crawl out and play. But he was too little then.

"It's called Starseek," she said, "and this is the star."

"Is it a real star?" Picket asked, his head cocked sideways and his whiskers twitching.

"No, little one," Heather said, "a real star hangs in the sky at night, along with a million others. This is just a game."

"A game?" Picket said. "Maybe they're all for games."

Now that they were both older, Heather near maturity and Picket not too far behind, the two of them had played Starseek hundreds of times. It had been fun to play alone for a little while, but that got old pretty quickly. So Picket had played, with Heather's patient instruction, from the time he could walk. Now he was older and, as much as Heather hated to admit it, getting as good as her at the game she had invented. He had a keen eye and was agile on the ground.

She was faster. She could still beat him at a straight-run race, but he was quick.

Today she was in danger of losing every match. But it wasn't over yet.

Picket flung the star, and it sailed, red ribbon against blue sky, far into the meadow. Finally falling, it disappeared into the tall golden grass. The moment it touched down, they were off.

Picket darted back and forth amid the tall grass. He had an uncanny knack for doing a sort of quick math in his mind, and his estimations were almost always spot-on. He liked to stay low, close to the ground. But Heather's chance lay in her experience and flat-out speed.

She bolted for the spot she was sure the star must be, running full-out, heedless of the hidden dangers that might send her sprawling. Let Picket dart back and forth all he wanted, dodging roots and stumps. She would fly.

Heather sailed up and over the grass with each leap, rebounding to soar once more above the heavy kernelled tips. She loved the feeling of the wind pushing against the fur of her face and her long soft ears. She was marveling at the power in her legs and feet, thrilled with the feel of the wind against her face, when she struck a stone, well-hidden in the thickest part of the grass. She lost her balance and fell hard, rolling several times. *Surely it's over now.*

Heather popped up quickly and stretched her long neck to look around. She ignored the pain in her leg; she could tell it wasn't serious enough to stop. She saw grass giving way in a zigzag to her left and knew Picket was closing in on the star. She quickly scanned the grass ahead, hoping to catch any evidence of the star's entry.

She saw it before he did, but he was closer, tacking back and forth. He stopped and popped his head up, trying to peer above the tall grass. He saw it and quickly swiveled to see where Heather was.

By then, she was already pounding toward the target. *Just the delay I need.*

Heather never stopped, but their eyes met. She saw Picket's eyes narrow, his whiskers twitch, and his brows furrow. He launched into the effort.

It was going to be close.

He led 2 to 0, and if he got the star this time, the match was over. Heather put all her energy into the last few feet, determined to snatch victory away from this young upstart. She smiled.

Picket was closing fast, she saw, faster than she expected. She watched him coil for the final spring at the star. He lunged for it, propelled through the air like a skipping stone rising from the dimpled surface of a lake. His hand opened to grab the star.

Heather's hand closed on it a moment sooner. They collided in the air, rolling over and over in a blurry heap of fur and red ribbon.

Heather bounced up first, her fist clenching the star.

Picket rubbed his head and leaned on his elbow. "That," he began, pausing to catch his breath, "was amazing."

"It was," Heather agreed, panting and trying not to giggle. "Closest finish ever, Picket."

"Yeah," he agreed, gasping for air and grinning wide. "That was even closer than the infamous Snow Match of last winter."

She laughed, remembering. That had been a cold, crazy day.

But this day was fine. There was no snow, no chill, nothing whatsoever to dampen their joy. At least, not yet.

Heather glanced at the sky over East Wood. Purple clouds pulsed with irregular stabs of light in the distance. A rolling rumble signaled the storm's approach. Pretty fast approach, if she knew anything. She looked away. After all, it was still sunny here, at least for the moment.

"Great match, Heather," Picket said, rising to his feet. "You were going faster than I've ever seen you."

"Thanks," she said. "But you still have the lead."

"Let it fly," he said, eager for a chance to win the overall match.

She leaned into it, her heart still racing, and flung the star with all her strength. It took flight, sailing high into the sky, its red trail rippling in the wind. The game depended on each player throwing it as hard as he or she could and both standing still until it landed.

The rabbits watched, eyes tracking the red ribbon, while their bodies prepared to bolt as soon as it disappeared in the grass. As soon as it landed.

But it didn't land.

The breeze caught it up, and it sailed wide to their right and stuck high in the branches of the old maple tree that bent on the edge of East Wood.

"I can't believe this," Picket said, kicking a stone. Thunder boomed in the distance.

"Let's go see if we can get it," Heather said.

Picket frowned but followed behind his sister.

They weren't allowed to go past this tree to the east. They could go into West Wood, sure. But Father had strictly warned them never to go past this maple tree, never to come a step closer to East Wood. He had also told them to run full speed back to the house if they ever heard anything whatsoever from the eastern forest, even as small as a twig snapping. So, on top of their game being delayed or ruined, they had to go near the creepiest place they knew.

They crossed to the meadow's edge quickly, an eye on the approaching storm. Heather looked up at the tangled mess of the maple tree. Its limbs stretched out like the brittle arms of a lanky monster; its hollow middle was a crevice of decay.

It was a young tree, nowhere near as big as the wide elm the rabbits made their home in. But the monster maple was dying. This seemed wrong to Heather, but Father had confirmed it.

"Yes, it's a very young tree. But it won't last two more winters. It's doomed," he had said while walking with them last year in the spring, "just like everything in the east. It used to be alive and beautiful. But now it's bent, dangerous, and dying."

Heather had felt a chill as he said this, a rare display of sadness by their father. But, come to think of it, Heather thought she could see this more and more in him. Was Father getting sadder, or was she just getting old enough to see it? She hadn't asked him then, or since, the questions that continued to bubble up in her mind: *Where are we from? Why did we come here?*

She knew that Father was from the east and that none of Mother's family still lived in Nick Hollow. But any time the subject of their moving to Nick Hollow—far away from almost everyone—came up, her parents grew sad, grave, and silent. She had learned to leave those questions unasked.

They reached the roots of the maple tree and stared up at the tangle of ribbon that surrounded their star.

"We could make another," Picket said, looking from side to side.

Heather knew why he was nervous.

"That ribbon isn't so easy to find, Picket," she said. "We can get it if we work together."

"You know I'm scared of heights," he said. "There's no point in teasing me."

"I'm not teasing you," Heather said, snapping back. "I just think you need to get over it. We're not that far away from being old enough to be on our own, Pick."

"I'm sorry I can't be as grown-up and brave as Heather the Magnificent," he said.

"Let me boost you up," she said, fighting off the urge to really sting him with her words. She cast an uneasy eye at the forest, which lay just a few yards away down a gentle slope. She found a good spot and folded her hands together, making a place for Picket's foot to step up and reach the lowest limb. From there, she knew, he should be able to reach the next limb and climb up carefully to reach the star.

She watched him hesitate, first glancing at the wood with a wince, then looking up fearfully at where the star was stuck in the branches. Beyond the branches, the blue sky was turning to purple as charcoal clouds churned above.

Heather could tell that he was embarrassed, that he was fighting off the urge to run away. She felt nervous as well.

This lanky monster of a tree had their star in its heights, and it looked determined to trap them in its branches.

The sky thundered suddenly, an ominous, brooding doom. Heather felt panic growing inside her. "It's nothing," she said aloud. "I'm not afraid of this—" But she couldn't finish her defiant words.

A bone-rattling boom ripped open the sky, sending a jagged javelin of gold crackling down.

The rabbits were knocked back as lightning struck the maple with a deafening crack, followed by a spray of sparks and shards of bark. Lightning ripped through the limbs, circling the brittle trunk of the maple in a braided tangle of fire.

Heather got to her feet, dazed. Her vision cleared. She looked up.

A huge limb, one of the monster maple's bending arms— heavy and ablaze—cracked off and hurtled toward them. She stole a panicked glance at Picket.

Picket was on his back, eyes closed.

He wasn't moving.

Chapter Two

HOME IN THE HOLLOW

As the burning limb descended, Heather sprang. She dove onto her brother, gripping him tightly and rolling them both down the sloping grass, away from the blazing maple's limb. The singed fingers of the outmost branches pawed at them as the monster maple's arm smashed into the ground in time with another thunderous boom from the sky.

They rolled into a thorn bush on the edge of East Wood as the rain began to fall. Like the blazing branch they had only just escaped, the rain came down suddenly, with no pitter-patter of polite introduction. Lightning split the sky again, this time a little farther off. Picket woke, eyes wide, and gasping for breath.

"It's okay, Picket," Heather said in a rush, loud above the noise. "You're all right."

Heather checked him over quickly to confirm her words. For a moment they sat there, staring dumbly at the burning tree, smoke twisting up into the sky as the rain extinguished the blaze from the top down. After another boom of thunder and a crackling flash, they ran for it.

Even though it was the middle of the afternoon, it was hard to see. With the storm's arrival, a frightening darkness out of the east had descended. The two rabbits ran, hand in hand, slipping and tripping in the driving rain. They were shadows of what they had been only a short time ago when they had crossed the meadow like comets chasing after a star. They were shaken and afraid.

They had the whole of the wide meadow to cross in the darkness, soaked and fearful, but in flashes of lightning they could see their elm-tree home.

Flash! Father and Mother appeared on the little porch between the wide, smooth roots of the tree. *Flash!* Mother was holding Baby Jacks, her face showing worry. Father peered into the darkness.

"Here!" Heather shouted. *Flash!* Picket shouted too, but their voices sounded small in the pounding rain and irregular claps of thunder.

Flash! Mother pointed. *Rumble ... flash!* Father dashed into the storm. The younger rabbits ducked as the sky was split and lightning fell. Heather saw Father in the bright bursts, never ducking, always moving toward them in the darkness. Eager. Determined. Confident.

He met them halfway across the meadow. Father paused before them, and they stopped. He looked from Picket to Heather and, after a moment's hesitation, put his arm around Heather and motioned for them to follow him back. Heather thought he had almost meant to pick her up, to fold her in his arms and carry her home. But he seemed startled, or half-embarrassed, that she wasn't really small enough to carry like that anymore. Nor was Picket, who was almost her size now.

Nearly to the porch, Father glanced down at her. She smiled up at him.

Finally, they were on the porch and through the door. Baby Jacks cried in the corner, while Mother met them with blankets, towels, and hugs.

"What a fright you've had," she said, unable to keep from making the pleasant chattering nonsense sounds she used to comfort Baby Jacks.

Heather received a blanket gratefully, felt it wrap around her, and sat down at the table along with Picket. Father hugged them each and then hurried across to the stove and built a hasty fire. He returned and took up Baby Jacks, who stopped crying when Father rocked him. Father grabbed the poker, still rocking Jacks, and poked at the fire. Heather watched him toss another log in, and it sputtered to life.

"You're soaked!" Mother said to Father, "And you're getting little Jacket wet now too."

"We're all in this together," he said, shaking his head so that water sprayed at her. She laughed, grabbed the kettle, and set it to boil above the fire.

"Now, both of you come sit by the fire, and I'll bring you some dry clothes," Mother said. Heather smiled. She was already feeling easier, safe within the walls of their elm-hollow home. She and Picket crossed the floor, dodging Father, who was trying to retrieve his glasses from Baby Jacks without breaking them or hurting him.

"All right, Jacket, son, please ... not my spectacles," he said as Jacks cackled mischievously.

"Spectacles," Picket laughed, taking Jacks into his arms. "Why do you call them 'spectacles'?"

"That's how most of them talk in the east, where your fancy father is from," Mother called. "They sound awfully sophisticated and clever out that way. Not like us perfectly ordinary folks raised in Nick Hollow."

Picket smiled and tickled Jacks. Mother often teased Father gently about his prim way of speaking. Picket sat on the hearth, Jacks in his lap, his back to the growing blaze. Heather poked at the fire, and it brightened. Picket smiled, and Jacks scrunched his shoulders in delight at the wave of heat.

Heather watched her brothers happily. "Why won't Jacks sit with me like that?"

"We have a brotherly bond," Picket said, "based on mutual promises of protection. I will always be there for Jacks, and he will always be there for me. Right, Jacks?" Jacks smiled up at Picket. He was never more relaxed than when Picket held him.

Heather frowned. "Where was Jacks today when that burning limb was falling on you and you were out cold?" she teased. She had meant it to be funny, but Picket looked down, then into the fire.

"I'm sorry, Picket," she said. "I was teasing. I didn't mean anything by it."

"I can't believe I fainted," Picket said, shaking his head.

"Never worry, my lad," Father said. "It's a weakness of our kind. Rabbits often faint before we even can think about it. And then we take a long time to recover. It's just a weakness."

"I don't want to be weak," Picket whispered. He looked into his baby brother's eyes. "I'll never let you down, Jacks. I'll be strong for you."

Heather frowned. It was sweet, yes, but when Picket talked like that, something twisted in her stomach.

Soon the kettle was boiling, they were in fresh, dry clothes, and they all sat around the fire, at ease as the storm raged outside. Mother poured tea while Father tried to fix his glasses.

Mother brought them each a raisin cake, and Father, setting down his glasses in surrender, began to fill his pipe. Heather loved the smell of Father's pipe. When he blew smoke rings, she always thought of it as magic.

"Mother can fix your glasses, or, your spectacular spectacles," Heather said primly. "Why don't you tell us a story?"

"Yeah," Picket said, perking up. "'Goofhack the Blabber and the Tattler's Dungeon'? Jacks and I vote for Goofhack."

Heather frowned at him and Father noticed.

"Perhaps something a little more grown-up for my adventurous children," Father said, cocking an eyebrow at Heather. She smiled, then panicked.

Did he want her to tell a story? *Oh, no.* She wasn't ready. She needed time. She could never tell one like Father told them.

"Heather?" Father asked. "Would you like to tell us a little tale?"

She looked down, blushed, coughed, and stammered. "Well, I don't know." She did know. *Not now. Not yet.* "Maybe next time?"

Father looked at her with a hint of disappointment and seemed about to say something; then he just looked into the fire. After a while, he spoke.

"Heather, I think you are very brave. What you did today, out there in the storm, took courage. All of life is a battle against fear. We fight it on one front, and it sneaks around to our flank." He paused, looked kindly at her.

"Yes, Father. I understand."

"I regret many things I've done," he said, "but most of all I regret those moments when I said to Fear, 'You are my master.'" He suddenly looked terribly sad.

"What is it, Father?" Picket asked as Mother tenderly took Jacks from him.

"It's only that, when you're older, you hand out wisdom to your children like you know everything, but it is sometimes hard to follow your own advice."

"I don't think you're afraid of anything," Picket said. "You wouldn't ever faint."

"Well," Father said, looking down, "I'm sorry to say that's not true. I'm not proud of everything I've done, son."

Mother's soothing noises could be heard from across the room where she quieted Baby Jacks for bed.

"What about that story, Father?" Heather said. "A story

about bravery?"

"A story to make us brave," Father said, nodding and laying down his damaged glasses. He rubbed his eyes, cast a glance at Mother, then stared into the fire.

Heather and Picket exchanged quick glances. This felt different than their father's usual fireside tales.

"How about if I tell you a true story?" Father said, still staring into the fire as if searching for the thread of the tale inside the bobbing, jagged edges of the flames.

Mother came to stand beside Father, Baby Jacks asleep in her arms. Father looked up at her, and a knowing look passed between them. Heather had seen this many times, how they spoke without words. Father's eyes asked a question. Mother nodded, smiling sadly. She sat down in the rocking chair and hummed the beginning of a sad melody. Well, Heather thought, the melody was something more than sad, but not less than sad. She tried to find a word for it, but Father was talking again.

"All right, my dears," Father said. "I will tell you of 'The Rise and Fall of King Jupiter the Great.'"

Chapter Three

KING JUPITER

The weariness vanished from Father as he closed his eyes, focusing on the tale. He smiled as if the memory of the story was sweet. There was a long, silent pause. Just when Heather and Picket began to wonder if he would ever speak again, he started.

"Long ago in The Great Wood there lived a rabbit king named Walter. You have heard many tales of Whitson Mariner and the First Trekkers. I have told you of the escape from Golden Coast, the calamitous sea passage, the discovery of Natalia, and the battle of Ayman Lake. You know of King Whitson, of brave Seddle, of loyal Captain Blackstar and the others of our first heroes. Over a hundred years separated King Walter from his famous ancestor Whitson Mariner, and a thousand tales lay between them. Many kings were born, lived, and died in Natalia. Some of them were good and some bad. King Walter was so well-loved that his small number of subjects called him the good king, or King Good. This name came to distinguish him from his father, a cruel lord who served himself all his days. King Good had not only goodness but also ambition. He tirelessly built back all that his father had lost, and more besides. He called his small kingdom the Thirty Warrens, though, in truth, there were only twelve when he came to the throne. But he aspired to build and create, to secure good for all those who would follow. Jupiter, his third son and heir, took all his father's vision into his heart. He was like his father, only—to King Good's delight—far more jolly and wise. Jupiter Goodson ascended to the throne when his aged father was killed by raiding hawks.

"By the time King Jupiter had been on the throne for five years, the Thirty Warrens—as the kingdom was still called—included nearly a hundred warrens and spanned almost the entirety of the Great Wood. He was a great lord, humble and happy. He sought justice and went to war to get it. He was magnificent in battle; the world had never before seen such a noble king—and never has since." Heather noticed Mother looking sadly at Father, a tear streaking down her cheek.

Father went on. "He had a powerful army and great captains to lead it. One captain was Perkin One-Eye, perhaps King Jupiter's greatest friend and most valiant warrior. There was also Stam the Stout, Pickwand, Fesslehorn, and Harlen Seer, the Wizened Warrior. Nine great wars were fought over twenty years. They are all worthy of great tales. Of course King Jupiter was there in every battle, leading from the front, with a fierceness rarely ever known in rabbits.

"In the Red Valley War, King Jupiter came to the aid of a small collection of warrens under siege. They were threatened by a pack of wolves led by their wicked king, a ruthless wolf named Garlacks. King Jupiter swept the wolves from the Red Valley. He fought Garlacks himself, ending him in a spectacular battle as the red sun set. Oh, they sang songs of his victory for years! He was a wonder."

Father paused to collect himself again. Heather and Picket waited, wise and silent, eager for more. Heather wondered why such a happy story could make Father so sad, but she didn't ask. Then she remembered that Father had called this tale "The Rise *and Fall* of King Jupiter the Great."

Father went on. "He became known as the greatest fighting king of the age. It was his glory for a while but eventually began to trouble him. The laughter in him quieted, and he became graver. He believed he had always tried to achieve peace and was sad that he so often had to find it at the end of his sword.

"So King Jupiter the Great, Lord of the Thirty Warrens, bent all his energies to diplomacy, to avoiding any wars that could be prevented. Thanks to his many victories and his great army, he was successful. He forged alliances with the last holdouts of the old inter-warren wars and brought home the rogue clans of Tarvan Bluff. He became Sovereign of the Great Wood. He worked for peace in the forest, using his allied forces to rid the land of the most troublesome elements, including the fairly small number of birds of prey.

All the awful raptors were banished back to their haunts in the High Bleaks, for the forest was vigilantly protected by the vaunted army of Jupiter Goodson."

In the firelight, Heather watched Mother cross the room and lay Jacks in his crib. She stayed there for a while, watching him sleep, as Father went on.

"All the energy he had earlier given to war he put into gaining peace—and keeping it. As his army had great captains, so too he had a Council of Seven Ambassadors." Here Father stopped again, walking to stand in front of the fire, as if a sudden chill had found him.

His back to the children, he went on. "These councilors served as his own voice in the far regions of the forest and beyond. One rabbit he called to be their chief: Garten Longtreader. He lived up to the great name of Longtreader, making countless journeys into the deeps of the forest on missions to make alliances for the king. It was he who was credited for much of the expansion of the rule of Jupiter Goodson. It was said that King Jupiter held the world together, but Longtreader was his thread. The king was happy and just," Father said, his voice cracking, "ruling with wisdom and building the idyllic kingdom his father had dreamed of.

"When the Great Alliance was forged and the wars seemed a glorious memory, King Jupiter finally rested from his adventuring and married. His family grew and grew, and he was truly happy." Father stopped again, closed his eyes, and rubbed his chin. Mother slowly crossed the room again, her head bowed.

"The king was asked during this time by a faithful subject, 'What, Lord Jupiter, is the greatest joy in the peace you have won?' He did not answer suddenly; that was not his way. He was a philosopher king, so he thought on it. Finally, after several moments in silence, he answered with a wide smile, 'That I am my father's true son.'" Father bent then, sobbing quietly, and Mother came to his side. She put her arms around him, eventually kissing his cheek and whispering in his ear. He nodded and laid his hand on her shoulder gently. "You are always right, my dear," he said. "I couldn't keep it from them any longer. Who knows what may ..." His voice trailed off.

Mother nodded. "I know."

"I'm sorry for my tears, children. They are not all sad, but some are. It's a story that ..." he began, but he could not finish.

"It's lovely, Father," Heather said into the quiet, her voice soft.

Father whispered thanks to her, then stood. "He was magnificent, children! I wish you could have seen him standing at the head of his forces in gleaming golden armor. Like the dawn, children! All who knew him loved him without reserve," Father said, but he stopped, struggling to go on. Mother hung her head, and Father managed to say, "Well, I should say that *almost* everyone loved him loyally."

"Father will tell you more another time," Mother said, taking his arm. "For now, it's time for sleep. It's a happy thought that there could be such a king, isn't it?"

"It is, Mother," Heather said, her mind overflowing with questions and answers, gleaming armor and flashing swords. "It's too good to not be true."

* * *

A few minutes later, Heather and Picket lay quietly in their beds upstairs. Their father had whispered his blessings on them, and Heather could hear his footfalls as he descended the winding stairs.

Heather stared out the small window beyond Picket's bed at the bright white moon. The storm was over and it was almost chilly. From below she heard Mother humming the song she'd begun to sing earlier. Then she and Father were singing softly, sadly, together. But it wasn't all sad. She couldn't make out the words, though she strained to hear them. But she understood something of what it meant.

It was sad, yes. But there was a note of hopeful longing woven into the aching heartbreak of the tune. She closed her eyes on tears.

Chapter Four

THE LADY

Heather woke early, though she had not slept well. All night she dreamed of King Jupiter, tall and strong with golden armor gleaming in the sun. She had woken often, only to sleep again and continue the dream. Now she got out of bed and crept past Picket, who was still asleep, and made her way down the winding stairs.

Father had hollowed out the elm years ago and made this beautiful stairway. She loved the smooth feel of the railing and the beauty of the pale grain of the carved elm. Breakfast smells found her as she descended, making her smile even as she yawned.

She heard shifting chairs and low conversation and paused a moment to listen. She heard an unfamiliar voice, female and ancient-sounding, say in a hoarse whisper, "They are on the move now; it is certain. I risked much coming here, I know. I think he may decide this place is safe."

Heather waited a moment; then she heard her father speak. "He may well. He's one of few who know we're here.

35

Are you sure you weren't followed?" Father sounded worried, which worried Heather.

"I usually am. He knows Morbin is seeking the Green Ember," she said. "Morbin has set his wolves on the hunt."

Heather went on, rounding the last of the spiral steps to find her parents at the table with the stranger, whose back was to Heather.

"Good morning, Heather," Mother said, changing her face from worried to welcoming in an instant. "Go back up and wake Picket, dear. Then come and eat something. We have a guest we'd like you to meet."

The unknown lady and Father were hunched over some papers, some of which looked like maps. The guest was short and appeared to be much older than Mother. She wore the same sort of sweeping dresses Mother often favored—the kind almost no one in Nick Hollow wore. Hers was black, and she wore elegant long black gloves fringed with lace.

She sat up straight. Her fur was grey, peppered with black. She turned her head slightly and raised it to peer, slit-eyed, at Heather. She nodded Heather's way and then returned to her papers. She resumed her conversation with Father in hushed, insistent tones.

Father winked at Heather and gave her an encouraging smile before returning to attend to the maps and the mysterious lady.

Father's worried. What does that mean? She returned the smile but did not mask her concern. She ran back up the stairs and crossed to Picket's bed.

"Wake up, Picket," she whispered.

He didn't move.

"Wake up, Picket!" she whispered louder.

Nothing.

This time she got right next to his right ear, which was sagging over the side of his bed.

"Picket! Wake up!" she shouted.

He spun out of his bed, knocking Heather back and rolling over on the floor twice before bouncing up.

"I was already awake!" he said, staggering.

"Right," Heather said, laughing at him. "And I'm a woodpecker."

"You're almost as irritating as one," Picket said as he dug at his still sleepy eyes.

"Let's get downstairs," she said. "There's a lady down there who seems—I don't know—kind of important. She's talking to Mother and Father about something serious."

"I wonder what it is," Picket said.

"Let's go and try to find out."

"They never tell us anything when stuff like this happens," Picket said, stretching.

Picket was right. This sort of thing happened every few months but lately more and more. A stranger had come last month. It had been happening a lot since little Jacks was born six months before.

"You're right, Picket." Heather sighed. "They'll probably just send us for berries again."

"At least there's a built-in snack to that job."

"True," Heather agreed, smiling. "Hey, Picket, did you dream of King Jupiter last night?"

"I tried," Picket said, shrugging, "but no such luck. You?"

"Yeah," she said. "Amazing ones."

"You always have great dreams."

"I always have vivid dreams," she said. "Sometimes they're not the good kind."

"I'd take it," he said. "I dreamed I was riding on a blind cardinal's back, and he kept flying into things."

That'll be the day, she thought. *He's afraid to climb a tree, let alone go soaring in the sky.* "That would be a funny story," she said.

"Why don't you make up one about it?" he said.

"Sure I will," she said, smirking.

"Heather, you should," he said, stifling a yawn. "You tell the best stories."

"Better than Father?"

"Well," he said, "maybe not quite the very best. But really, awfully, terribly good ones."

"Terribly awful?" she asked, scowling.

He laughed. "That's fair."

"I would love to write down these King Jupiter stories," she said.

"Hopefully we'll hear the rest today," Picket said.

"I hope so too. But we'd better get down there. We can ask Father later."

They descended the spiral stairway to the bottom floor. Picket had more to say.

"I wish I could have dreamed about him," he said as the kitchen came into view. Picket was looking up at Heather. "What a story! Do you think it's true, Heather? It must be, right? King Jupiter, Lord of the Great Wood. It must have been a lon—"

Picket stopped short when he saw the guest, who was standing beside Father at the foot of the stairs, looking at the two young rabbits.

She was short but graceful, stern-looking, with serious eyes. She crossed slowly to where they stood and looked each of them in the eyes in turn. Heather felt like she wasn't looking at their clothes or the color of their fur, but inside them.

The guest bent in front of Picket. "Would you like to think there was such a king in this world as Jupiter Goodson?" she said, peering into Picket's eyes.

At first Heather feared he wouldn't answer. He didn't like to be put on the spot. But he did answer. "More than anything, lady," he said, bowing.

Heather wasn't sure why, but it seemed the right thing to do. So when the lady looked at her, she curtsied, bowing her head.

"What about you, young maiden?" the lady said, peering into Heather's eyes. "Do you long for such a king?"

"With all my heart," she said without hesitation.

The lady turned to face Father and Mother, who stood arm in arm beside the table. She nodded to them. "You do well, my friends."

"Thank you," they said together.

"My dear young rabbits," the lady said. "King Jupiter is gone, but others take up his cause, and another fills his place."

Chapter Five

EASTERN WINDS

I don't think King Jupiter's cause is picking berries," Heather said. She and Picket had, as they had predicted, been ordered to make the trip into West Wood and pick berries after breakfast.

The stranger, who introduced herself as "Lady Glen," had said little at breakfast. They ate quickly, feeling the unspoken urgency in the air. Lady Glen eyed them sternly throughout, but before they left on their errand, she had given Heather a quick smile.

"You're right, Heather," Picket said, hurling a stick into a tangled bramble off the path. "But it's our job anyway. We may as well enjoy it."

Heather slumped her shoulders and pushed out her bottom lip, walking as if heavy with gloom. Then she burst off running with a laugh. "Last one to Gladeberry is a turtle!"

"No fair!" Picket shouted, running after her.

Heather was upset about being left out of the important talk back at the house, but it was hard to be sad on a day like this. All around them, Nick Hollow was coming alive.

The spectacular rainstorm of the day before had made everything greener and brighter. Never mind the broken limbs and downed trees; it was a perfect spring day, breezy and bright. The air was warm around them, and above them lay a deep blue blanket of sky. The sunlight sparkled through the wind-bent boughs of trees, dancing in an ever-shifting pattern of shadows along the path.

They ran for a long time, around Evergreen Row, along the widening stream, and even straight past Seven Mounds. Seven Mounds was always an enticement to distract them from chores, but not today.

Last summer they had discovered what appeared to be a hidden cave entrance at the base of the third mound. It was a small crack, almost impossible to see. They weren't sure if Heather could fit through it, and Picket had been too afraid to go in alone. They had agreed to try it again sometime but hadn't yet gotten up the courage.

"What a day!" Heather shouted as Picket caught up to her at Gladeberry Crossroads. They stopped to catch their breath. Heather looked down the lane that wound to their right—the way to Gladeberry. To the left, it was only a minute's run to Elric's Farm. She considered going down to check on old Mr. Elric but decided they'd better stick to their instructions. Plus, she hoped to see Lady Glen again. That parting smile had stuck with her.

"You ready?" she asked after a minute.

"Of course," he said, still puffing. "I was just stopping … for you."

Heather smiled, shaking her head. *Why do bucks have to pretend to be so tough?*

"All right," she said, clapping. "Let's—"

A faint but distinct scream came from the direction of Elric's Farm.

"Was that—?" Picket whispered, but Heather held up a hand for silence. She waited, hoping they would not hear it again. All she could hear was the beating of her own heart and Picket's labored breathing.

Another scream! This time louder and more urgent. There were more noises, voices gruff and insistent, followed by more screams.

"The house!" Heather shouted, grabbing Picket's arm. "Run!"

She darted off back in the direction of their home, running hard. Picket followed quickly, though they were both tired from their long run of just a few moments before. They moved fast, Heather in the lead. Every terrible possibility flashed before her eyes as she ran. She imagined their elderly neighbor, Mr. Elric, being attacked by enormous bloodthirsty hawks, talons razor-sharp and beaks gaping. Then she imagined them attacking her home, Baby Jacket, Mother, and Father.

Father would know what to do. They had to reach home. She noticed that Picket had lagged behind her, clutching his side.

"We have to move, Picket!" she screamed at him, stopping to let him catch up. Heather didn't know what to do.

43

She considered running on ahead to warn their parents but heard the insistent voice of Father inside her head saying, "Always stick with your brother." But was this different? "There's no time!" she cried. "We can still make it in time to warn them, if we hurry. Think of Jacks!"

Picket nodded gravely, and, gasping for air, they launched into a full run once more. Heather smelled something awful. This day, which had been so bright and lovely only moments ago, felt suddenly heavy with doom. Even the sky seemed to darken and grow grey.

The smell was worse now, burnt and foul, and the grey haze thickened above. Heather's foreboding grew. They raced past Seven Mounds and through Evergreen Row, worry filling their fast-beating hearts.

They turned the last corner out of West Wood, preparing to sprint across the meadow to their home. Heather skidded to a stop. She was not prepared for what she saw.

Their elm-tree home was on fire. Grey smoke pumped out of the upstairs and downstairs windows, spilled through the door to the porch, and gathered into the sky. Orange flames licked the higher branches and played at the edge of every opening.

Heather barely stifled a scream. In the smoky haze, she saw large black-clad figures in the meadow. Wolves, she realized with amazement. *Here? How?* She was incredulous. She had never seen a wolf but recognized them from her reading and her parents' descriptions.

These wolves were organized. They clearly had captains

among them. She saw some barking orders and others in formations. They were all in uniform, dressed in black, with a red diamond symbol on their chests. The right side of the diamond fell away in a fang. Their arms were marked with what looked like a hideous brand, a wound standing out bare against their coarse fur. It looked like an M. She saw a terrifying scene of confusion.

She hesitated only a moment, then grabbed Picket and dragged him back into the woods. Then she darted sideways, hauling her terrified brother into a thorny thicket. Once inside, they got a look at some of what was happening in the meadow. Their meadow.

Heather strained to see through the smoke, trying to find her parents and Baby Jacks. She saw a collection of around fifteen wolves in the foreground, about halfway up the meadow, near the fallen maple limb. The maple tree, half-burned with a tangled scar of black char where the lightning had ripped through it, somehow still stood. The hard rain had doused the flames that would have surely overtaken it.

It struck her as almost funny that she noticed the red ribbon of their starstick wedged in one of the still-intact limbs of that dying, damaged tree. Trapped forever in the clutches of a charred and crippled monster.

Some of the wolves were prowling around the edges of the pack, looking in all directions. Teeth bared, their harsh, snarling voices polluted the air. Heather viewed them as a foul offense. They looked, she saw with terror, very hungry. In the hazy distance near the house, she could vaguely see

what looked like a struggle. She tried to make out the forms darting around through the smoke and flames. Was that grey form Father? She strained her eyes.

Picket interrupted her focus, sobbing loudly. She pressed her hand over his mouth, then shook him, finally lifting his chin to look in his eyes. She was stern, serious.

"Not now, Picket," she whispered. "Later! What would Father want?"

Picket nodded, raking his hand across his nose and sniffing. He took a deep breath. Heather gave him another stern look of confidence, nodding. Then she bowed her head, collecting herself to look again at the awful scene of her ruined home. She turned, then gaped in terror.

Five wolves were running straight at them.

Chapter Six

RED EYE AND SMOKE

They had heard Picket. The wolves closed in on them.
Heather hissed, "Follow me!" to Picket and dove
deeper into the thicket. The wolves crashed in after them.

She turned to Picket and said with all the authority and
confidence she could muster, "Third mound! Don't look
back!" She slapped his back, urging him on, as she slowed.

Picket bolted, changing direction swiftly, like a leaf in
a sudden strong breeze. He zigzagged through the maze of
thorns and brush and disappeared.

Heather turned to face the wolves, who were having a
harder time of it in the dense thicket. She only saw two. *The
other three must be trying to head us off.* She let go of the idea
that she could do any more for Picket than she was doing
now. The longer these two were delayed, the better chance
he stood of making it to safety. She stopped in a hollow of
the thicket. The wolves crashed in, brutal, hulking creatures
breathing hard.

The two wolves slowed as they neared. They looked
surprised to see her standing still.

Heather smiled. Perhaps they didn't realize there had been two rabbits.

Go on, Picket!

"She's smiling, soldier," the wolf in back said, his voice like grated gravel. He appeared to be the leader. Plainly older and calmer, he carried himself with a cruel dignity. As he slowly crept closer, making no sudden movements, Heather saw a long, dark scar across the left side of his face. It went right through where his left eye should have been. His right eye was bright red. He laughed a guttural, sneering laugh. "She is, perhaps, honored to be eaten by us?" His smile, hideous and hateful, vanished. "Give her the terms," he growled dismissively. Heather could see he had measured her and dismissed the possibility of a struggle. He looked out of the clearing back toward the meadow, his mind clearly moving to other concerns.

"Yes, Captain," the nearer wolf said. "Hello, Food," he said to Heather, his voice higher, filled with excitement. His eyes were wide and wild. "Come with us easylike and you'll live—for now. Struggle, and we're allowed to kill you."

"Please, do struggle," the second wolf said, moving slowly to flank Heather. His calm manner compared to the frenzied eagerness of the younger wolf was even more frightening. He was wicked and cold, and she saw he had done this kind of thing many times.

Heather decided to try to imitate his calm. "You believe you have me, but you don't. Not yet," she said, trying to keep her voice even and low. "I know this thicket. I can disappear before you know which way to look."

The awful captain laughed, but she now had his attention. *Maybe this is a mistake. I should have let them underestimate me.*

"So, it talks?" the red-eyed captain sneered. "That's precious."

"I talk, yes," she said. "And I'll not go quietly. I'll bite back before I'm finished."

Now both of the wolves laughed and exchanged looks, blinking in amusement.

"Well, Captain," the younger wolf said amid high-pitched laughter, "at least we've had some entertainment." They moved to widen their distance apart, and now the two of them formed two parts of a triangle, with her as the third point.

She looked from side to side. These were no fools. She was cornered. "Your pride is your weakness," she said.

The younger wolf let out a howl of fury. "Let me finish her, Captain," he begged. "She shames us."

"Only if we let her," the captain said, motioning for the other to remain calm. "I'm intrigued by you, little rabbit doe. There seems to be quite a bit of fight in the rabbits of these parts."

Heather felt a jolt of fear. What had they done to her family? The older wolf went on. "It's odd that traitors and deserters would be the least bit bold."

"We're not deserters, or traitors," Heather said quickly, her voice cracking.

"Then what are you doing so far from home?" he jeered. "And in such questionable company?"

"This is home," she said, not knowing what he meant by "questionable company."

"They have given you lies for every meal, child. You have swallowed them and kept asking for more," he said, his voice crackling like dry thorns in a blaze. He smiled. He savored this as much as the attack. "Your father is a coward and a liar and a traitor," he said, finishing in a proud, toothy snarl.

She looked down for a moment, sad resignation on her face. The wolves looked at each other. Their faces read of satisfaction at breaking her. But just as they looked from her to each other, Heather acted.

She pretended to be deeply wounded by the captain's words and crouched down, showing she was beaten. Then she erupted between them in a flash. The two wolves, seeing their mistake, recovered quickly and lunged for her. She narrowly avoided their snapping jaws and felt the stirred air of their missing strikes, their hot breath. They collided as she dashed between them.

She had only bought a few moments but planned to make the most of them. She had rested as they talked and had planned her next moves. Now she went to work.

Behind her she heard another piercing howl, high, terrible, and fierce. She recognized that this was from the younger wolf. The howl was followed hard by a cursing, guttural roar of orders. Her fur raised at the sounds, but she ran on. She darted back and forth through the thicket, emerging far from where she had entered.

She left the thicket and ran across a small opening for the cover of nearby trees. She heard a loud barking command. She couldn't make out what it was but soon saw its effects as she peeked out from behind an oak tree. The sky, already acrid with twisting plumes of smoke, filled with flaming arrows, which plunged into the thicket she had only just escaped. The thicket burst into flames, and even more smoke filled the air.

Good. Let them think I've burned. She prepared to flee, eyeing the great wall of grey smoke passing before her. She waited for it to thicken a bit more as the fire kindled to a blaze. She stared into the smoke. Then, through the wall of grey a gust of wind opened a slim, wispy window. She saw, across the clearing, a single red eye.

And it saw her.

They stared at each other for a moment. Heather was still. In this moment she felt that all the meaning of her life was to escape and so frustrate this wicked one-eyed wolf. She could have run right then, and he could have called his wolves, but neither moved. Neither blinked.

Then the smoke thickened, closing the window in grey, and the moment was gone. Heather looked quickly from side to side, then darted along the smoke wall toward Evergreen Row. She moved by instinct and memory. She couldn't see much at all. She knew if she ran as fast as she could, she would be in the row of evergreens in a minute.

The great walls of smoke surrounded her like an ever-shifting house, changing shapes all the time. She inhaled a gulp of smoke, unable to avoid it. She slowed, coughing and spluttering. *I can't stop now!*

Heather winced and wavered, the thick grey air closing in on her. She ran on, still trusting her way. But doubt crept in. The scene was so confusing, and she was tiring again. The smoke burned her lungs. Maybe she was running the wrong way? When she coughed, had she turned? Where was she headed? Any wrong move would likely mean the end. She needed to be perfect.

Minutes went by. *How many?* She couldn't tell. She could hardly breathe. The blanket of smoke was covering her, and there was nowhere to turn. She ran on but was running out of air. Her eyes stung. *I won't make it.*

Coughing, she looked up and saw a break in the smoke above, revealing a clean blast of sunlight before a brilliant blue sky. She smiled. For the briefest moment it occurred to her that this would make a happy last sight.

But the air began to clear in a sudden strong breeze. She saw the tops of evergreens in the near distance, the ever-widening circle of blue brightness as the heavy clouds of smoke retreated.

She knew where she was.

The ground was still heavy with smoke, though it was clearing. Her eyes stung; the smoke began to blind her. Tears came, filling her eyes, and she saw more clearly.

The smoke on the ground was twisting in the wind

and being carried off like sheets jerked from a clothesline. She saw the tops of the trees, knew she had made it near Evergreen Row. She smiled, throwing herself into the last yards, gathering all her energy for her greatest possible speed, then looked straight ahead.

The last of the ground smoke cleared to reveal ten waiting wolves at the bottom of the first pine of Evergreen Row.

Chapter Seven

FATEFUL DECISIONS

T*his is the end.*

She was pounding the ground, hurtling towards Evergreen Row and the snarling, sickening smiles of the waiting wolves. At their head, somehow, stood the awful captain with the single red eye.

He had outsmarted and outmaneuvered her. How could she have thought she might escape?

She made a decision. She would not, did not, slow down. Heather sped toward them, hoping to plow into Redeye with one powerful leap and kick. Rabbits were capable of great force when they struck with their legs at high speed. She had never done it, of course. But she wasn't about to quit.

She was seconds away from the gang of wolves. They crowded around the trunk of the first pine, panting, their lolling tongues dripping saliva. As she hurried their way, some tensed and took a few steps back, but Redeye advanced. He stood in front of his soldiers at the edge of the first great evergreen, beneath the drooping branches. The rows of green pines stretched back beyond them, nearly all the way to Seven Mounds. Heather prayed that Picket was safe. There was nothing else she could do for him now.

The last few yards. A final burst of speed. That single red eye. It became a target, and she, a hurtling arrow. He barked for the wolves to spread out, cut off the possibility of her darting sideways in an attempt to escape. They obeyed at once, fanning out in a wide arc behind Redeye, extending like a giant mouth ready to snap closed on her.

She readied herself to launch at him, noticing at the last moment the low limbs of the pine above the snarling face of her enemy.

She coiled, in stride, her powerful legs ready to propel her forward at an even greater speed. The wolves at the flanks closed in on her, but Redeye stood firm. He rose to his full height and drew a long spear from where it lay hidden behind him.

Too late!

She launched.

* * *

Picket reached Seven Mounds with some difficulty. He had done his best to calculate the quickest route while accounting for the need to cut back and forth as often as possible. As he fled, he had been tortured by the conflict in his mind.

Should I go back?

He had slowed a few times but always remembered Heather's charge, "Don't look back!" He didn't know what to do. *What would Father say? What would King Jupiter have done?* Finally, he decided that, for the moment at least, he would do what Heather asked and trust to her plan. Seven Mounds came into view, an odd, almost-natural looking series of large hills that ran, all seven, in succession.

Running hard, he crossed between the shorter rise that separated the second and third mound and sprinted into the small, narrow clearing he and Heather knew so well. He removed the broken limbs and brush that disguised the small cave-like opening. He looked from side to side, confused and afraid.

He slid roughly inside the opening. All was dark. He closed his eyes and sagged onto the cold, damp floor.

Opening his eyes, he looked around the cave. His eyes had adjusted to the dimness, and the slim opening let in a glowing seam of light. The room was small, with a high ceiling. It could hold maybe five or six more rabbits his size. He heard a faint trickle, like a small stream. As his eyes grew more and more accustomed to the dark, he noticed what looked like another fissure in the rock at the back of the cave wall. There was no light coming through it.

He crossed back to the entrance and peered out, fear and guilt gnawing at him.

He hung his head. He didn't know what to do. He felt as if he was responsible for all that had happened. It was certainly his fault the wolves had found them. "Don't look back," she had said. Was that because she knew if he did, he would see her—what? What did she not want him to see? It didn't take much imagination to know. She had given herself up to save him. He was alive because of her.

Despair mingled with gratitude within him. Guilt rose in his throat like a gag, and he slumped to the ground, beating the rock floor of the cave. His father had tried to teach him courage, had told countless tales of great rabbits who sacrificed and did brave deeds for those they loved. He knew his Whitson Mariner, Captain Blackstar, and, though only a beginning, the tale of King Jupiter Goodson. He was supposed to be like those very real heroes who had gone before. He was supposed to protect his sister, to never leave her. He was supposed to protect Baby Jacks. He should have run into the danger and done all he could to rescue Jacks, no matter the cost. Hadn't he promised as much? Instead, he was a cowering, crying rabbit staying safe in a cave. Heather had been the one who acted heroically. Heather, his only sister and dearest friend in the world.

Will I ever see her again? Will I ever see my Jacks?

He rose and looked out the cave entrance. He peered down the flat, level stretch of ground running a short distance from the mound to the thick trees straight ahead. The trees and brush were heavy on both sides of the short clearing, and Picket imagined wolves and hawks waiting inside them to strike the moment he left the cave. It was like a tunnel, the overhanging limbs and leaves forming the top, with the roots of the trees curving back toward the path. Trying to ignore the terrors that might lurk on either side of the thick brush, he set his gaze on the trees beyond.

That way led to Heather, to Jacks and their parents. If any of them were still alive.

Chapter Eight

HEATHER'S FLIGHT

Heather was flying. She had never put this much energy into anything. All her years of playing Starseek felt like effortless exercise in this moment of extreme action. Her legs stretched out behind her, then rotated slowly over her head as she flipped in midair to present her powerful feet as a weapon.

The red-eyed wolf stood firm at the base of the pine tree, the low branches brushing his haughty, hideous scar-crossed face. He snarled viciously, extending his spear. Heather hit the ground just short of the wolves, inches beyond the lunging thrust of Redeye's spear. Like a spring, she shot up, feet barely escaping the claws of the desperate diving wolves.

Heather struck the low branches of the tree, grabbing on for dear life. The low-hanging limbs were thick and did not snap as she clung to them. They bent wildly with her weight, crashing into Redeye and the nearest wolf soldiers as the others dove in after her. She glanced down to see Redeye's shocked, furious expression.

The tree was her only hope of salvation. She clung to it as teeth and spears, swords and claws sought her. The branches, having bent in with her impact, now sprung out with equal force, shoving back the wolves who had waded in to destroy her.

As the pine tree resumed its natural shape, shaking out its arms like a stretching giant, she held on. The wolves nearest were almost all scattered, but two of the hysterical soldiers clung on just below her. Heather didn't hesitate. She leapt into the thick of the tree, dodging swiping blows and snapping teeth as she ascended the pine.

The two wolves recovered quickly and chased her through the limbs. She calculated as best she could, building momentum as she bounced back and forth between limbs, then ran full speed across a long, sturdy limb. One of the wolves was inches behind her. As the limb bent with their weight, she once again coiled and launched as powerfully as she could. The wolf's snapping jaws closed on the air where, a moment before, Heather had been.

She sailed through the air, this time from partway up the giant pine. Beneath her, she saw the wolves reforming and the terrible glare of Captain Redeye. He was shouting orders, and the wolves on the ground were forming up. They were recovering from the surprise she had given them.

The second pine in Evergreen Row loomed before her. She landed much like she had before, though this time she was more prepared for the impact. She clung on hard, but when the limb snapped back she used the momentum it carried to propel herself up farther into the tree. She did not stop for a moment. She could hear howling and barked orders below. She knew that if she stopped for even a second, she would never see Picket again. Would she anyway? Had he made it? No time for worry now. Every ounce of her concentration was required.

Once again she bounced back and forth, up and through the limbs, until she landed on a long sturdy branch and darted across it at speed. She coiled to launch and leapt with all her might. She sailed through the air between the pines again, looking down on the scurrying wolves. She saw Redeye pointing at the trees ahead and knew she needed to think fast.

She landed and again held on, springing into the heights of the tree. She knew she had no chance if she simply scaled to the top. The wolves would easily trap her. She had to keep going. Locating a strong long limb close enough to the next pine, she leapt skyward.

As she sailed through the air, a spear rose to meet her. She twisted, and the spear narrowly missed her. She turned again, unbalanced, and crashed into the next tree. By inches, she managed to cling to the springing branch as it reformed and launched her into the heights of the tree. She decided to go up higher on this tree and leap to the next from a distance where it would be more difficult for her enemies. As often as she could glance at the scrambling wolves below, she did. It filled her heart with dread. They were already ascending the next tree, and Redeye trotted along beneath her, barking commands and looking wickedly intent.

With a glance, she saw three of the wolves standing alongside Redeye in the gap between the tree she was in and the next one in Evergreen Row. Her heart skipped as she saw what was in their hands. But it was too late. She coiled and launched.

She heard the twang of bowstrings as speeding arrows split the air in their flight toward her. She couldn't do much. Ahead of her, the tree was occupied by three more wolves, who were scurrying to meet her when—if—she landed there. They climbed higher and higher to intercept her. She twisted in the air, trying to move, if only a little bit, from her natural flight.

Two arrows sailed past, whipping the wind around her, and the third struck her right ear, splitting it at the top. She focused, reached out for the limbs of the next pine. She made contact, and the limb swung low, just beneath the ascending wolves, who growled and bared their teeth. This time, instead of letting the limb spring back and carry her up again, she let go, falling down a few limbs lower, so that she landed beneath the waiting wolves.

The wolves were on her in a moment. But she had surprised them again. She scampered across the lower limbs and, as quickly as possible, sprang to the ground again.

The wolves were in disarray now. Many had lost track of her, and some were panting or wounded from the chase. Heather noticed she was cut in several places, not just her split ear, and felt bruised all over. But she knew she couldn't stop.

She stole a backward glance and saw that three wolves were chasing her on the ground. One was right on her heels.

Redeye.

She was losing energy fast, but she leapt into the next tree, found a footing on a sturdy low limb, and zigzagged up as Redeye lunged for her. He received a face-full of prickly pine but recovered quickly and ran along the ground. His eye never left her.

One of the other wolves followed her into the tree at great speed. He barreled toward her with all his strength, leaping at her. She dove out of his way at the last moment, and he careened, with a sickening crunch, into the trunk of the tree.

She recovered quickly, striking out to snag a limb, and sprang back into a full run along the branches. The next tree was the last in Evergreen Row, and, as far as she could tell, there were only two more wolves in close pursuit.

She ascended and ran along the longest limb that was closest to the next pine, as she had each other time. Redeye ran ahead, anticipating her next move by hurrying to the next tree. But as she ran, full speed, along the limb, she suddenly stopped and dropped like an acorn from the tree.

She landed behind them.

As they slid to halt and churned in the dirt to recover, she shot off into the clearing that led to Seven Mounds. She could hear the gurgling brook now closer and knew she had a chance if she could only make it to the third mound.

Her strength was nearly gone. She had, in fact, gone far beyond anything she had believed herself capable of. But now it truly was the end of her energy. She was wounded and exhausted and had been through what felt like a lifetime's worth of danger in only a few minutes. She thought of Picket, safe but worried, in the cave. At least, she hoped he was there. If only she could reach him and if only she could fit through the small opening, they might survive. She and her brother. They could figure things out from there. *He needs me. Only let Picket be all right.*

She plunged into the woods, Redeye and the other wolf trailing her in. For a moment she thought she saw something in the thicket ahead, but when she looked again, there was nothing. *Please don't be Picket. Please, be in the cave.*

She was finished with diversion, done with subtle maneuvers and clever turns. She only had energy for one final straight run at the cave.

She came in sight of the third mound through the woods, entered the small tunnel-like clearing, and hurtled towards the cave entrance. She heard the heavy footfalls behind her, felt the instinctual sense that a predator was upon her.

She only had eyes for the cave entrance, which came into view before her, illuminated in a blast of sunlight breaking through branches that waved in a sudden gust. She stared hard at the cave entrance, hoping, praying, that she would see Picket's face. But there was no one there. Despair grabbed at her, but she ran on. She would not look back, though the grunting, wheezing wolves felt close enough to reach back and touch. She focused on the cave entrance like it was the only thing in the world. *Please, Picket. Please!*

Then she saw something. A face appeared at the entrance. *Picket!*

It was him. When their eyes met and she knew he was all right, beyond hope a last jolt of energy filled her. She sped toward the cave entrance, putting a short distance between herself and her attackers.

She slowed for a moment at the small entrance and turned to slide in.

Rock closed on fur. Panic rose as she found she could not move.

She was stuck tightly, unable to get into the narrow opening.

"No!"

Redeye and the second wolf slowed to a trot, a triumphant sneer forming on the leader's mouth.

"Stuck, are we?" Captain Redeye said, glowering even as he panted. The other wolf made to lunge, but Redeye barked a short, insistent order, and the wolf resisted. "Ending this little troublemaker will be my pleasure, soldier. Fall back." The wolf obeyed and trotted back behind Redeye.

Picket shouted and pulled and dug at the walls. He was desperate to free her and pull her inside. But he could not move her.

Heather was incredulous. It would really end like this? No matter how hard Picket pulled and she struggled, she knew she was truly and finally stuck.

I'm dead. After all that. Inches from safety.

* * *

Picket was beside himself, his moment of exultation turning to terror as he pulled at his sister with all his strength. He would have run out and faced the wolves himself if he could have, but Heather was lodged in the opening, and he could not get out, even to die in a futile effort to protect her. He was stuck as well. Stuck safe.

It was unbearable.

He didn't give up but kept pulling on his exhausted sister, tearing at the rock to break open a path for her. But it was too late.

* * *

Heather looked up wearily at Redeye, too exhausted now to think clearly. Was she imagining the faint hint of pity in his eye? She must have been, for when she shook her head, it was gone. He crept upon her with a cruel, gloating sneer.

"This is the end, little rabbit," he growled, baring his razor-sharp teeth. "Thank you. The sport was … exhilarating."

Heather closed her eyes and whispered, "I love you, Picket," but just when her eyes had almost closed, she saw a grey blur over Redeye's left shoulder. Her eyes shot open again. It was a grey rabbit, hurtling towards them with his powerful feet coiled to kick. *Father! Can it be?*

Redeye couldn't see the grey shape, because it sped toward them from his blind side. Surely the wolf behind Redeye had seen it. Heather waited for the powerful kick to land on Redeye, hoped it would come in time, but the rabbit passed the attacking wolf and stretched out his powerful feet and struck her. She felt the terrible blow on her shoulder, and everything went black.

Chapter Nine

Salvation

Picket had seen far more than Heather had.

He had pulled at her with all his strength, knowing somewhere inside that he could not pull her free but refusing to heed that voice. He had torn at the rock until his nails bled. He tried everything to rip her free and pull her inside the cave, but the one-eyed wolf was upon her, and there was no time left. She had whispered her farewell, and all he could say was, "No! No, no, no!"

Then Picket saw him, soaring through the air over the shoulder of Heather's attacker. *Father?* he thought, but all was a grey blur. Behind Heather and the first wolf, the one whose jaws were wide to strike, the second wolf was now charging, intent on intercepting the soaring grey rabbit.

Picket's brief moment of hope dissolved. He tried to get an arm out past Heather to strike the red-eyed wolf bearing down on his sister. Then he saw another form, a white blur, launch from the bushes and tackle the second wolf. The grey and white tangle of teeth and blades rolled away into the thicket and out of Picket's vision. He heard the sounds of a terrible struggle.

Then, to his shock, he saw that the soaring grey rabbit was headed for Heather. *No!* He stepped back without thinking as the rabbit's powerful feet connected with Heather's shoulder, sending her crashing—into the cave!

In. The rabbit had hit her hard, yes, but had put her out of danger of being killed. The wolves could never fit inside. Picket was thrilled and confused at once. He knelt by his sister, listened to her heartbeat, and felt her breath. She was knocked out cold, but alive. He sprang over to the cave entrance, his heart racing. What had happened to Heather's savior? Was it Father? And what of the white rabbit, the one who had attacked the second wolf?

When he peered out the cave's entrance, he saw the grey rabbit's back to him, standing guard over the entrance, a gleaming sword in his hand. There were three long red lines across his back. Rescuing Heather had cost him. He stepped back and forth as the red-eyed wolf with the horrible scar stalked him. The wolf was sizing up the sword-bearing rabbit and looked eager to strike.

"You again," Redeye said, a guttural growl growing in his chest. "This makes me very happy. My mission, you know," he finished, laughing.

Picket knew the grey rabbit had little chance against this powerful wolf. Redeye bared his teeth, crouched to spring.

Then out of the bushes came the white rabbit. He was injured as well, Picket could easily see, but had overcome the other wolf. Picket could not believe it! The white rabbit was dressed in ordinary traveler's clothes, as was the bigger grey rabbit, but his neck was crossed in a flowing black scarf. He strode out of the thicket, his sword bared.

He said, "Unless you would die like your father died, Redeye Garlackson, leave now."

Redeye's lone eye widened in shock. He was taken aback, then seemed suddenly eager. A look of frenzy was in his eye. But he could see that his opportunity had passed. For a few tense seconds, Picket believed he would strike anyway. But, after a moment's hesitation, he stole away with a bitter growling hiss. Picket saw mingled triumph and disappointment on his face as he left. When he disappeared into the woods, they heard a terrible, menacing, and mournful howl.

"The howl of shame," the white rabbit said, lowering his sword slowly.

"It's not the first time I've heard it," the grey rabbit said, slumping. Picket thought he knew that voice.

"Father?" he said, emerging from the cave.

The grey rabbit turned slowly, and, at first, Picket thought it was Father. But looking closer, he wasn't sure. Everything seemed hazy.

"I'm not your father, lad," he said gently. "I'm the next best thing. I'm your uncle."

Picket could see it clearly now. He needed no confirmation other than to look at his uncle's face. There were, he realized, some fairly easy differences to spot. Where Father was soft, perhaps a little pudgy, this rabbit was lean and powerful. In fact, he was more muscular than anyone Picket had ever seen.

"I'm Picket," he said, smiling wearily.

"I know your name, lad. I'm your Uncle Wilfred," he said, winking.

"Heather!" Picket said, running back inside. He knelt beside his sister. He wanted to hug her, to hold her and weep. He couldn't believe she was safe. It was too wonderful. And he owed it all to his uncle and the white rabbit.

The white rabbit slid easily through the cave entrance and noticed Heather on the floor, unconscious.

"We need to move her," he said, taking in the cave through squinted eyes.

Picket didn't like this idea at all. She was tired, needed to rest in safety. "When she's better," he said.

"No, lad," the white rabbit said. "Now."

Picket bristled. It was one thing for his uncle to call him "lad," but not someone who looked to be about his own age, even if he was a fighter.

"We can't move her," Picket insisted.

"I'm not asking," he said, looking back and forth from Picket and Heather to the cave entrance.

"And she's not moving," Picket said.

"How long until Redeye Garlackson gets back with his wolves and brings an army crashing down on us?" the white rabbit asked.

Picket couldn't think of anything at first, but he was determined to take care of his sister at all costs. "The wolves can't get in here."

"And what about your uncle? He can't fit in here," the

white rabbit said, his tone growing sharper with urgency. "Should we leave him to the wolves? He didn't leave your sister, did he?"

"Didn't leave her?" Picket asked, furious. "Just what are you getting—"

The white rabbit held up his hand, motioning for silence. "Listen," he said.

Picket fumed but was silent. They heard the soft gurgling of a stream. The white rabbit crossed the cave, found the fissure on the other side, and went in, without hesitation.

"Wilfred," the white rabbit called, trotting back into the section of cave where Picket sat holding Heather's head.

There was the chirrup of a whippoorwill, a hurried call, which made Picket flinch; then Uncle Wilfred's face appeared in the door. "That's my call, Picket. You'll know it's me if you hear it. I do it a little faster than is quite right."

The white rabbit went on. "There's a stream in here, Wilfred. Must be another entrance where the water comes out."

"Right," Uncle Wilfred said.

"Where's the stream, lad?" the white rabbit asked. Now Picket was sure—he hated being called "lad" by a rabbit who appeared to be about the same age as himself.

"Past the seventh mound," he said curtly.

The white rabbit nodded at Uncle Wilfred, who disappeared with another wink at Picket. "See you soon," Picket heard his uncle say.

The white rabbit bent and dug into his satchel. He rummaged inside for a moment, then made for the cave entrance.

"What's going on?" Picket asked, allowing some of his anger to bubble up.

"Just a moment."

Picket watched the white rabbit leave the cave and heard rustling in the woods. Picket paced, anxiously watching Heather's dim form. *Wake up, Heather. Please.*

In a few moments, the stranger returned with two long, thick sticks. He bent to apply some cloth to the top of the staffs, squinting as his eyes again adjusted to the darkness. In a few minutes he had two blazing torches going, and the cave lit up. He tossed one at Picket, who caught it. He held it close to Heather, examining her face. He saw the torn top of her right ear and noticed multiple other scratches and cuts. He winced at each one.

I should have been with you.

"We have to get moving," the white rabbit said, his eyes flitting between the cave entrance and Heather, then back to the opening deeper in the cave.

"We have time to take care of her, I'm sure," Picket said. But just as he spoke, they heard urgent, gruff voices and heavy footfalls. "They can't get in here," he added nervously. But it was almost a question. He disliked deferring to the white rabbit, but fear crept in, and he would do anything to protect Heather, even following this white rabbit's orders. He would never leave her again.

"They won't be alone," the white rabbit said, all business. He was calm but collected his things quickly. "Can you carry her?" he said.

"I think so," Picket began, handing over his torch and trying to lift Heather. He laid her gently down again and said, "No. I can't. Please help me."

The white rabbit looked at Picket, laid a hand on his shoulder, and nodded. "It's all right," he said. "Please carry the torches and go on ahead."

Picket accepted both torches and stepped forward, glancing back again and again.

"I'm right behind you," the white rabbit said. Lifting Heather off the ground with surprising ease, he moved behind Picket into the interior fissure of the third mound. The noise outside grew louder then began to fade as they disappeared deeper inside the darkness.

Chapter Ten

RULES OF THE LABYRINTH

Picket charged ahead with torches aloft, the white rabbit carrying Heather right behind him. They moved through a narrow rocky passage into a wider room. Picket noticed vaguely that there were drawings on the walls and some crumbling tapestries hanging. He tripped over what felt like cups on the floor. They waited here a moment; then the white rabbit ran on into another passage, which led to another and still another room, similarly strewn with a sparse assortment of neglected objects. Picket followed behind, or beside, the white rabbit from room to room, providing the light needed and looking, always looking, at Heather with concern. The white rabbit stopped to listen, grew frustrated, and hesitated at each turn.

Picket was sure he heard voices inside the caverns, but they were distant and indistinct.

They raced on and on. Picket stayed quiet, but he heard the white rabbit's mumbling sighs, saw his eyes darting all around in futility. Finally, after speeding through countless corridors, they came to another cave that looked like the first entrance at the third mound, where Heather had been rescued. They crept up, and Picket looked out the tiny entrance, which had been covered with large rocks and was impossible for any of them to get through. Picket peered out but didn't see any sign of the wolves or Uncle Wilfred. He shook his head.

The white rabbit hesitated. He seemed to be deciding between trying to force an exit—which seemed impossible to Picket—or surrendering to the frustrating hunt for another exit in the dim and dank passages of the cave. He was also struggling with Heather. He was surprisingly strong, but he had his limits.

Picket heard scraping and clawing coming from deep inside the cave. Had it been there the whole time? He was unsure. But it was there now. The only other sound was the constant noise of water, which would increase or decrease depending on where they went.

The white rabbit ran back inside the passage, bearing Heather, with Picket following hard on his heels with the torches. They stopped to listen again and again. They found many similar rooms but no way out. The white rabbit finally collapsed to his knees and laid Heather down. He sagged, gulping air and heaving deep breaths. For the first time, it came to Picket that he and Heather weren't the only ones who were exhausted. He had no idea how long Uncle Wilfred and this rabbit, whose name he did not know, had been without rest.

"What's your name?" Picket asked.

"My name?" the white rabbit gasped. "I'm … I'm Smalls."

"Smalls?" Picket asked, surprised.

"I know," Smalls said with a weary, wheezy laugh, "it's strange. But I've always been little."

Then it occurred to Picket that, though they were roughly the same size, he might still be younger. And Smalls had the same lean, muscular frame that Uncle Wilfred had.

"Smalls," Picket said, motioning in the air, as if counting, and concentrating hard, "I'm good at math."

"That's fantastic, Picket," he said. "I wish we were in lessons right now," he said, "working on a massive math problem." He sounded completely spent.

"We are, Smalls," Picket said. "This is a labyrinth. But it has rules."

Smalls stood up. "Go on."

Picket furrowed his brow, thought for another moment. "Well, I know this area. I know Seven Mounds, at least from the outside. And while we've been running around in here—"

"Wasting time," Smalls finished.

"No," Picket said. "It hasn't been a waste. I've been getting to know the inside." He paced back and forth as he spoke. "When we looked outside I recognized the second entrance, the blocked up one, as being outside the fifth mound. We came in the third mound. Now, by the way we came, it seems clear to me that there was no similar room in the fourth mound. We have been going around inside through these three mounds. The third, fourth, and fifth. I think, if there's no entrance in the fourth mound—and there isn't—then maybe there isn't an entrance for the second and sixth mounds."

"Okay. I sort of follow," Smalls said.

"So, I know there's the stream up near the first mound. And there's the stream you heard, which comes out and must join the brook that runs right past the seventh mound."

"So," Smalls said, "you can find the stream entrance and—"

"Uncle Wilfred," Picket finished. "I think so."

"Lead on," Smalls said, bending to scoop up Heather once more.

Picket ran, with Smalls right behind him bearing Heather, who was still unconscious. They heard noises in the distance, what sounded like wet wings flapping and terrible screeches. Every noise echoed, and the caves resounded with pounding steps.

They ran on harder, Picket making some adjustments in their route, until they came through a long tunnel, longer than they had been through before. "The seventh mound!" Picket called. "There's a longer distance between the sixth and seventh mounds!"

"Great," Smalls whispered, "but keep your voice down."

Behind them they heard a growing noise of hurrying figures, shouting and cursing. Closer and closer.

Picket led them through still more rooms and passages, always ascending higher and higher, before finally coming to a halt before an open space. In front of them were three entrances to separate passages. Heather stirred in Smalls' arms.

"Please tell me you know which one is ours," Smalls said, looking back as the noise behind them grew louder.

Picket paced and rubbed his eyes, shaking his head. "I don't have it, Smalls," he said, peering over his shoulder down the corridor, as if he expected it to burst with birds and wolves at any moment.

"Get it quick!" Smalls cried over the crashing noise echoing in the endless series of cave passages.

"I can't," Picket cried, crouching to the ground and rubbing his head, defeated. "If we choose badly, there's no telling what's down the wrong passages. Have you looked at some of the tapestries in here? This is not a safe place."

"Agreed."

"I'm sorry," Picket said. "I can't solve it."

"Then we'll do what I usually did in math," Smalls said.

"What's that?" Picket said.

"We'll guess!" Smalls cried, and he shoved Picket into the middle tunnel. Picket heard him slide in with Heather behind him.

Sliding. Unable to slow down. Smooth, slippery rock. Spiraling down and down. More and more water seeped into the tunnel the farther they slid, so they picked up speed on the increasingly slippery surface. Picket tried to see if Heather was okay behind him, but as he twisted to look, one of the torches he was holding was extinguished. He threw it ahead of him and worked to protect the flame of their last torch. He would have to trust Heather to Smalls' strong little arms. He could not let their only light go out in the middle of an underground labyrinth.

They picked up more and more speed, and the tunnel steepened. Picket tried to control how fast he slid, but he couldn't. It grew wetter still as more water rushed in from unseen underground streams. *This is a drain. How full will it get?* Picket struggled to stay upright and keep the flame of his torch from going out. But it was impossible. He squirmed and gripped for the sides, trying to shield the flame. But he could not.

A quiet hiss and all was black.

They were underground, almost underwater, hurtling down a narrow tunnel of rock, and the fire of their only light was quenched. Picket cried out as he slid wildly in total darkness. The tunnel grew steeper still, until it finally ended and Picket shot into thin air.

Chapter Eleven

Trapped and Attacked

Midair. Blind and frightened. Picket hung like a flightless bird out of his element. The moment passed, an endless fraction of a second.

And now he was falling fast, plunging through blackness into he knew not what. He closed his eyes. He flailed wildly, as if it might somehow slow him down. But he came down and down like a sack of stones. One moment he was surrounded by nothing but air; then he was submerged in ice-cold water.

Picket sank deep in the water, kicking frantically to reverse his downward momentum. Finally, he fought his way up and up in the darkness to break the surface of the water and take in great gulps of air.

He opened his eyes. In a few moments he could see, albeit dimly. He was in a huge cavern, the bottom of which formed the large pool in which he found himself. Above, there were cracks in the walls that let in small shafts of light. After total darkness, it seemed almost bright. He strained to see a shore but couldn't locate anything. Steep walls arching into a dome surrounded him. He was still confused, and his eyes were adjusting to the room's dim light.

Heather!

He twisted, paddling in place, searching the water for his sister and Smalls.

"Heather!" he shouted. "Smalls!"

He looked all over, desperate to find them. He could not lose Heather again. In his frantic searching, he saw a little shore of pebbles in a corner barely illuminated by two low lights from the cave wall.

He saw that the pool he swam in was formed from an excess of water pouring into the cavern, with the water escaping through some unseen route deep below them. He thought he could hear the water pouring out somewhere, but he couldn't tell where. "Heather!" he shouted, shivering. His voice shook.

He swam hard for the pebble shore, then heard the water stir behind him.

He turned to see his sister, struggling to stay above water. She was clutching the slumping form of Smalls, who appeared to be finished. "Help," she whispered.

Energized by the sight of his sister alive and awakened— no doubt by the cold blast of water—he crossed to her in seconds.

"He's …" she said, but she wasn't able to finish.

"Come on," he said. "I have to get you to the shore."

"We can't leave him," she said, treading water with difficulty. "He's alive."

"But we have to," Picket said. He couldn't save them both. "Come on!" he screamed, trying to grab on to her.

"We can do it," Heather said, teeth chattering. "Together. I can help you."

They each took hold of Smalls under one arm. Heather winced as she strained, and they swam desperately for the shore. The whole time they swam toward the distant beach of pebbles, Picket wondered when they would all sink for good.

Somehow, they at last fell heavily onto the shore, freezing and out of breath. They lunged forward and together dragged Smalls out of the icy pool.

Picket collapsed beside Smalls, shivering and coughing. His mind blanked for a while, and he almost lost consciousness. Then he came tearing back to life with flashing images of their flight.

Picket crawled to Heather and wrapped her in a hug.

"I thought—" he began.

"Me too," she said shakily.

They held each other for a little while longer, warming up a little and saying nothing.

"How are you?" he asked.

"I think I'll be okay," she said. "I was spent, for sure. I'm all right, besides being a little rattled and cold. My shoulder is hurting, but I don't think it's broken. I can use it." She stood up and looked around wearily. "What happened to us? And who is that?" She indicated the slumped form of Smalls.

"His name is Smalls," Picket said. "He helped Uncle Wilfred rescue us."

"He was our uncle?" she said. "I thought he might have been Father. Where is he now, this uncle of ours?"

"He's nearby, but we have to get out of here," he said, crossing to the wall of rock. "We need to act fast. There are cruel things in this place. They're after us."

"Of course there are," Heather said, shrugging and shaking her head. "Of course they are."

"Uncle Wilfred's out there somewhere. We need to find him and get as far away from Nick Hollow as we can." He stumbled across stones, seeking in the shadows for any hint of a way out.

Heather crossed to the slumping form of Smalls. "I think he hit his head," she said. She felt the bump on his head and frowned. She left him and went to the water's edge. She plunged her hand into the water and retrieved a small stone.

"What are you doing?" Picket called.

"Helping," she said. "I think." She placed the icy stone on the bump and held it there, despite the numbing cold she was feeling. Picket looked away, scanning the rock wall and feeling for anything that might be a way out.

"Hey!" he shouted.

"What is it?" Heather called. But Picket's answer was drowned out by loud screams from the caves above. It sounded like dozens of creatures were sliding down the tunnels overhead. "That sounds bad," she whispered to Smalls' unconscious form. "Will this never end?"

"Heather," Picket called. "Come help me!"

A boat was leaning along the wall. A rusty chain trailed down to the ground, where a heavy anchor lay. "Let's pull it down," Picket said. There was an odd assortment of things all around the boat: ropes, oars, pans, all sorts of gear strewn out on a rotting table.

Behind them, they heard shrieks and an awful clamor as the cavern roof shot dark shapes into the air, then the cold pool below. They searched for a way to lower the boat as the cavern filled with loud, piercing wails, then silenced again in terrific splashes.

The rabbits heaved on the boat and pulled it down by the old anchor chain. It smashed to the ground as they clambered out of the way.

"What now?" Heather asked, her eyes on the pool and the desperate creatures splashing and flailing in it. "We have no time," she said, trying not to let panic creep into her voice.

"I don't know exactly," Picket said, throwing the rope, oars, a net, and a few small items he couldn't identify into the boat.

Into the silence the call of a whippoorwill echoed, faintly, in the cavern. Picket ran to the wall.

"What are you doing?" Heather asked as the bird call was repeated.

"Uncle Wilfred!" he called, running toward the sound, which seemed to come from one of the nearby shafts of light.

Beside the beach, the pooled water moved into a small channeled stream, which appeared to have an outlet somewhere deeper still beneath them. He couldn't see how it worked, but he heard the release of water outside and below them. It must lead to the stream outside. How? He had no idea. The piled-up rocks of the wall, in which there were a few openings marked by shafts of light, served as a dam against the great store of water in the cavern. Picket considered swimming deep down and trying to escape that way, but he had no idea how they would get Smalls out.

He clambered up the part of the stone wall above the waterline and found a foothold that allowed him to see outside one of the light-filled openings. It was like a small rectangular window. He peered out.

There was his uncle, looking worriedly up at the stone wall from a spot near the stream. Uncle Wilfred was right outside the bottom of the seventh mound. Between his uncle and the three of them stood a high, firm wall of built-up rocks, forged together by art and age. It was like the entrance to the cave on the fifth mound, blocked intentionally, the wall apparently unmovable. The stream flowed steadily beside Uncle Wilfred.

"Uncle!" Picket shouted.

"Picket?" Uncle Wilfred said, moving with great speed to the small opening. "Is Smalls all right?"

"He's injured, knocked out," Picket said quickly. "We've got to get out of here."

"You have to protect him until I can get inside!" Uncle Wilfred shouted. "Don't let anything—"

But Picket cut him off. "Uncle Wilfred, they're coming! We have no time!"

Picket tore at the small opening, and Uncle Wilfred threw his shoulder into the wall with furious desperation. It was a crafted wall, and Picket thought it could be torn down, given enough time.

"Smalls!" Uncle Wilfred cried. The wall shook a little, and some small stones plopped into the pool. Uncle Wilfred was strong, but Picket knew it would take much more time than they had to do it that way.

"They're almost here!" Heather shouted. Picket turned to see her dragging Smalls up the bank of the pebble shore, the sheath of his sword rattling against the cold stones. Picket glanced at the boat.

Then he shouted to Uncle Wilfred, "Save your strength! Wait here!" He ran to the water's edge.

"Help me drag him, Picket!" Heather yelled.

But Picket did not help her. He knelt beside Smalls and drew his sword. Heather thought he had gone mad and was preparing to fight their attackers, but he ran away as soon as he had it. He crossed to the boat and swung the sword with a grunt. A metallic clink sounded. Again and again he swung the blade.

Finally, there was a sound of snapping chain, and Picket cast the sword into the boat. He gripped the chain and ran for the cave wall.

Just before he reached the wall, the heavy anchor on the other side of the chain dug in, stopped him short of the wall. "Help!" he shouted. Heather, who had begun to drag Smalls toward the boat, ran to Picket, grabbed hold of the chain, and helped him drag it the last few feet. Picket climbed the rock wall again and fed the chain through the rectangle window. Uncle Wilfred looked puzzled, perplexed, as the piles of chain fell at his feet.

"Picket!" he shouted, "what is this?"

"It's an anchor," Picket puffed out. "Pull with all your strength!"

Realization dawned on Uncle Wilfred's face. He didn't hesitate a moment but sprinted away, twisting to wrap the chain around him as he ran. Picket climbed down and ran back to the shore.

The creatures were coming ashore. It was hard to see more than vague, slippery shapes, some of which shot into the air and flapped wet wings. Others lurched across the pebbles.

He didn't care. He was exhausted and cold and had no time to watch. The attackers would need only a moment to recover before descending on them. They had only a few precious seconds now. Picket hoped it was all they needed.

Heather struggled to drag Smalls to the little boat. Picket joined her, and they quickly moved him nearer. As they breathlessly pulled him toward the old boat, they saw the chain tighten and the heavy anchor begin to drag. It skipped and clanged along the ground and then lifted into the air. The anchor struck the rock wall with a tremendous crash.

The wall held. He heard a sound of grinding stone, the rattle of rocks crumbling down the wall and disappearing in the water. Dust clouds filled the shafts of light, but the wall stood.

Picket looked back. The beach was filling with creeping creatures bearing down on them. The noise of their cursing threats and screeching cries filled the cavern. They would reach the boat in seconds.

The anchor slid down the dam wall, slumping into the water. Picket imagined Uncle Wilfred, the jarring he would have endured to pull the anchor so hard without result. Picket made ready to defend his sister for as long as he could. He grabbed the sword, which was chipped now, and held it up with trembling hands. He stood in front of the boat, hopeless and afraid. He watched Heather pull Smalls into the boat and turned to see their attackers only a few steps away.

"I'm sorry, Heather."

Chapter Twelve

WATER ISSUES

Hopeless and cold, Heather watched her brother raise the sword with trembling hands. It didn't feel real; it couldn't be real. They were just two ordinary rabbits, children really. *This can't be happening.* The beasts swarmed toward them with a hatred on their faces she couldn't comprehend. She closed her eyes.

All was noise now. The uneasy breathing of Smalls beside her, the anxious mutterings of Picket, the screeches of the attacking creatures, and she couldn't tell what else. Then a rattling, chinking sound made her open her eyes.

The anchor chain jiggled and Heather gasped. The anchor moved again, now racing up the slope of the rock wall. Uncle Wilfred was trying again.

The anchor rose in a terrific arc and once more stabbed the piled stones of the dam wall.

This time, it smashed through! For a second, only an anchor-sized hole appeared. Then rock chunks broke apart, spraying mortar and gravel in a great tear that avalanched down from the breach to the bottom of the wall, gushing water into the brightness outside. The breach in the dam wall caused the rest to crumble and collapse outwards in a terrific noise of crashing, splashing stone. A blast of sunlight filled the cavern, blinding them and their attackers as the enormous pool of cavern water shifted in a moment.

"Picket!" Heather cried, reaching out for her brother. She clasped his hand just in time to pull him into the boat as the massive pool rose and rushed for the gaping hole in the wall of the seventh mound. Water overwhelmed the small pebble shore, surging up to meet them.

Picket made it into the boat with Heather and the still-unconscious Smalls just in time. The boat rose with the swell and raced forward on the crest of a wave that smashed into their attackers, scattering them in the swirling pool. A few of them escaped upwards, but they flew back quickly, unsure of what was happening. The rabbits held on as best they could while the boat sped forward with a roaring rush of water.

Outside the seventh mound, the once-humble stream that had been slowly fed by a small flow of water from under the rock now raged like a river, overflowing its banks.

Heather gaped as they issued through the cave wall, their eyes nearly blinded by the daytime sun. She saw Uncle Wilfred twist out of the chain, dodge flying debris, and dive for the rushing boat before the bank he stood on disappeared in the gushing flood. He snagged the boat's edge with one hand, and Heather fought to pull him in. Picket dove to the side of the boat where she held fast to Uncle Wilfred's wrist. The boat tilted wildly, and Heather believed for a moment

it would tip over. But she leaned back, steadying the vessel, as she and Picket strained to hoist their uncle in amid the gathering rapids of the gushing stream.

At last he was in, soaking wet, wide-eyed, and smiling.

"Adventure!" he cried, shaking his fist at the creatures scurrying near the cave, all desperately trying to swim ashore all along the swollen bank. As they sped still farther down the teeming rapid, Redeye Garlackson and a squadron of wolves rounded the corner of the seventh mound. Heather saw how the mound was broken open and water issued as from a spewing mouth. Broken stone was sprayed all over the swollen banks, and trees stood waist-high in a sudden flood. The wolves appeared on peninsulas of land, pawing the earth and rushing back and forth in a frenzy. The scene was disappearing behind them with remarkable speed, shrinking in the spreading distance. Then the air was split by a long, bone-chilling howl. First one, then many. Heather looked away quickly.

They floated in silence for a few minutes, catching their breath. Heather closed her eyes and shook her head, as if she could wake up from what felt like a dream. But when she opened her eyes again, she saw the familiar sights of Nick Hollow sliding past her on the shore. She and Picket were passing the borders of the only place they'd ever known. The stream raced on, now passing long open fields dotted with small clumps of trees. Behind them the sky grew grey as rainclouds hovered ahead. But they sped on into cloudless skies and sunshine.

"I think we're safe, for now. We should be well clear of them in an hour," Uncle Wilfred said, gasping for breath but grinning defiantly in the direction of the tiny shapes. Heather managed a weary smile. She had never been as glad to see anything disappearing behind her as she was those horrible creatures and their wicked captain, Redeye. They had caused terror and destruction and had done who-knew-what to her parents and baby brother, as well as her friends at Elric's Farm. But they had been robbed of some of their plunder. They had fewer victims than they intended to get. Heather took grim satisfaction in that.

The boat steadied as the stream, which was still wide, grew calmer. They had a great burst of momentum and were moving along at a good clip, but the water was more predictable here, and they began to relax. Ahead the stream joined with Whitmer River, which rolled away south for unknown miles.

"Garlackson," Picket said. "Smalls called him 'Redeye Garlackson.'"

"Yes," Uncle Wilfred said through gritted teeth. "That's his bloody name. Redeye Garlackson," he said, spitting, "is as evil a creature as you'll find in the world. As Morbin Blackhawk is among the Lords of Prey, so Redeye Garlackson is among the wolves. And Morbin has got him for an awful alliance."

Heather's mind, now that she really was relaxed for the first time in a long time, filled with questions. "Is it the same Garlacks who fought King Jupiter in the Red Valley War?"

Uncle Wilfred's brows rose in some surprise. "Yes, that's his son back there, dear. I'm impressed," he said. "I wasn't sure your father would be telling you those tales."

"He hadn't really begun, until last night," she said, tears starting in her eyes. She still hadn't had time to cry over losing her parents and brother. It all began to weigh on her, and she turned her head away, sobbing softly.

Picket put his arm around her and said, "I'm not sure if it'll be all right. But I'm glad we're together." She put her head on his shoulder and nodded.

Uncle Wilfred said, "It will be all right, I think. We'll talk about a plan a bit later," and he crawled up to care for Smalls, who still lay unconscious in the prow of the little boat. "Smalls has had quite a knock. Don't worry; I know where we're going, and we'll be safe, at least for a little while. Please, try to rest."

Heather let herself be held by her brother, and they both watched Uncle Wilfred care for Smalls. He lifted the white rabbit's head gently and examined the knot there, nodded to himself, and searched in his satchel. He consulted a small book and made Smalls as comfortable as he could. Uncle Wilfred then sat beside him, holding his hand and looking at the young rabbit with the kind of concern their father showed when they were hurt. They looked so alike, Father and Uncle Wilfred.

"We didn't know we had any cousins," Heather said as their little boat slid from their swollen stream into the larger Whitmer, drifting quickly down the middle of the river.

Uncle Wilfred's eyes widened, and he looked around, not meeting her gaze. Eventually he nodded, saying nothing for a long while. He worked to straighten the boat in the increasing current of the river, then returned to attending Smalls.

Finally, he spoke again. He wasn't looking at them but from Smalls' peaceful face to the wide lands on the shore and the sinking sun above. "Smalls is a fine rabbit. As fine as any I've known. And that's saying a lot. I don't think you saw it, Heather, but he saved you. Without him, I never could have stopped Garlackson and that other wolf."

Heather wanted to ask about Uncle Wilfred's wife but was afraid to. There was too much of loss and sadness already in this tiny boat. She was afraid to raise another ghost to haunt them. *Perhaps,* she thought, *our aunt has been killed, along with who-knows-who-else? It is,* she considered gravely, *a terribly dangerous world.* She supposed it always had been, but she was only now really experiencing it.

"Heather," Uncle Wilfred said quietly. He nodded at Picket, who Heather could see, as she turned, was fast asleep. Finally able to relax, Picket had fallen asleep with his arm around Heather. He was leaning against her. She leaned into him with her head, snuggling against him, then laid him gently down and patted his hand.

Heather realized she was more exhausted than she could ever remember being. Her eyes drooped.

"You should get some rest too, Heather dear," Uncle Wilfred said, and he never looked more like Father, sitting there, smiling kindly down on her as the sun sank behind him. She half expected him to kiss her cheeks and whisper a blessing in her ear.

But he went back to caring for Smalls.

Then she did feel lost. *Where are you, Father? Where are you, Mother, and Baby Jacks?* She turned to look behind as all the world she knew disappeared in the far distance.

After the mad rushing and horrible noise of the last hours, the river was gentle and the surrounding country quiet. She crumpled beside Picket and fell asleep before the first star appeared.

Chapter Thirteen

BOAT ANSWERS

Heather could tell the sun was high in the sky even before she opened her eyes. She lay still, trying to remember where she was and why she was hurting all over.

Then it all came back to her: the storm, Lady Glen, the terrible fire, the wolves, her family killed or captured, and the wild flight to escape from Redeye Garlackson and his horrible band. So much had happened.

She felt the gently bobbing rhythm of the river as they continued to drift down it on the old boat. She felt Picket's presence beside her. Judging by the sound of snoring in her ear, he was sleeping deeply. At least that hadn't changed. She didn't want to disturb him, so she lay still a little longer. She opened her eyes for a moment and saw that Smalls was awake and huddled with Uncle Wilfred at the prow of the boat, their backs to her and Picket. As Uncle Wilfred shifted to look back at them, she closed her eyes.

She wasn't even sure why she did it. She just did. The two of them were talking. She felt like it was wrong to eavesdrop on these two who had been so kind to her, but now she wasn't sure what else to do.

"I think we should make for Cloud Mountain," Uncle Wilfred whispered, "wait it out a little while."

"That's what they want," Smalls said, anger just touching his words. "That's what they'll expect, for us to go to cover, to hide somewhere. Which is why I say we don't do it. What if we head straight for First Warren?"

"First Warren?" Uncle Wilfred said warily. "I don't like it. It would be so dangerous. Even if we somehow got in, the protectorate won't listen to us anymore. Winslow as good as banished us. Morbin's been in his ear too long. And anyway, what about these two?"

"Can we set them up somewhere—somewhere they can get up the mountain? Wouldn't Tommy Decker take them up?" Smalls said.

Heather could feel their eyes on her, and she tried to breathe easy and not move. Picket's sometimes raucous snorting snores made it hard to hear.

"We could leave them at Decker's and go on," Uncle Wilfred said. "But nowhere's really safe if Morbin's willing to send wolves this far out. I think we'd do best to go up ourselves. There'll be a citadel congress soon, and we should be there. Anyway, this is my family, these two. I think we'd all be better off to go on up."

"Maybe you're right. I want them safe, Wilfred," Smalls said, and there was a heaviness to his words. "I really do. But we have more than just them to think of."

"I know," Uncle Wilfred said. Heather squinted and saw that Uncle Wilfred had his hand on Smalls' back. "You know I'm on—" But he stopped talking as Picket snorted, stirred, and yawned loudly.

Heather was irritated. She wanted to hear more. Picket sat up, stretching, and Heather did the same.

"Welcome back to the land of the living," Smalls said.

"I was already awake," Picket said, rubbing his eyes and looking around, confused.

Heather shook her head. *Of course you were.*

"Good morning, shipmates," Uncle Wilfred said. "You're true sailors now, having passed a night on the water and under the stars."

"Add that to the list of firsts," Heather said, smiling weakly.

Smalls smiled back at her. "You were amazing yesterday, Heather," he said, crossing and extending his hand. Heather took it. He said, "I'm Smalls. I'm so glad to finally meet you when both of us are awake."

She laughed.

"My pleasure to meet you, Smalls. How's your head?"

"Nothing life-threatening," he said. "I've had much worse."

"Thank you so much for rescuing me," Heather said. "I would have been finished, for sure, without you, and you, Uncle."

"And Picket was very brave as well," Uncle Wilfred said.

*   *   *

107

Picket didn't believe he had been brave. He believed he had been saved, had stood by as his sister had been saved, and then had been lucky to be saved again. He was losing count of how many times he'd failed and needed rescuing. He saw Baby Jacks in his mind's eye and squinted against the rush of tears. He shook his head.

"You *were* brave, Picket," Heather said.

"Of course," Smalls said, laughing and turning to him. Smalls slid over and slapped him on the back. Picket pitched forward a bit but rebalanced quickly, looking sideways, back and forth. "You," Smalls said, pointing at him, "are my favorite mathematician. When ... well ... I'd love to see you as an engineer. Building things, solving problems."

Picket frowned. The dislike for Smalls he had felt when they first met was creeping back. Little things about the white rabbit irritated him. His fancy black scarf, the plain sword sheathed at his side, his strength. Why these things should bother him, he couldn't say. They just did. Picket imagined himself like a magnet and Smalls as another magnet, turned the wrong way. He looked at Smalls for a moment, then looked down and said quietly, "Thank you, Smalls. You saved Heather when I let her down, and I'll never forget that."

"C'mon, Picket," Wilfred said. "You never let anyone down. We all did what we could yesterday, and it turned out all right."

Picket wanted to argue, but he kept quiet.

For the next few minutes, Uncle Wilfred looked them each over, consulted his little book, and offered advice or encouragement about their many pains and wounds. He had clearly been around wounds of many kinds and was not alarmed by anything.

"You both should be fine with some rest and food," he pronounced, smiling at them. How much he looked like Father. It was both comforting and sad. Pain settled down deep in Picket. Since the disaster of yesterday morning, everything he saw and heard felt like another chapter in an awful story of pain.

"I am so sorry about your ear, Heather," Uncle Wilfred said, taking a small strip torn from a cloth in his satchel to bind the split ear together. "It's not anything that will hurt your hearing, but I'm afraid it may always be like that."

She smiled, but her eyes unfocused for a moment, and she winced. Picket saw that she was remembering a terrifying trial from yesterday. *So much pain.*

"It could have been much worse," she said.

"It's a mark of distinction," Smalls said. "It in no way diminishes your beauty."

Picket bristled.

"Uncle Wilfred," Heather said quickly, "where have you come from? How did you know we were in trouble? Why have we never met you?"

"Well, Heather dear," he said, "I know you have these and more questions. You're far too clever to be satisfied with ignorance. I like that." He grinned at his niece. "But we really need to get some food and rest. How about I give you the quick and almost totally unsatisfactory version?"

"Fine," she said. Picket realized he was starving.

"We're about a mile from Decker's Landing," Uncle Wilfred said. "It's run by an old friend, name of Tommy Decker. We'll see if old Decker has a meal for us. Later, we may have a chance to talk more."

"Thank you, Uncle," Heather said. "I don't know where we'd be without you and Smalls."

"Don't mention it, dear," he said, smiling down at her.

"I'll paddle," Smalls said, hopping to the oars with unexpected energy. He displayed his surprising strength as the lolling boat shot forward. Picket sniffed.

"Well, well," Uncle Wilfred began, "where to start?"

"Why not tell us where you and Smalls met?" Picket asked.

"Picket," Heather said, "can't you tell that Smalls is Uncle Wilfred's son? He's our cousin."

At this, Smalls faltered at the oars. Uncle Wilfred stammered a moment, then said, "Well, my dear nephew and niece, Smalls isn't …"

Smalls picked up as he trailed off. "I'm not his natural son. He has … adopted me."

Uncle Wilfred paused, then said, "Right."

"So you don't have a wife and kids?" Picket asked.

Heather shushed him. "Let him talk, Picket."

"No, Picket," Uncle Wilfred said sadly, "I don't have any family like that. Not anymore."

There were a few moments when no one spoke and the splashing of the oars was the lone, insistent sound. Smalls worked on, his black scarf trailing in the breeze.

"Uncle," Heather said, "what can we do to get Father and Mother and Jacks back? If they're still ... you know. If they're all right."

Picket sat up and clenched his fists.

"I'm sorry, dear. We can do nothing at present," he said. "We will alert those who need to know. But I'm sorry to say that they are best considered gone for now. And probably forever."

Picket's insides churned. He leaned over the side and was sick. He looked back to see Heather hang her head and cry. Picket closed his eyes, gasping. He saw a vision of Jacks looking up at him and, with an expression of unbearable sadness and confusion, wordlessly asking over and over, *"Where were you?"*

A long silence followed. The only sounds to be heard were the plunge and splash of angry strokes as Smalls tore at the water.

"They'll be taken to the Great Wood, or worse," Smalls said.

"What's so bad about the Great Wood?" Heather asked softly, tears standing out in her eyes.

"It is a ruin, Heather," Uncle Wilfred said. "And the crumbled wreck is ruled by pathetic puppets. Smalls and I came from the Great Wood. We were on our way to see you. I haven't seen my brother for a long time and haven't seen you, Heather, since you were a baby."

"You've seen me before?" Heather asked.

111

"Yes," Uncle Wilfred said. "I've seen you, but never Picket. Your parents are very dear to me. But I had work to do, and when you were born, they decided to leave, along with most families who could."

"We're coming up on Slender Bend in a few minutes," Smalls said.

Picket looked ahead at the bending river, then up and away to the right. He noticed how much the scenery had changed from when they sped away from Nick Hollow the previous day. There were high hills rising in the distance, the highest of which were ringed with mist.

"Ah, good," Uncle Wilfred said. "Up around this bend, our friend Decker has a home on the Whitmer. He's been here for years, gardening and living his own way. He was like your parents. He left the Great Wood for the safety of the wider world. Of course it used to be the reverse. Free rabbits would never have thought to leave the Great Wood for safety elsewhere. They would flock there for protection."

"And now you've left the Great Wood as well," Picket said. "Why?"

Uncle Wilfred and Smalls exchanged a knowing glance. "Because," Uncle Wilfred said, "things finally got so bad that we had to get out as well."

The oars bit hard into the water, and they shot forward. Smalls seemed to be seething.

"I'm sorry," Heather said, as much to Smalls as to Uncle Wilfred.

"We didn't know about the wolves at first," Uncle Wilfred went on. "We were away up north of Nick Hollow for a little while. But when we came south, we saw some signs of trouble. We made good time trying to get to your home. But we were too late. When we arrived, the elm was burning, and we knew there were too many enemies to attempt a rescue."

"You saw Mother and Father?" Heather asked, and Picket's breath caught.

Uncle Wilfred nodded sadly. "And the baby."

"Jacks!" Picket said. "How were they?"

"They were hurt," Uncle Wilfred said. "I won't lie. Your father looked bad."

Picket's head drooped. He sniffed and said, "I'm sure he kept fighting until they made him stop."

"I think so," Uncle Wilfred agreed. "That would be like him. But they were all alive. At least, they were then."

After a few more moments of silence, Smalls said, "Nearly to Slender Bend."

Picket saw ahead that the river started to shrink, bent a couple of times, and then disappeared around a corner.

"What will we do, Uncle?" Heather asked.

"I'm not sure yet," he said.

Picket shook his head. "I can't believe they've been taken."

"Get used to it, lad," Smalls said, rowing harder and harder.

"I'm not your lad," Picket spat, his anger and resentment boiling over. "Sorry if I'm upset that we just lost our family."

Smalls laughed bitterly and shook his head.

"Picket, don't—" Uncle Wilfred began.

But Picket's pain was rising inside him like bile, and this sword-bearing, scarf-wearing little rabbit was going to hear it. "How would you know," Picket shouted, "how it feels to lose those you love most? I'm sick of your charming, stuck-up attitude and your 'lad' this and your 'lad' that. I'm not a kid anymore. I don't need permission from you to think or talk. I don't like you, and I don't want to hear you talking to me like I'm a little child."

Uncle Wilfred made to speak again, but Smalls shook his head. He stopped rowing for a moment as the river narrowed around them. He turned to look at Picket, and there were tears in his eyes. "Picket," he said quietly, "stay angry. It's okay if it's at me, for now. If you aren't angry about the wicked things happening in the world all around, then you don't have a soul."

There was silence as they rounded the S curve of Slender Bend. Then Heather screamed. Everyone looked ahead.

Decker's Landing was on fire.

Chapter Fourteen

FOREST FLIGHT

We need to get to shore," Uncle Wilfred said. "Now!" Smalls stabbed the water with one oar, and the boat spun quickly to face the shore. Then he dug in with both oars, and they shot forward. The boat raced ahead to the rocky shore of the Whitmer River a little ways upstream of Decker's Landing. Heather could see it was once a pretty little place with a long, wide deck and a cozy home on a high frame above the water. She thought of home and clenched her fists.

"Stay low," Uncle Wilfred said, though he didn't need to. They had all shrunk low as if an owl was flying above. He was looking all around, and Heather did the same, searching for signs of movement anywhere. She saw them first.

"There," Heather whispered sharply, pointing to several loping wolves on a ridge above and behind the burning home. "Seven."

"Yes," Uncle Wilfred said, nodding. "Well-spotted, Heather." He motioned for quiet and pointed at some reeds near the shore.

"It's not Garlackson, is it?" Heather whispered.

"No," Uncle Wilfred whispered back. "It's his wolves, under his command, but a different company. It would take Garlackson a while to get here."

"Decker?" Smalls asked.

"No sign of struggle from them," Uncle Wilfred whispered, squinting to see through the haze of heat and swirling smoke. "Maybe he got out in time."

They reached the shore, and Smalls, shedding the oars with ease, deftly hopped from the boat to the water with barely a splash. Uncle Wilfred did the same, and the two of them pulled the boat to shore quickly. They dragged it in among some reeds and hid it as best they could. Heather saw that Picket was looking this way and that, uncertain of what to do.

"Let's go, Picket," she said, taking his arm. He shrugged off her help and hopped to the stony shore.

"I'm not a child," he said.

"Quiet," Smalls said, not looking back. Picket bristled.

Smalls crept forward and made hand gestures to Uncle Wilfred. He pointed ahead and to himself, then to the rest of them and to the ground. Heather assumed he meant "Stay here, while I go ahead."

Uncle Wilfred huddled with Heather and Picket while Smalls crept ahead. They watched Smalls dart quickly through an open patch. He dove, landing behind a large oak on a knoll near what was left of Decker's Landing. Smalls found cover and peered around.

"What's he doing?" Picket whispered.

"He's scouting their location," Uncle Wilfred said. "Seeing if we can slip past them unseen."

"He'll do anything for attention," Picket muttered, then quickly winced.

"That's unjust," Uncle Wilfred whispered sharply, frowning, "and ungrateful. If it weren't for Smalls, Heather'd be dead, I'd be dead, and you would have had a time of it yourself."

Picket looked down and muttered something indistinct.

Heather ached, but she wasn't sure what she could do for Picket. He was having a hard time, she knew. But they had bigger things to worry about.

"Okay," Uncle Wilfred said, "he's tracking them now."

Heather looked up to where Smalls was peeking out from behind the oak. His scarf flapped behind him, and his sword dangled at his side. Smalls' hand, when it wasn't busy in some other way, went instinctively to the hilt of that sword. Smalls signaled "seven" with his hands, then gave a thumbs-up. The number of enemies was confirmed. He pointed at Heather, Picket, and Uncle Wilfred, then to a rock formation a hundred yards inland to their right. It stood on the edge of the forest, as well-concealed a place as any. Uncle Wilfred extended his own thumb in a signal back to Smalls. Smalls nodded and resumed his watch.

"The rocky ground, over there at the forest edge," Uncle Wilfred said. Heather and Picket both nodded. "We're going to run for it. Soon. It's our best bet to get past these wolves."

"So we're running from them; is that it?" Picket said, shaking his head.

"Of course we are," Uncle Wilfred said, his frown returning.

Heather looked back at Smalls. He extended a flat hand, which she took as a signal to wait. Then came one finger lifted and waved up and down, almost bouncing.

"Be ready," Uncle Wilfred said. "We have to run full-out, do you understand? We cannot be seen. You have to run hard and focus on the woods. Run for the woods! We go when Smalls points to us." As soon as the words were out of his mouth, Smalls pointed urgently at them.

They ran.

* * *

Picket saw that Heather led them in the sprint. She would make it safely if any of them did. Behind her was Uncle Wilfred, who was slowed by looking back at Smalls, to make sure he was on his way. Picket came last. He also kept checking back to see where Smalls was and looking beyond to where the enemy wolves were. He wanted to prove he wasn't afraid, that Smalls wasn't the only one with courage.

After a few seconds of watching, Smalls left his tree knoll and pounded the ground toward the cover of the thick trees. Picket was amazed at how fast Smalls was. His scarf blew behind him as he raced towards them with incredible speed.

He may even be faster than Heather. Add that to the list of his irritating perfections.

Picket stole one more glance at the wolves on the ridge. He saw the silhouette of a wolf half-turn toward them. Heart racing, Picket turned his head quickly toward the forest edge and tried to increase his speed.

It didn't work. He tripped awkwardly on a jutting rock. He somersaulted, out of control, and fell heavily in a long slide.

He was in the open.

His foot throbbed, and he barely stifled a cry of pain. He shook his head to clear it and saw Uncle Wilfred ahead in the forest, holding Heather back. He lay there, exposed to the view of the wolves. Anger rose in him once more, resentment at this whole horrible situation and how useless he felt. The wolves would have him, and probably Heather and the rest as well. It would all be his fault.

Then he felt a blow. Strong arms grabbed him roughly; he was being lifted and carried. He saw white fur and a blur of black cloth waving.

Smalls was carrying him to safety.

Chapter Fifteen

Picket's Check

Picket knew he had a chance right now to get past his resentment of Smalls. He had done it before, inside Seven Mounds, when he had managed to forget his resentment during the crisis of their escape. Danger still hovered around them; enemies were everywhere. Why not just apologize to Smalls, to everyone, and move on?

But he couldn't do it. It would feel too much like surrendering ground he felt entitled to. To give it up would cost him too much.

They were running again. Well, most of them were. Picket was limping through the forest. His foot screamed for attention. He had jammed it on the rock, but he rejected any help offered. Smalls had saved him from being spotted by the wolves. At least, they hoped so. Once Smalls set him down, Picket wasn't about to let the white rabbit carry him even one step farther.

"We have to hurry," Uncle Wilfred called back. "If they saw us, then we have almost no time." He squinted at Picket and looked down at his foot. "We're not safe yet."

They made their way carefully but quickly deeper and deeper into the forest. Picket had no idea where they were and even less idea where they were going. The only place he had heard mentioned on the boat trip downriver was Decker's Landing. Of course, that place was turning to ash and cinders right now. He knew of nothing within miles, and almost nothing he knew of in the world was as it had been. Nowhere felt safe.

The branches flicked him as the others moved ahead. He hobbled on, hoping they were close to escaping. But escaping to where?

Uncle Wilfred darted past trees and through unfamiliar paths. They moved quickly back and forth, on the trail for a time, then off again. The forest grew denser, and tree limbs bent low and heavy all around and over, hovering like a worried mother. Picket felt smothered. Nick Hollow was so open and full of sunlight. At least it had been. Now the memory of the place was as grey as the sky had been yesterday, when the world he knew had disappeared in flames. He could still smell smoke in the air. For all he knew every home in the world was burning.

They ran on. Picket's foot throbbed. He tried to hop on one foot for several steps, then risk one excruciating step on his bad foot, but it was becoming impossible. He lagged behind. He thought he might have to shout out, to scream that he couldn't go on, but he limped on, biting his hand to keep from crying out. What frustrated him most was that this darting between path and brush was something he was usually good at. He could have rivaled the agility Smalls was showing, maybe even outmatched him, if he knew the way and hadn't been injured. Instead he hobbled along, bringing up the rear. Heather kept dropping back to make it seem like he wasn't going much slower than she was, but he knew she was just trying to make him feel better. He managed to be angry at her for this, though he knew it was unfair.

They cut through a clearing, then shot down a steep slope, thickly wooded once more. Picket was getting dizzy with the pain and confused about where they were. His foot ached so badly that he almost fell, catching himself on a tree. He restarted quickly, though Heather had seen.

"I have to stop," she called out ahead.

Smalls, who was directly in front of Heather and behind Uncle Wilfred, spun and ran to her. "Are you all right?" he asked.

"I'm okay," she said. "I just need a moment to rest."

Smalls looked at her with a question in his expression. He didn't buy it, Picket knew. She cast a quick glance back at Picket. Smalls nodded. Picket was thankful for the rest, but he hated being the one who needed it.

"I could use a rest too," Smalls said, sinking to the ground, puffing loudly.

Picket turned his back to them and sank onto the turf. He grabbed a thick stick and squeezed it to distract his mind from the pain.

"What's up?" he heard Uncle Wilfred say. Picket's head was down. "Why're we stopping?" Then there was a silence.

Picket was aware that these two—the new best of friends, Heather and Smalls—were subtly pointing at him.

"Well, I needed a puff as well," Uncle Wilfred said, walking back to Picket.

Picket quickly wiped his eyes and looked up as Uncle Wilfred came to sit in front of him. The pain was agonizing.

"Let me have a look at that foot," Uncle Wilfred said.

"It's nothing," Picket began. But, not waiting for permission, Uncle Wilfred knelt in front of him, taking hold of his foot firmly.

"Ouch!" Picket cried, snapping the stick he was holding.

"Yes, son. It's clearly nothing," Uncle Wilfred said, frowning. He lowered his voice so the others couldn't hear. "You're stubborn, Picket. And you're acting like a fool."

Picket's head dropped and tears slid from his eyes. It was true; he knew it.

"I know you're hurt and life is not a meadow picnic right now, but there's the kind of foolish that's forgivable and the kind that gets good rabbits killed."

Picket looked up. "What do you mean?"

"Well, young sir. If you'd done as I said, your foot would be fine. But you're too preoccupied with fuming at Smalls to pay attention and follow orders. And you're so maddeningly proud now that you can't even admit your foot's hurt."

"I can handle the pain," Picket said.

"No, you can't," Uncle Wilfred said, feeling the foot again. "Your foot is fractured. I can feel it. So your arrogant insistence that you can run means you're making it worse with every step. With every step, you make the time it'll take to heal that much longer, putting everyone, including your sister Heather, in terrible danger."

Picket looked away, not bothering to wipe away the tears that slid down his face.

"Now, son," Uncle Wilfred said, taking Picket's face in his hands. "I'm for you. I'm on your side, and I love you. But there's something you need to know. As much as I love your parents, Baby Jacks, and you and Heather, I have to protect Smalls. And right now, you're making it very hard for me to do that."

"I'm sorry," Picket said. "Just leave me here and go on with Smalls. But please, take Heather with you."

"Don't be a fool, son," Uncle Wilfred said. "I'll carry you on my back. We don't have much farther to go."

Picket bowed his head again and his jaw tightened. *Will I be humiliated at every turn?*

"Be careful of resentment and pride, Picket," Uncle Wilfred said. "They've been the undoing of many a great rabbit."

"I can't seem to stop," Picket whispered, looking away.

"Your father only began to tell you of King Jupiter, I know, but do you know your Whitson Mariner?" Uncle Wilfred asked.

"Yes," Picket said. "We've had those stories from the crib."

"Do you remember about the first boat, about the resentment Whitson felt when Rangel's crowd laughed at him?"

Picket was silent for a while. Finally, he managed to say,

in a hoarse whisper, "But I'm not like Whitson Mariner. I'm like Rangel."

Uncle Wilfred looked into Picket's eyes. "Do the stories say if Rangel eventually joined the trekkers in the boat and made the crossing with Whitson?"

They didn't, Picket knew. But his throat felt tight, and he could only shake his head.

"Interesting," Uncle Wilfred said, getting to his feet. "Then we don't know how his story turned out either."

Chapter Sixteen

STRANGERS IN THE MIST

Picket rode on Uncle Wilfred's back, silently sulking all the way. He felt like a small child, like Baby Jacks. A burden. His foot hurt, but Uncle Wilfred had wrapped it tightly, and that was some help.

Heather and Smalls followed behind them. Whenever Uncle Wilfred turned in the path, Picket caught glimpses of Heather. Sometimes she was looking up at him with worry; other times she and Smalls were talking. Smalls had his sword drawn some of the time, eyeing the woods carefully. Picket couldn't really explain, even to himself, why he resented Smalls. Part of him was ashamed of the way he was acting, but he just couldn't stop. It felt so very right to be angry, and there was Smalls, just asking for it.

They went on and on, tired, hungry, and sore. The trees hung heavy and low. They were climbing, Picket realized, slowly and steadily upward. The air was moist, and the moss around the tree bottoms grew thick. A mist rose and hung all about the trees like a garish white cloak. They took many hidden paths through concealed hedges

127

and up haunted hollows. Picket closed his eyes.

He must have dozed off. When he awoke, they were ascending a steep rocky hillside in the heavy mist.

They slowed. Uncle Wilfred nodded to Smalls, who unrolled a cloak from his pack and draped himself in it. Uncle Wilfred, after lowering Picket, did likewise.

"There it is," Uncle Wilfred said, stopping on a small stretch of flat ground partway up the mountain. "The Savory Den."

Picket saw a thick mist settling around a cave mouth overhung by gnarled ancient trees. A small stream ran beside the wide cave mouth, and water trickled over the entrance, splashing onto the stone below, before sliding down into the stream.

"Can we drink?" Heather asked, pointing to the stream.

"Let's make sure it's secure," Smalls said, passing in front of Wilfred and drawing his sword once more. He pulled a hood up and over his head, folding his ears beneath it. He was hard to recognize, but by now Picket could have spotted those deft movements from across a ridge. Picket watched him closely. Smalls moved like a soldier who had done this a thousand times. He seemed to be aware of everything. His arms were strong, Picket knew, but he gripped his sword loosely, almost casually. He seemed almost at ease but on the verge of springing into action. It was mesmerizing to Picket, who had dreamed a thousand times of moving just this way. Then he saw Heather watching Smalls with admiration, and the all-too-familiar resentment, like a stomachache, gurgled up inside him again.

Uncle Wilfred looked at Picket. "Please don't move," he said. "Just wait here a moment." Uncle Wilfred drew his own sword and passed beyond Heather to just behind Smalls. They crept silently, looking everywhere. Picket didn't understand this, as there was nowhere to hide, either behind or in front of them.

"Stand fast!" they heard a voice cry out. In the heavy mist, Picket couldn't see where it came from or who said it. "Take another step, and it'll be a bellyful of arrows for you."

"I'm so hungry," Smalls said calmly, "I'd eat about anything now."

"Make a sudden move, little one," the voice called out again, "and you'll have your wish."

"Have anything savory or dennish?" Uncle Wilfred said.

The wind picked up, blowing a swath of mist away like a drawn curtain. There, beyond the cave, a tall brown rabbit stood on a rock. He had a bow, though it wasn't nocked with an arrow. Several rabbits stood behind him, arranged in staggered rows on each side, like a V.

"Is that Wilfred?" the stranger asked, an edge to his words.

"It is," Uncle Wilfred said, squinting up. "Is that Pacer?"

"The same," the stranger said, bowing. He straightened and descended, his eyes on Uncle Wilfred, with an occasional uneasy glance at Smalls.

Pacer was a long, lean rabbit, with weary eyes and a voice that was quiet but hard and cautious.

"It's been a long time," Pacer said, crossing to Uncle Wilfred. Smalls drew even with Uncle Wilfred, his hand playing at his sword-hilt. They stood apart, Uncle Wilfred and Pacer, and Picket thought this was a very cold reunion. Pacer's small gang of rabbits, all dressed in green and all with arrows ready on their bowstrings, stood behind him.

"We've come far, and we're very hungry," Uncle Wilfred said. "We need to get inside."

"No one enters unless Lord Rake gives the word," Pacer said, nodding to a rabbit just behind him. The rabbit moved quickly into the cave.

"How long has that been the law?" Smalls asked. Picket noticed some irritation in Smalls' tone. He enjoyed it.

"Since our most recent betrayals," Pacer said. "It's hard to trust anyone, regardless of their family connections."

They looked on in silence. Picket was confused, but part of him reveled in the quiet anger simmering in Smalls. But Smalls stood still, looking cautiously around.

"It is an evil age when old friends aren't welcomed quickly," Uncle Wilfred said. "But I understand your caution."

They heard footsteps, and Picket felt a surge of panic. *This is not how I imagined this happening.* O   ve came a tall rabbit with grey and white f   He w   an Uncle Wilfred, well-dressed, and wore a gold c .ain around his neck with a bright pendant. His cape was grey and his bearing elegant. He wore a long sword with an elaborate silver hilt. His white tunic bore a simple crest, two diamonds side by side, touching, the left one red and the right green.

He walked quickly to Wilfred, glancing at Smalls. Wilfred stepped forward, and Picket caught his breath.

The two rabbits embraced, wordlessly, and Picket thought he saw the beginnings of tears in the lordly rabbit's eyes. He breathed again.

"I am so glad to see you," the new rabbit said to Uncle Wilfred as Pacer bowed and stepped back. "You are very welcome, friends."

"Thank you, lord," Uncle Wilfred said. "Lord Rake, may I introduce my niece and nephew, Heather and Picket?"

"I am delighted to meet you both," Lord Rake said. "All that I have is at your disposal. I see you are injured, Picket. Pacer, please send someone for Emma. And Gort as well, while he's at it." Pacer nodded, and another of his lieutenants disappeared inside the cave. As Pacer turned, Picket noticed that the twin-diamond crest, here set on a white field, was stitched on the shoulder of all the rabbits they were meeting.

"And this," Uncle Wilfred said, "is Smalls."

"Smalls," he said, nodding. "It's my pleasure to meet you."

"I'm sorry to cut short the introductions, Lord Rake, but is Tommy Decker here?" Uncle Wilfred asked. "The landing is destroyed, and there are wolves down there."

Lord Rake looked down, his smile vanished. "Decker's gone. He sent a message to us, but he didn't make it. The wolves—" he started, but he didn't finish.

Heather gasped and Picket winced. Uncle Wilfred's face fell. Smalls crossed to him and put a hand on his shoulder.

The small crowd around the cave entrance—Pacer and his rabbits, the newcomers and Lord Rake—bowed their heads. Picket could see that Decker had been loved by all. Lord Rake looked up at last and took in the scene of bowed heads. He glanced at Smalls, then said in a strong, defiant voice, "It will not be so in the Mended Wood!"

Then the group, all but Picket and Heather, each struck the air with a fist and called out in an echoing reply, "The Mended Wood!"

Chapter Seventeen

FOOD AND FRIENDSHIP

Heather was surprised at how each face had changed at the call of "The Mended Wood." She knew neither what it meant nor why it should be any comfort to them after the death of their friend.

"Decker was a kingsbuck, loyal always," Uncle Wilfred said, and Lord Rake nodded. "He'll be missed."

"That's right. There was never a doubt about *his* loyalty," Pacer said. Lord Rake frowned at him.

Heather saw that Smalls wanted to speak, but after almost beginning a few times, he settled into silence.

"He has been our lookout for many years," Lord Rake said. "Now we are more vulnerable than ever. Instead of a lookout, we'll have a garrison of wolves down there."

Then two more rabbits emerged from the cave. One was short and nearly as wide as he was high. He walked out, swaying back and forth, almost as if he might fall over and start rolling down the mountain each time he took a step. The other was a lovely auburn-red rabbit with white spots, dressed in a plain white frock, carrying a black bag.

"Ah," Lord Rake said, "Emma, will you see to this young rabbit, please?" He motioned to Picket, and she bowed, then walked over quickly. Lord Rake and Uncle Wilfred then joined in conversation with the wide rabbit called Gort.

"Hello," Emma said, smiling wide.

"Hello," Heather said, crossing to greet her. She stood beside Picket, who still sat on the ground and looked more uncomfortable than ever. "You're Emma, are you? Well, it's not fair that we know your name and you don't know ours."

Emma laughed. "No, not fair at all. But I shall endeavor to overcome this devastating calamity," She looked to be of an age with Heather.

Heather pointed to herself dramatically. "I'm Heather, and this sour grape here is Picket," jabbing her elbow in his direction.

"Well," Emma said, laughing, "I'll see what I can do for his bad foot, though there's nothing in my bag that cures pouting." The girls laughed again, Heather urging Picket to laugh along. She had only meant to try to lighten his mood. He attempted a smile, but then his head drooped again. She had often used this method to cheer him up, but he appeared to be beyond help at present.

"All right, Captain Grouchypants," Emma said. "Let's have a look at that foot of yours."

"It's fine," Picket said stubbornly.

Emma raised her eyebrows, "It is?" She flicked his foot with her finger, and Picket cried out. "I see, yes. It seems perfectly fine. No problems. I'm glad young bucks are always honest." She exchanged a look of disapproval with Heather, then set to work on the wrap that Uncle Wilfred had hastily made in the forest. "That's a fine wrap. Did you do that?" she asked Heather.

"No," Heather said. She wished she had known how. "It was Uncle Wilfred."

"He's no stranger to doctoring," Emma said.

Heather watched and Picket winced as Emma deftly undid the field wrap and made a careful examination of Picket's foot, feeling for the bones and wincing along with Picket. She opened a wide, short pot and dipped some goo out and slathered it on the foot. "For the pain," she said; then she redid the wrap, carefully but quickly. "We'll help you inside," she said, motioning for Heather to take one of his arms around her neck while she took the other. "Now, listen, Grouchy. I'm commanding you to never put weight on that foot until I, or one of the doctors, say it's okay. We'll have some crutches made in no time."

Picket grunted assent.

"Will Lord Rake make them?" Heather asked as they hobbled along, supporting Picket, toward where Lord Rake, Uncle Wilfred, Gort, and some others clustered around the cave mouth.

"No," Emma said. "Lord Rake is no craftsman. There'll be craftsmen lined up to make them."

"Really?" Heather asked, but they had reached the others.

"All right now, Master Picket?" Lord Rake asked.

"Fine, sir. Thank you," Picket answered softly.

"Well done, Emma," Lord Rake said. She curtsied as best she could without knocking Picket over. "Emma's an apprentice now, but Doctor Zeiger says she'll make a fine doctor soon. I'm very proud of her."

Emma made as if to smooth her ears dramatically and look pompous. Then she laughed. Lord Rake joined in and theatrically frowned at her, shaking his head. Heather smiled. She definitely liked Emma. Then she caught a whiff of something wonderful. Her stomach growled loudly.

Lord Rake laughed and said, "You must be starving! Gort says we're ready to eat, so come on in, and you'll be served first."

They passed through the cave mouth and were sprinkled with bursting pellets of falling water. Thick mist mingled with the fetching smell of soup on the fire. The swirling clouds of appetizing aromas filled the recesses of the cave.

"I could eat a house," Picket grumbled.

"You're in luck!" Gort shouted, wheezing with laughter as he waddled through the cave. "I have prepared a culinary castle for your bellies."

It was dark inside the cave and the mist was gone. There were lighted torches along the wall once they had gotten far enough inside. They were following a long passage. The smell was incredible. Heather hadn't realized how hungry and weak she was. She sagged. Half-carrying Picket was using the last of her energy. But she pressed on. How many times in the last two days had she believed she was at the end of her strength, only to somehow find more?

The cave's long passage opened into a larger room, wide and deep, where many rabbits were seated at tables and eating. Many of them wore the same green that Pacer wore; others varied. Some were dressed elegantly, like Lord Rake, but most were dressed simply. Heather saw one tall, strong rabbit in the corner, eating alone. He alone among all those there did not raise his head and look when they came in. He was dark in color and, it appeared to Heather, in mood. He brooded in the corner while others chatted happily. But some frowned when they saw the strangers.

"My friends," Lord Rake said, bowing slightly to his guests, "the Savory Den." He motioned with his hand, and all the rabbits inside, except one, made a short bow. Most appeared friendly, but a few stared hard at Uncle Wilfred, concern blooming on their faces.

"Thank you," Heather said. Smalls and Uncle Wilfred, both hooded, returned the bows.

Emma helped Picket to a seat, then smiled. "I'll be right back with your soup," she said to them all. She walked away from them and disappeared down another passage.

"Thank you!" Heather called after her. She sat down beside Picket. Uncle Wilfred and Smalls sat across from them at the wooden table, their backs to most of the room.

* * *

Picket winced again at the pain shooting through his foot, but he tried to conceal it. What would it be like if he'd been hurt like this at home? Father would have carried him to his bed. Mother would have fussed over him for days. Heather would have … but Heather was right here beside him. At least there was that. A ray of light in a dark cave. Baby Jacks, Father, and Mother were gone, but he still had his sister. He looked up at her, a smile forming on his lips. But she was looking at Smalls. The ray of light went dark, and he slumped.

It was in this dark frame of mind that Picket first saw someone in the corner, a tall black rabbit. Another rabbit was walking toward him, a wary courage showing on his face. "May I sit down?" the approaching rabbit asked. The black rabbit said nothing, only looked up from his soup for a moment, stared coldly at the friendly rabbit, then went back to eating. The friendly rabbit walked away, dejected.

Picket was impressed, right off, by how physically imposing the black rabbit was. But Picket also felt a kinship in his furious loneliness. It was exactly how Picket felt. If he could wordlessly push everyone around him away, he would.

"How are you holding up, Picket?" Uncle Wilfred asked.

"Fine," Picket said softly.

Smalls took the room in, a smile on his lips. Emma appeared in a corner of the room with a tray bearing four brimming bowls of soup. Picket's mouth watered.

"Here you are, friends," Emma said, serving them.

Slurpy thanks were said as the four hungry travelers dove into their bowls. Emma smiled at them, then at Gort, who was hovering not too far away. Emma raised her hands and mimed clapping for Gort. He looked down, trying not to smile. The contented sighs and quickly emptied bowls seemed to serve Gort the same way the meal was serving the weary four. He beamed.

Bread was brought, along with refilled bowls of soup. Picket tried to decipher the ingredients in the soup, knew they included mushrooms, potatoes, and carrots. He could get no further. It was the best thing he'd ever eaten, and he had never needed to eat so badly.

Uncle Wilfred and Smalls, after eating a few bowls, removed to a corner to talk privately with Lord Rake. The three younger rabbits ate in silence, though occasionally Emma had a question for them about where they came from.

Then a group of young rabbits, about Heather's age or older, entered the room. There were five of them, and their leader was a tall handsome rabbit of a strange and familiar color. He was grey and gold, kind of like Picket. A rare coloring. He was taller than Picket, however, and his attitude was definitely different. The others seemed to defer to him, copying his gait and exuberant manner.

The tall rabbit deftly swiped a long slice of bread, whipping it casually to an accomplice while he mesmerized Gort with a joke. While Gort wheezed, a few more items were pilfered from the food line. They left Gort and, noticing Picket and Heather, came sauntering over.

"I'll catch up with you at the well, gents," the tall one said to his four friends. They nodded and left.

"Poisoning the well tonight, Kyle?" Emma asked. "That would get you some attention, since you're so desperate for it."

"Great to see you too, Emma," Kyle said. "Not poisoning the well, no. Just going to throw somebody down it."

"Great," Emma said, "That's an escalation even of your already profound immaturity."

"We're just going to teach somebody a lesson, that's all," Kyle said, smiling like he was put on earth for the purpose of smiling. "Won't you introduce me to your new friends?"

"I probably shouldn't," she said.

"I'm Heather," Heather said, shaking hands with Kyle. "This is my brother, Picket." Picket waved.

"Kyle's the name, and the game is—well, it's all a game," he said, bowing slightly. "At your service. If you need information on a rival, mishap on your masters, escape from your duties, or are looking to have a reckless ramble, I'm your rabbit."

"Go on, you rascal," Emma said, shooing him away.

"Nice to meet you, Kyle," Heather said, smiling.

"Hey," Kyle said, catching Picket's eye. "Don't let this crummy place get you down. There are ways to have some fun here." He winked at Picket, bowed slightly to Heather and Emma, did a smooth shuffle-dance toward the door, and walked slowly away, bobbing as he went. He stopped and chatted with Pacer, Lord Rake's lieutenant, casting sideways glances back at Heather and Picket. Soon Pacer was smiling and whispering back. Bowing to Pacer, then clapping him on the back, Kyle headed for the door with one backward glance their way.

"Sounds like a real sweetheart," Heather said, giggling. "Everyone he talks to breaks out in a smile. Except Picket, of course."

"Because I'm not a silly doe," Picket said sourly.

"No, you're a very mature grown-up, that's for sure," Heather said, frowning.

"He's charming, true," Emma said in a scolding tone, "but he's also a wily, arrogant, mischievous, self-centered hooligan. Other than that, he's fine."

"Sounds terrific," Picket said absently.

"He's actually pretty harmless, I think," Emma said. "Just cocky and restless. But there's something about him …"

Smalls and Uncle Wilfred made their way back to the table, resuming their meal. They tried to act normally but were clearly troubled by their talk with Lord Rake. Their silence was heavy with questions.

When they had all eaten their fill, Picket felt more exhausted than he could ever remember. He yawned loudly. It spread to Heather, and she also yawned, apologizing afterward. Then it couldn't be helped. Smalls and Uncle Wilfred yawned as well, and soon they were all blinking as the room grew dark.

Lord Rake crossed to their table. "You'll need rest, of course," he said, pointing to the door from which Emma had brought the soup. "Emma will show you to your rooms. My friends, there is much more to this place, our Cloud

Mountain, than you have seen. Please know you are welcome here for as long as you should like to stay. I hope you shall decide to join our community. I speak for the entire council when I say you are most welcome."

"That's very kind," Heather said, and Picket bowed. "Are you the lord here?" Heather asked.

Lord Rake smiled. "I am," he said. "But I answer to the council. And we are all loyal to the fallen and the future king."

"Who is that?" Heather asked.

"King Jupiter is dead, Heather," he said sadly, "but we remember what he built, and we look for his heir to rise and recover what's been lost." He absently fingered the crest on his chest. A red diamond alongside a green diamond.

"Then we are in the right place, I think," Heather said, bowing.

"You are," he said, laying his hand gently on her head. "I'm sorry that answers will come a little slowly here. So that we might be as free as possible, we live under certain laws. An important but frustrating one is the law of initiates. You will be initiated into this community, but there is a trial period before anyone is allowed to give you very much information. I beg your pardon for this, as I'm certain it is frustrating, but I assure you it is a law of good cause and consequence. We are all bound to it. Now, you must be exhausted."

Emma bowed quickly to Lord Rake and said, "If you'll follow me, friends."

"We'll talk more later," Uncle Wilfred said to Lord Rake, then quietly, so no one else could hear, "I didn't know he was here," he said, nodding to the corner where the black rabbit brooded.

"We'll talk about it," Lord Rake whispered back. Then louder, he said, "I'll wake you if there's trouble. My scouts are in the forest."

"I know it's vitally important to keep this place safe, Lord Rake," Smalls said. "If we need to go, we will."

Lord Rake nodded his acknowledgment, and they followed Emma to the passage in the corner.

"Where does this cave lead down to?" Heather asked.

"Not down," Emma said. "It leads up."

"Up?" Heather asked.

"Yes. Up and up."

"What is this place?" Heather asked as they reached the doorway.

"This," Emma said, turning to face them all and raising both her hands, as if to indicate all around them, "is a seed of the new world."

Smalls smiled at Uncle Wilfred. Heather and Picket wore puzzled expressions.

Emma went on. "We are the heralds of the Mended Wood."

Chapter Eighteen

An Orphan World

Heather came awake slowly, her eyes still closed, trying to remember where she was and how she had gotten there. She opened her eyes and found she was in a small, neat room, and Picket was asleep on a bed across from her. In the fog of waking, she noticed that the beds were arranged much like their room on the second floor of their home at Nick Hollow. She smiled. Then it began to come back to her—the terrible ordeal of their flight, the fiery end of the life they had known.

It started again, the now-familiar churning of sadness, anger, and hopelessness in her stomach. She looked around the small room, and what she saw had a settling effect. There were, she saw by the faint light streaming in, paintings on the wall and subtle beauties all around. Her mother painted, but not like this.

Heather had been so tired and it had been so dark the night before, she had barely cared if there was a bed. She was asleep when her head hit the pillow. Now, she stared long at each painting, captive to the beauty on display and the curious feeling of hope it stirred in her.

"Who could make such things?" she heard. She turned to see Picket, leaning on his elbow, staring past her as the colorful wall came alive in the growing light of morning.

"I don't know," she said. "But I'm very glad they have."

Picket said nothing more and both rabbits looked on. One painting in particular held Heather's attention. It was large, colorful, and amazingly realistic. It depicted a hollow home in a forest surrounded by several others, with a great garden between all. Heather felt as though she might easily walk into it. She wanted to.

It appeared to be the same small glen depicted in the painting above the fireplace at their Nick Hollow home, the painting Mother had often stared at, weeping. It wasn't from the same angle, but Heather believed it might be the same place. The longer she stared, the more sure she was. She noticed in a corner what she guessed must be the painter's initials: "F. S."

There was a knock, and Heather crossed to open the door.

"Good morning, Emma!" Heather said, delighted to see her. Emma had led the exhausted rabbits to this room last night, where they had fallen asleep immediately.

"Good morning, friends," Emma said cheerfully. "I hope you slept well. You have certainly slept long enough."

"I feel rested, thank you," Heather said. "And thank you so much for taking such great care of us."

"I'm delighted to serve," Emma said, reaching an arm around Heather. "And how's the Fractured Footfellow?" she said, smiling at Picket.

Picket did not smile, but he replied with reserved politeness, "I'm feeling well. Thank you, Emma."

"I am glad to hear it," she said, raising her eyebrows at Heather and crossing to where he sat. "May I take a look at it?"

"Of course," he said.

She undid the wrap and examined the injured foot, then redid the bandage as Picket winced here and there, always trying to pretend it didn't hurt as much as it clearly did.

"Doctor Zeiger will be in later to see you, Picket," she said. "He's a bit strange in the way he talks—he's from far away from here, farther still than you two and your funny way of speaking. But he'll take good care of you."

"Thank you," Picket said. He was still sullen, Heather noticed, but some of his anger appeared to have subsided. He seemed not so much resentful and angry as regretful and weary. She worried for a moment that he would never be anything but the sullen, dour rabbit she saw before her. Where was the carefree brother she had always known? Gone, along with all their past life, she supposed.

"I have something else for you," Emma said, disappearing out of the room for a moment. She returned with a pair of ornately carved crutches. Heather was amazed at how beautiful they were. They featured intricate carvings of interlacing patterns, a clever design of whittled wonders marking them from top to bottom. "Now you'll be able to get around on your own, without two girls lugging you about." Emma smiled at him, and, to Heather's surprise, he smiled back.

"Thanks, Emma," Picket said, and he looked truly grateful. *Maybe there is hope for the old Picket*, Heather thought. *Until he sees Smalls again.*

"Okay, friends," Emma said. "Would you like me to bring you some food, or can you hobble down to the Savory Den?"

Picket started to speak, but Heather beat him to it. "We'll come down." She did not want to stay cooped up and didn't think it would do for Picket to have that option. More than his foot needed healing.

"As you like," Emma said. "I'll be back in a few minutes to fetch you starving pilgrims. There are clean clothes in the drawers—including clean drawers," she said with a mischievous wink. She made to leave.

"Emma," Heather said, "may I ask you something?"

"Of course."

"These paintings," she said, indicating the wall, "who did them?"

"Oh, so many," Emma said, her eyebrows knitting in thought. "I'm not sure of all their names. They'd know every one of them up in the galleries and at Lighthall."

"Lighthall?" Heather asked.

"A place set aside for this sort of thing. The best of them, I think," Emma explained. "Though it's shut up at the moment for repairs."

Heather looked them all over. "There are a thousand untold tales in these places."

"I suppose so," Emma said. "Are you a tale spinner?"

"No," she answered quickly. Too quickly. Emma eyed her doubtfully.

"Heather has great stories," Picket said, examining his crutches. "She's told them to me since I was a baby. She's told them to our baby brother as well. You should hear her story about why the leaves change color in autumn. She's an amazing storyteller, but she doesn't like being put on the spot. It's the one way it's actually possible to shut her up."

"We'll see about that," Emma said slyly. "I'll have you," she pointed at Picket, "walking, and you," she eyed Heather, "telling tales, in no time." Emma crossed her arms. "You poor, weary, pathetic, sad, happy, strange, and wonderful travelers shall be my project."

"Grand," Picket said with a sigh.

Heather laughed, a little nervously, then turned again to the paintings. "What about this one?" she said, pointing to the large painting in the center of the wall at the foot of her bed. Heather was sure it featured her family home in the east. "Do you know anything about this one, like what place it's showing?"

Emma crossed to look with Heather as Picket tried out his crutches. "I'm sorry, Heather; I don't have any idea," she said. "I mean, I know it's from the Great Wood before the fall of King Jupiter, and before the afterterrors. But I haven't been in here much, and I wasn't the best for listening to the lessons on art. I know some of the major ones." She sounded embarrassed by her limited knowledge. "I've been working so hard to become a doctor, you see."

"And you'll make a great one, I'm sure," Picket said, successfully crossing the room with the crutches after a few stumbling efforts.

"Of course you will," Heather agreed.

They looked at the painting together. "Does it mean something to you?" Emma asked.

"I think it's a picture of our old home," Heather said quietly.

"Away in the northwest?"

"No, in the east. In the Great Wood, I suppose. Where our parents lived and where I lived, when I was a baby."

Picket shuffled over to join them. He stared at the painting, longing written on his face.

"It's lovely," Emma said.

"Yes," Heather agreed. "Mother had a painting of her own that showed this glen. At least I think it's the same one. It hung over our fireplace at Nick Hollow. One day I found her crying, looking at it. She told me then, if we ever couldn't find her, to look there." She pointed at the tree home depicted in the lower corner of the large painting.

Emma nodded.

Picket noticed the initials at the bottom. "Who is F. S.?"

"That I *can* tell you," Emma said. "I'm not such an ignoramus that I don't know the leading artists of the Great Wood's golden age. That'll be Finbar Smalls, the Mage of Meadows. The painters here all adore him."

Heather and Picket exchanged a brief questioning glance. "Is Finbar Smalls here?" Heather asked.

"No. He was killed in the afterterrors of the fall of King Jupiter, along with so many others." Emma swallowed. "Including my own family."

"I'm so sorry, dear friend," Heather said, squeezing Emma again. "Do you ever go back to the Great Wood? It looks so lovely."

"The Great Wood is a ruin now," Emma said hoarsely. "It's charred and decaying, in both its appearance and its soul. I think rabbits love Finbar Smalls because he reminds them of what it was."

"Finbar Smalls?" Picket asked into the silence. "Is the whole world orphaned?"

Chapter Nineteen

LIGHT FROM ABOVE

At breakfast in the Savory Den, Heather and Picket ate sliced peaches in maple syrup, with sweet bread for dipping. Gort found excuses to be near them as they ate, checking on this and that, fussing over some detail of the breakfast. When the young rabbits sighed with delight over this, the beginning of another wonderful meal, he beamed and turned away quickly to hide his face. He waddled away soon after.

Heather was amazed at the care they gave to every detail of the meal, from the food itself to how it was presented. It was almost too lovely to eat. Almost. She dug in with relish and left her plate, and a few more besides, spotless. Picket, sour as he was, seemed to sweeten with every sugary bite. He ate four platefuls and looked likely to never stop, until Emma spoke up as he rose from his seat to get still more.

"Seeing the doctor over your foot is enough," she warned. "If you carry on you'll have to see him for a burst belly, too."

Shyly, Picket settled back into his seat.

"Anyway," Emma went on, "I want to take you newcomers on a little tour. There's so much I want to show you."

"But, I can't," Picket said, pointing to his foot.

"A bit of movement won't hurt you," Emma said. "As long as you stay off it. Don't put any weight on it," she commanded in mock seriousness. "Future doctor's orders," she added with a wink at Heather.

"Yes, Pick," Heather said, putting her arm around her younger brother. "We've got to get you back on your feet."

"Plenty of rest," Emma said.

"And lots of food," Heather added.

"And lots of laughs," Emma said.

"Yes," Heather said, "lots and lots and lots of laughter, while resting ... with food."

"You'll recover that much quicker when they're all combined," Emma said.

"Recover for what?" Picket asked, almost to himself.

* * *

Picket looked over at the corner where the black rabbit had sat the night before. His place was empty. There were a few rabbits nearby, whispering and glancing up at them. They looked upset, almost offended even, by the newcomers' presence. Or maybe Picket was just seeing things. Maybe it was the girls' laughter.

"'Recover for what?' For life, Picket," Emma said. "There are lots of trades here for an eager young rabbit."

"Emma's said she'll get me started with the healers," Heather said. "She thinks I might even be a doctor someday myself."

"And maybe the storyguild as well," Emma said.

"Are there actually storytellers here?" Heather asked.

"Sure there are."

* * *

Heather faltered. Fear rose up inside her. She felt both delight and terror at the thought of sharing her stories with such rabbits. "That's their job?" Heather asked. "Storytelling?"

"Of course!" Emma said. "Now, they do other work like everyone else: gardening, cleaning, teaching—whatever's needed. But all the crafts are honored here. We're heralds of the Mended Wood."

"You keep saying that. Everyone keeps saying it. What does it mean?" Heather asked. "Heralds of the Mended Wood?"

"Let me show you what it means," Emma said, smiling and dragging Heather to her feet. "C'mon, Shuffler," she said, urging Picket to follow.

Heather waited for Picket to get his crutches in place, and the three crossed to the little door in the back of the Savory Den. They walked past Gort, who waddled around, fussing over the early lunch preparations. "Too much salt!" he cried after dipping his finger in a simmering pot and tasting it. "It's the Savory Den, not the Salty Saltstation of Salty—er, uh … Salt … er, uh—Saltland! I've warned you of the dangers of over-salination, Welton. Oh, how I've warned you."

"Sorry, Master Gort," Welton screeched, ducking to escape a ladle Gort had whipped at his head.

"What do I always tell you? 'Not enough salt is an in-salt,' and 'Too much salt is an as-salt!'"

"Yes, Master Gort," the entire kitchen said together, some hiding giggles behind carefully raised bowls and towels.

Heather tried not to laugh herself but was unsuccessful. She turned to Picket as they walked. "What job would you like to train for?"

"Soldiering," he said quickly.

"You'll want one of the citadels for that," Emma said. "There's only the Forest Guard here, and they are the elite of the elite. Everyone starts soldiering in the citadels, and, whether you'd like to or not, almost every healthy buck serves for a time. But I'll have a word with Lord Rake and see if he can speed it up, if you'd like. It's a noble career."

Picket nodded.

Heather didn't like Picket's answer. She wanted him out of danger, happy, and his old self again. But it appeared that the events of the past few days had hardened his resolve. "Why do you want to be a soldier, Pick?"

Picket didn't answer, so Emma broke the silence. "I know you are waiting under the law of initiates, but I will tell you that I believe there will be a great need for soldiers very soon."

"What do you mean?" Heather asked. Picket's eager expression troubled her. "Will this place be attacked?"

"It may be, Heather. I hear that the wolf patrols get closer every day. I'm sorry, dear. The world is not very safe."

"And yet we wait to be told everything important," Picket said.

"That's the reason you must wait," Emma said. "But I am sorry for it. Please, don't get too upset. I want to show you more of our community."

They came to a wall, and Emma tapped four times soft and quick, then twice hard. After a moment, the wall gave way, revealing a passage and a wary guard. Heather must have been too tired to notice this code the night before. Passing through the door, they did not, as Heather expected, turn to the right. That way, she had learned, led down the long hall, which then turned again into the corridor of rooms where they had stayed last night. They turned left, which led them through a series of clean-cut stone hallways, ending in a steep grey-green stairway.

Heather was unsure how this place worked—how it was laid out. It made her uncomfortable, not knowing which way led out. She felt confused. It appeared to be a series of caves, something like what Picket described Seven Mounds as, but it was different too. There was so much light here. It was so lively and clean.

"Emma," she asked, "where exactly are we? Is it like a cavern inn, with a restaurant and rooms?"

"It is that. But that is really only a sort of secret entrance to all of Cloud Mountain," she said, motioning above them.

"Cloud Mountain?" Picket asked.

"Yes. This mountain is always covered in a heavy mist—at least there is almost always a great belt of cloud near the top. You came into the Savory Den, which is a restaurant, meant to appear ordinary. There's been a salt lick there for centuries, they say, so it makes sense. But it also serves as a cover for what happens beyond and up the mountain. That's the real life of this place. If enemies come, it's our hope—admittedly a faint one—that they'll just see the restaurant and won't realize there are more of us hidden away up here."

"The exiles from the Great Wood?" Picket asked.

"Yes. Many of us ended up here."

"Clever," Heather said.

"It is," Emma agreed. "We have only the Forest Guard for protection. There are ever so many orphans here. Like me."

"And us," Heather said, patting her arm.

"Anyway," Emma went on, "above the cloud belt there's plenty of sunlight, and though mountainside gardening is hard, especially with all this rock, we've found a way to survive."

"They couldn't have made this place after the exile," Heather said, running her hand along the smooth-cut walls of stone.

"No. They just restored it a bit," Emma said. "It was here all along."

"Like Seven Mounds," Picket said.

"There's a place kind of like this back in Nick Hollow,"

Heather explained. "No one knows where it came from, but it's massive and full of carved-stone rooms."

"It's a great mystery here as well," Emma said. "Rumor has it that two of the hidden citadels are like this, though I'm told the one nearest here, Halfwind Citadel, is just an old-fashioned warren."

"How far is it?" Picket asked.

"Most of a day's journey," Emma said. "But you don't need to worry about that yet, Shuffler. You need to worry about this." She pointed up the seemingly endless stairs, which led up and up a dark stairway to end in a curious light glowing around the topmost stairs. It was so bright at the top, it looked like the sun itself might be sitting on the top step.

Chapter Twenty

MYSTERIES ON THE MEND

Heather was intrigued. How could it be so bright?

She glanced at Picket, who squinted at the shimmering light up what seemed like an endless number of stairs. He looked at his crutches, then doubtfully at Emma. Emma didn't know about Picket's intense fear of heights, and Heather wasn't about to reveal anything that would embarrass him further.

"It's worth it, Picket," Emma said, smiling. "There's a rail. Let me have the crutches, and just lean on the rail and hop up each step. There's only a hundred or so." She snatched the crutches and, grabbing Heather's hand, pulled her into the stairwell.

Heather rushed up with Emma, while Picket made slow progress behind them. She glanced back to be sure he was okay, and he nodded for her to go on. She did.

About halfway up, she noticed there were large chains crisscrossed along the ceiling of the stairway. These all appeared to be tied together and ended near the top. She couldn't see what they were for. The bright light above was so alluring, she was too distracted to ask.

As she reached the final few steps, she noticed that the light was more than just bright; it was many-colored. She saw blues and greens, oranges and reds, splashed along the top of the stairway like illuminated paint.

When she crested the stairs, she gasped.

Before her ran a short walkway of beautifully laid brick, almost as if the stairway continued, now level. This walkway split a sprawling garden bursting with bright flowers and small trees. But it was, Heather saw to her astonishment, indoors. Above them, as she and Emma walked slowly along the path, was a clean, clear glass ceiling, something she would have thought impossible. Sunlight descended in waves, covering the little garden walk with a faintly hazy glow.

Ahead, she saw the source of the colors. It was an octagonal room, wood-framed, with large glazed glass panels of every color. Above a dark brown door, a banner was mounted. It was a white field with two diamonds, side by side. The left one was red, the right, green. This was the same symbol she had seen on Lord Rake's tunic. *It must be his own coat of arms.*

The building was lovely. Somehow the sunlight erupted through the multicolored glass and into the garden walkway. She now saw that only some of the light came in from above. The octagonal room was brimming with sunshine, casting magic images along the walkways and the grey-green stone walls. It washed over them, and they gazed at the shimmering garden of colorful light.

Picket joined them, his mouth gaping. Emma relished the wonder written on her friends' faces and was silent for a long time.

Finally, she spoke. "This is who we are here, Heather. You asked what it means to be heralds of the Mended Wood."

"Yes."

"It means this," she said, motioning all around. Heather listened closely, and Picket, breathing hard, turned away from his amazed appreciation to attend to Emma. "And it means much more. Follow me."

They kept to the path but didn't go into the octagonal room with the glass panes bursting with light.

"They're still working on Lighthall," Emma said, motioning to the room. They heard sounds from within, a light hammering and what sounded like glass being cut. "Our best artists are getting it ready."

"What's the name of this garden?" Heather asked.

"I'm not sure anyone's named it, officially. But everyone calls it King Whitson's Garden, or King's Garden. You'll see why."

They followed the path around tall trees and found that the walkway widened into a circular space featuring large statues on stone pedestals. The statues were of two rabbits, swords drawn and faces strained in action. Heather understood that this was why the garden was called King Whitson's garden. There he was, his image in bronze, cape caught up in the wind and sword aloft. What a hero. She glanced at the other statue and walked on behind Emma.

"Do we know what King Whitson Mariner looked like?" Heather asked.

"I don't know," Emma said as they crossed under an archway leading to a large wooden door. A tall rabbit in green stood by the door, gripping a long spear. "Maybe they just imagined it."

Heather nodded. "Are there sculptors—"

"Where's Shuffler?" Emma interrupted.

Heather looked back. He hadn't followed them. They walked back along the path, reentering the statuary space. There was Picket, looking up at the statues with tears in his eyes.

"What is it, Picket?" she asked, coming alongside him.

"It's him, Blackstar," he whispered hoarsely.

"Is that story important to you, Picket?" Emma asked.

"Very important," he said. "Father loved to tell it to us. I loved to hear it."

"He was a real hero," Emma said, touching the statue's foot. They saw the black star patch on his shoulder, his place beside and in front of King Whitson, his sword frozen in flight.

"He was brave," Picket said, hanging his head.

"I always loved the tale of Whitson and Seddle best," Heather said.

"Me too," Emma said. "She was my favorite."

"It was always Blackstar for me," Picket said. "Even more than Whitson Mariner himself. I knew I'd never be a king, but I thought, maybe ..." He trailed off, shaking his head.

"It feels like there couldn't ever be heroes like them again," Heather said. "Those days are long gone."

"But King Jupiter reigned only a short time ago," Emma said, "and everyone says his was truly the golden age of rabbit civilization."

"I know it wasn't so long ago, but it feels as distant to me as their day," Heather said, motioning up at the statues.

"Let's go on," Emma said, moving along the path. "I have more to show you." They rounded the curve again, seeing the stone archway and the guard in green before the door. When he saw Emma, he smiled and opened the door for her. Heather thought she noticed his expression change when he looked at Picket and herself. But she wasn't sure. Heather noticed that he bore the double-diamond emblem, stitched onto the shoulder of his tunic.

She and Picket followed Emma through the door and down a long hallway, this one dark again, illuminated only by a few torches. Soon the hallway ended in a large round room with three large doors.

"This is called Hallway Round," Emma said. In the center of Hallway Round stood a large barrel of dark wood, hooped with bright brass clamping. Around the barrel paced three guards. All three bore the double-diamond crest, and the same banner hung from the ceiling high above. Two of the doors, the one to their left and the one straight ahead, were guarded. The third, on the right, wasn't.

"Where do the doors lead?" Heather asked.

"I'll show you." Emma motioned for them to follow and, smiling at another guard in green, led them through the door on their left.

Heather squinted as Emma passed ahead of them into sunlight. She followed carefully over the threshold and into a vision of green, gold, and white. The persistent mist hung about the edges of a green hillside, lit with glittering sunlight. There was a surprisingly wide, mostly flat area, but this soon gave way to the ever-tilting hillside. Around the rim of the village green, the hillside slanted up into stony outcroppings, ending in the mountain peaks that showed about the ring of Cloud Mountain. It looked like a broken bowl, with the green being the bowl's inside bottom. Heather saw row upon row of vegetables of every kind—cabbage and corn, potatoes and turnips. Her mouth watered, and she felt a little lightheaded. After the confining corridors of stone, it was unsettling to be out in the open like this.

There were rabbits all over, working and talking. Young ones played in groups dotting the hillsides, their laughter making Heather's heart ache for Jacks. Beyond the gardens, she saw a little village of wood and stone homes. Stone walls crisscrossed the grounds.

"I've never seen a village," Picket said as they crossed the flat grass along a row of hedges.

"Or this many rabbits at once," Heather said, smoothing her dress. "It'd be almost frightening, if everyone didn't look so friendly."

Well, Heather noticed wordlessly, *almost everyone looks friendly.* Beneath a nearby maple tree, the moody black rabbit they had seen at dinner lay on the ground, apparently napping. The maple tree was curious, stripped of most of its leaves and tangled with ropes and other odd-shaped things. She saw what looked like wooden wolves with great orange heads scattered all around the tree. More large shapes filled the tree, but she couldn't tell what they were. More orange and green, but it was too far and the shapes too crude to see clearly. The tree was scuffed and scarred in a hundred places.

"The village has come about in the time since King Jupiter fell, of course," Emma said, not paying any attention to the black rabbit. Heather thought this was deliberate, though Picket hadn't seemed to notice. "The farm has also grown as more and more of us have come here."

"It's beautiful," Heather said.

"It is," Emma agreed, smiling.

They walked along hedgerows and stone walls, marveling. Looking back at the door that had led them up onto this lush hillside, they saw only a great mass of rock. The door they had emerged from was nearly invisible. Heather wondered what lay behind those doors that she had not yet seen. *Were there endless chambers beneath them? What secrets are in this mountain?*

Her mind filled with the beginnings of tales, loose threads that could be woven by a skillful hand. She thought of what Emma had said about the storyguild. *Tale-spinners.* The all-too-familiar fear returned, telling her she didn't belong here and certainly couldn't tell stories with anything like the skill of those who had lived in this place for years. Her stories were unimportant, simple tales for little ones.

They reached a mossy area, set up with several stone tables, and sat down. They were only a short walk from the entrance back into Hallway Round.

"Do they all live in the village?" Picket asked, motioning toward the rabbits all around.

"Most do. I used to live up there," she said, pointing to a neat row of cottages. Heather squinted to see the small wood and stone homes; then her gaze returned to the hedges a few feet away. She had never seen such neatly cut hedges. Everything here was well tended; even the rabbits looked well. She felt the tranquility of the place wash over her as she imagined the many kind folks who must live here, rabbits of great character and serenity.

Then snapping blades were speeding toward her face.

She almost fell off her bench when she saw the long shears shoot through the hedge wall a few feet from her face. She regained her balance and saw a lanky rabbit emerge through the hedge, his long arms holding the shears, his face bent in a frown. Heather breathed a relieved sigh.

"You frightened me!" Heather said.

"I beg your pardon, Miss, but what's frightening is the state of these hedges!" he said, scowling at the row and holding his hand up carefully, closing one eye, trying to measure how straight they were.

"Hello, Heyward," Emma said. "You're absolutely, positively, without-a-doubt correct about the hedges. They're really quite crooked. I almost lost my balance just looking at them."

"I am genuinely mortified, Miss Emma!" he said, nodding his head in agreement and looking at her in sympathetic grief. "They shouldn't be allowed to stand. I think I shall cut them all down and start over!" He made to attack the row with his long shears. The shears seemed almost to be extensions of his lanky arms, so that he looked like a very tall rabbit with strangely incredible limbs.

"Don't be silly!" Heather shouted, while Picket laughed. "They look perfect. You could use the edge of those hedges to show what the word *straight* means!"

Heyward paused his attack, smiled for a mere instant, then quickly resumed his frowning. "What utter nonsense!" he puffed. Then he hustled away, hunched over the hedge, peering at it like it might run away if he took his eyes off it for a moment. Every few steps, he brought his enormous shears down on even the teeniest twig judged to be jutting out a mere fraction of an inch.

"He's a little bit … um …" Emma began.

"Dedicated?" Picket asked, trying not to laugh.

"Yes," Emma said. "He's that. You'll find that a lot of the rabbits here are devoted to their work, though not many are as—well, attentive, as Heyward is."

"He's a nut, and everyone knows it," Kyle said, appearing behind them and surprising them all. The tall golden-grey rabbit they had met briefly yesterday had come from out of nowhere, it seemed, flashing his casual smile.

"Where did you come from?" Heather asked, looking around.

"Oh, I hail from the land of Terralain," Kyle said with a wink. "Home of the long-lost Whitson Stone and birthplace of wonder and unity."

"Not that again," Emma said, sighing loudly. "Please, bring Heyward back. More about hedges, I beg you!"

"Well, I wish I came from Terralain," Kyle said, smirking at Emma. Emma looked as if she'd seen enough of his smirks and he might want to try a new expression out.

"Where's Terralain?" Heather asked.

"Not so far away as we imagine," Kyle said with another wink.

"Oh, Heyward!" Emma called, pulling on her ears. "Come back!"

"What are you talking about?" Heather asked, trying not to laugh at Emma.

"Oh, you're serious?" Kyle said. "Sorry. I thought everyone knew about Terralain. But you two are from far away and have lived sheltered lives. You've never heard of Terralain? Mysterious land of enchantment? Home of wizards and lost princes?"

"Is it real?" Heather asked.

Emma said, "No," and Kyle said, "Yes," at the same time. They eyed each other warily, Kyle imitating Emma's dismissiveness.

"Okay, sure," Emma said, "it's real. And they keep Jupiter's heir there in a magic bubble where he governs the rivers with his mind. Isn't that right?"

"No, Emma," Kyle said, "that's not quite right. They don't acknowledge King Jupiter in Terralain. But I do have some new information on the whereabouts of Jupiter's heir."

Picket and Heather both sat up and attended carefully to Kyle. Heather said, "The fallen and the future king, or so Lord Rake said."

"Oh no, you two," Emma said. "Don't let this rascal fill your head with his nonsense."

"This is reliable info," Kyle began, touching his nose. "I have come to learn that Jupiter's heir is kept hidden in the Deep Belows." He pointed to the mountain and then down. "There's a labyrinth down there unlike any you've ever seen. It's impossible to get to him without intimate knowledge of the passages. Only three know the way. One is Lord Rake, our Emma's secretive adoptive father and lord of this, *ahem*, flawless little community." He winked again. "As Lord Rake was a councilor and friend to the fallen king, so now is he the guardian of the future king. Another is the prince's bodyguard, a mute warrior who wears all black always and is never seen. And the last is the prince's scribe."

"And what does he need a scribe for?" Emma asked, smirking. "Does he write poems about your greatness, Kyle?"

"Not poems, exactly," Kyle said, rubbing his hands together. His eyes were wide and excited. "It's prophecies. You see, the prince, King Jupiter's heir, is very sick. He's in a sullen stone room, with only a bed to lie in and a table for his scribe. He lies there in a constant fever, never fully waking up, mumbling things in a semi-madness."

"A semi-madness?" Emma laughed. "So he's ahead of you on the madness scale. That's good."

"Hey," Kyle said, shushing her. "Listen, a few years ago they realized that the things he was mumbling about would later actually happen. Like, he mumbled about a rockslide, and the next week, a rockslide happened, and it killed somebody. Then the guard knew something was wrong, so they got this scribe to write down the prophecies. They are all kept in a book, *The Whispered Prophecies of Jupiter's Heir*, and it's read day and night by the council. They make their policies and plans based on it."

"Fascinating," Heather said. Kyle smiled, nodding.

"Don't encourage him!" Emma cried, slapping playfully at Heather's hand. "He's a rogue, Heather!"

"Listen," Kyle said, raising his hands, "I know a fellow who knows a fellow who brings water to the mad prince."

"I thought you said only three rabbits can get to him!" Emma said. "And if he's sick all the time, then doesn't he get seen by doctors?"

"Well, the doctor, obviously; it goes without saying," Kyle said. "But the water bearer is met by the guard at the entrance to the stone labyrinth. Then the guard, who knows the way, takes the water."

"And the doctor?" Heather asked.

"Is escorted by the guard as well," Kyle said, nodding

with authority.

"You act like you at least believe the story," Heather said.

"Liars always believe their stories," Emma said.

"*Liar* is an awfully strong word, Emma," Kyle said, looking wounded.

"I know," she said, scowling.

"What about Terralain?" Picket asked. "Tell us about it."

"It's a kids' story, Picket," Emma said, her anger rising. "It's a fantasy to distract us from our real work here."

"I want to hear, Emma," Picket said. "Can you let me decide for myself what to believe?"

"One more thing—then I'll be quiet," Emma said. "You can choose what you believe, Shuffler, but you can't change what's true. The land of Terralain is like Kyle's honor. It doesn't exist," she said, throwing her hands up in surrender.

"But it does exist," Kyle said, throwing another smirk Emma's way and half-turning away from her so as to exclude her from the conversation. "Greggor's aunt's friend from the Halfwind Citadel met a fellow who was out on patrol one night, and he saw it. He saw Terralain. One night, when the fog was thick and he was far away down southwest, he lost his way. After hours wandering, he crested a hill in the dark and saw in the distance a thousand torchlights, like stars across a field. It was the Valley of Stars, the lost land of Terralain. It exists. And this fellow supposed there were fairer things there than any we've seen here in this dingy den of sweaty labor."

"You haven't broken a sweat at work in all your life," Emma said.

"Because I'm smarter than that, Emma," he said. He ignored her and focused on Heather and Picket. "I'm going someday, heading out to find it. If you ever get tired of this place, you can come along." He kept their attention as he got up, bowed slightly, spun around, and sauntered off.

"Don't listen to him, Picket," Emma said. "He once tried to seriously tell me that he himself was really a prince, the so-very-secret heir to the true king. He was so, so convincing. It was like he really believed it. I'm telling you, he's good at sucking you in, but not so good at delivering on his word."

"But he sure is entertaining," Heather said, patting Emma's hand. "And no one tells us anything, so we're curious."

"I know," Emma said. "Lord Rake says you'll be initiated soon, and lots of questions will be answered then. I want to get you answers, but I think it's best to get them from the right sources. I want to follow the law of initiates, even if I'm also frustrated by it. Unlike Kyle, I don't think it's right to pick and choose which laws to follow. Your situation is, well, unique. Anyway, that's where we're headed next. To meet someone who can give you some answers. This place has many, many wonderful rabbits."

"Good rabbits, huh? Like him?" Picket asked, pointing to the brooding black rabbit under the maple tree. The hulking brooder had risen from his resting position and was fiddling with some long ropes and straps arranged around the maple. This complicated contraption looked like a tangled mess, but he drew a rope taut here and loosed one there. He adjusted the great orange heads on the wolflike wooden dummies.

Heather could see now that the orange heads were pumpkins. The things filling the tree were topped with pumpkins and other gourds too, though she still couldn't tell what they were exactly. They were at a distance where they could see him and the shapes but not make out exactly what he was doing.

No one was near him. The groups of working rabbits and their playing children kept an obvious distance from him. It was like they were afraid of him, which Heather understood. She certainly felt a strong sense within her that spoke clearly in her mind *He's not safe*. She noticed, now that he had risen, how many eyes were on him. The older ones watched out of the corners of their eyes and with subtle glances, but the young watched openly and whispered to each other.

"Pay him no mind. He's another troubler of the community," Emma said. But she did not take her own advice.

"We seem to be meeting quite a few of that type," Heather said.

"I know," Emma said, frowning. "I'm trying to fix that."

They all watched, rapt, as the black rabbit made his rounds, checking knots and hoisting a wooden contraption, tying a rope off, testing a knot, or making other mild adjustments. Then he disappeared behind the maple, only to emerge a moment later with a sword and a shield. The shield was black, as was the sword hilt. A single emerald shone out from the black hilt, glinting in the sunlight. He wore black clothing, which matched his color. His shield bore a red diamond—the same red diamond that Redeye Garlackson and his band of wolves wore, but there was no fang on this one.

Picket stood up.

"Who is he?" Heather asked.

"An endless frustration," she said. "Everyone calls him Helmer the Black. He's like the well-cut caves here, a bit of a mystery. The ones who know who he is won't say, and the ones who don't know aren't allowed to ask. At least that's what I get from my noble guardian, Lord Rake."

"Not allowed to ask?" Picket asked as the black rabbit stretched, then tried out the sword in practice strokes through the air. "Why? Why all these secrets?"

"You and everyone else would like to know," Emma said. "The rumor is that Helmer's a knight from King Jupiter's army, disgraced and angry, bent on revenge. But half the time you can't tell if he's madder at the Lords of Prey, who killed the king, or the Lords of Cloud Mountain. I can't imagine him being meaner to the Lords of Prey than he is to us."

"He's difficult?" Heather asked.

"He makes Shuffler here look like the pleasantest rabbit who ever lived," she said, giving Picket a smile. Heather was amazed that she could get away with making jokes about Picket's sullenness that she herself dared not try. "Where Kyle talks constantly, you won't hear ten words from Helmer in a year. And he won't suffer any interference in his exercises, which, if you ask me, really should be interfered with. Though he does work hard in the garden and does his share of the labor. But he's constantly—oh, wait. Look there!"

They all looked where she pointed. A very young rabbit doe in a blue dress was toddling toward Helmer as he practiced sword strokes. The rabbits nearby, even adult ones, gave up the pretense of other work and watched. He finished a striking slice, the sword disappearing into its sheath in a silent, swift motion.

"He won't hit her?" Heather asked, genuinely unsure.

"I wouldn't put it past him," Emma said, looking worried. Just then a mother ran after the little one, almost catching up to her as the black rabbit, Helmer, turned and saw them. There was a moment of silence as he eyed them both coolly. Heather was afraid he might attack them. But his sword remained sheathed.

"Leave me alone," he growled at them. His tone was gravelly, harsh, and bitter. It reminded Heather a little of Redeye Garlackson. Seeing the black clothes and the red diamond symbol, then hearing that awful voice, she panicked. The mother, frozen to the spot, couldn't say anything. She clutched her child and opened her mouth, but nothing came out. She looked terrified, couldn't seem to move.

"Hideous rabbit," Emma hissed. "He ought to be expelled." Heather nodded but looked over at Picket, who was entirely engrossed.

Then Helmer drew his sword and ran.

Heather screamed.

177

Chapter Twenty-One

SWINGING DEATH

Heather's scream joined with a hundred others. Helmer ran, but he broke away from the terrified mother. The mother found her feet and fled, wailing, back up the hill, clasping her child.

Helmer ran in an arc around the tree, slicing ropes as he went. The massive forms came swinging down in turn. In a moment, swooping down from twenty directions were what looked like giant birds. Heather gasped. Picket jumped, almost went to the ground.

It had taken only a few seconds, but Helmer had made a circuit around the tree. All his careful preparations were in motion. Sweeping down on him were the wooden birds of prey, which, free of their perches, now came into focus. Their talons, crude as they were, were set with razor-sharp knives. Many had beaks fixed with short swords, which shot out in all directions. One of these monsters, coming directly at a rabbit, would be deadly to deal with. In his initial arc around the tree, Helmer had cut loose nearly twenty of them. They all swooped down at different heights and with varying speeds, so that he had to move with incredible agility to simply avoid them. The birds were made to be deadly; the only vulnerability appeared to be their small heads of squash, melon, or pumpkin. His movements were further complicated by the various pumpkin-headed wolflike models, each of them featuring what Heather could now see were sharp blades from their sides. The terrifying gauntlet was set up to mimic an attack from birds of prey and wolves, all at once. An attack from all directions.

Immediately, he looked doomed. He sidestepped a swooping bird, only to turn as another swung straight for his head, blades pointing out like long monstrous teeth. The crowd—for it was now a crowd gathered—cried out together in terror. Helmer ducked only just in time, then whirled and struck out with his blade to slice in half the pumpkin head of a model wolf. As the pumpkin split, he kicked the model over. That was one enemy down. Only about thirty to go. They swarmed him as he dodged, dove, and struck out at them.

He dodged back from a low-swooping bird, receiving a nasty gash for his effort, and seemed to realize that two of the gliding attackers were converging on him at once. He looked to be crushed, never mind the blades. Heather was sure this must be the end of him. A scream died in her throat, and the crowd's voices rose in collective panic. Picket's eyes widened, and he stepped forward a few more paces.

At the last moment, as the two birds were almost on him, Helmer flipped backwards, his large feet barely missing the pulverizing blow as the two birds collided, breaking into pieces. Their shattered collision sent knives flying. Another dive, this time behind the body of a wooden wolf, saved him. Some shards flew over his head, and three speeding blades stuck fast in the wooden body he had barely gotten behind. He stood, already panting, and looked wildly from side to side. The crowd gasped.

Above him fell a massive bird, ten sharp points poised at his head. He had no time to move out of the way, and four other birds, each in a unique rebounded flight, were surrounding him. He had, Heather believed, no escape. But again, at the last possible moment, he kicked out his feet, not in a jump but to quickly give up his footing. He fell back, in sync with the diving bird, and landed hard on his back as the large wooden terror struck at him with its awful knives.

But it came up just short. The rope it was tied to went taut, and the bird rebounded back up with a snap. The cords must have had some bounce to them, for they never died but always sprang back up to fall or swing again with renewed pace.

He lay there a moment, watching the sky above him swarm with foes. Nearby, Heather, Picket, and Emma watched in terror. They heard a guard in green nearby talking anxiously to a farmer. "Too many this time, Gabe. Far too many. That'd be a right hard test for five well-trained soldiers. He'll be killed for sure."

Heather was frightened. She had no desire to see such a thing but felt powerless to do anything and too engrossed to look away. She cried out, "No!"

Others were shouting as well. "Stay down, you fool!"

But Heather could see that would not happen. Helmer rose and with his powerful legs sprang into action once more. Immediately he was in grave peril. As he lunged at a swooping bird, another two were converging on his back. He leapt up and swung his sword at the gourd-head of the bird, sending it flying. Then he sliced the cord, and it tumbled to the ground. The two birds from behind were nearly on him.

Heather closed her eyes and plugged her ears. She did not wish to see or hear the end of this barbaric madness.

She could avoid seeing, but she couldn't block out the noise entirely. The groans and screams of the gathered crowd were displaced suddenly by a growing clamor that almost sounded like a cheer.

She couldn't help it. She opened her eyes. Helmer had somehow evaded the two birds set to destroy him. He was wounded but fighting on. He was now in a more desperate spot, with nine of the birds converging on him from all sides at staggered times. He was backed against two of the model wolves. There was no escape.

But she saw something else.

Racing into the chaotic scene of careening blades came three figures. Lord Rake, Uncle Wilfred, and Smalls were diving into the fray.

Now Heather was truly frightened.

"No!" Emma shouted, running after them. Heather barely knew what to do, but she grabbed Emma's arm, slowing her down, as the crowd all pushed toward the wide circle around the maple where the deadly game was being played.

As Heather ran toward the fast-forming crowd encircling the tree, she watched, half-tripping, as the scene unfolded.

Lord Rake, in full run, soared through the air and clutched a rope, changing the direction of the attacking bird that he now stood atop. In the same motion, just as he found his footing on the deadly bird, he cut the rope free, sending it tumbling out of the circle as he held on to the remainder of rope, gliding out in a wide arc.

While Lord Rake swung wide of the converging birds, Smalls ran hard, shedding his hooded cloak. He never broke stride, running alongside Uncle Wilfred. With one hand he unsheathed his blade, launching it from its sheath toward Uncle Wilfred, who caught it by its hilt. Uncle Wilfred now carried two drawn swords. Smalls finished his unsheathing pass and, in the same motion, reached for an arrow from his quiver. This he nocked and loosed with amazing speed, never stopping.

The crowd broke out in fresh screams as they saw the arrow speed right for Helmer. But the arrow narrowly missed Helmer and embedded heavily in one of the wooden wolves that fenced Helmer in, setting it to gently rock. By the time that arrow had sunk, Smalls had sent two more in turn. Finally, he nocked three arrows and sent them all at once to the same target, a shout pouring out of his mouth with the tremendous display of strength. Heather was certain one would go amiss and find Helmer, but none did. They added their force to the rocking wolf, and it toppled over.

There was action all over. Uncle Wilfred was not idle. He had caught Smalls' sword in midair as he soared confidently into the fray. With a shout, he extended blades on both sides, slicing two of the ropes at once, sending the attached birds sailing into the ground. He turned and hurled his borrowed sword back to Smalls and finished by catching a low swinging bird's rope and allowing it to send him speeding toward Helmer.

He rode its momentum for just the right amount of time, then cut it loose, sending the bird to harmlessly crash to earth. Meanwhile, he let go of the rope and cut through the air, slicing two more ropes as he hurled past Helmer.

Helmer himself appeared half-mad with anger and joy. He only just dodged a deadly bird, slicing its rope as it passed, and made ready to face the remaining convergence of his brutal creations. Even with the intervention of Rake, Wilfred, and Smalls, he seemed certain to fall. Three of the last few birds were converging on him in such a way as to make his escape truly impossible. Uncle Wilfred had crashed into the crowd beyond, and Lord Rake swung back too soon, unable to recover in time.

Helmer dodged, avoiding the two he could while the third swung down on him with unavoidable speed. It was large and fast, with blades all over. But Smalls was there. Leaping, he sailed through the air and presented his powerful feet to collide with the swooping bird. Blades stood out on the monster. Heather screamed. Smalls kicked the bird, sending it spinning away. He spun and smashed into the ground. She saw that he was cut, but she couldn't see how badly.

Helmer's eyes were wide as he was dragged out of the circle over the fallen arrow-riddled wooden wolf. He looked shocked, perhaps from being saved from certain death, but Heather thought there was more. His shocked expression was tinted with a fresh shame.

Then the crowd swelled in a chorus of terrified screams once more. Heather looked and saw, to her terror, that as Smalls lay wounded on the ground, the bird he had knocked away was rebounding and crashing down on him with amazing speed.

Now it was Smalls who looked up in a haze to see certain death descending on him.

Chapter Twenty-Two

FEET AND FEATS

Heather lunged ahead, knowing it was hopeless. Even with her considerable speed, she knew she could do nothing. Despair filled her, along with anger at Helmer's grotesque, selfish folly.

Then she saw a flash of light. A sword sliced through the air, catching slivers of golden light as it sailed, point-first, toward the swinging blade-ridden false bird and the rope that it hung on. It would have to be a perfect throw.

Behind the sailing blade stood Uncle Wilfred, his arm extended and his face contorted by fear and determined concentration.

There was a moment when everything slowed down, and Heather froze in the unsettled middle ground between observer and participant. This was happening, really happening, and she could do nothing about it. Her hopes hung on a thin slice of cold steel.

The blade point found the narrow rope, unbinding the several cords in a beautiful snapping slice. Heather ran to Smalls as the last descending bird, cut loose from its propelling rope, fell to the ground and skidded, then sunk into the grassy ground, fixed by its disappointed blades.

Uncle Wilfred collapsed in relief just as Heather reached Smalls. He was wounded in his feet, both of them sliced by the knives of Helmer's horrid creations. Behind them came Emma, along with a strange-looking rabbit dressed in white.

"Making way! Out of mine get it, you crazed lookers-on!" the strange rabbit in white cried.

"Please, everyone," Emma said, motioning for the crowd to back up, "Doctor Zeiger needs room. Back up!"

Doctor Zeiger was a large brown rabbit with long wispy white hairs shooting out all over his head. One of his ears was bent sideways, while the other shot toward the sky. He wore glasses like Father, but these had large red frames that circled his huge wild eyes, one of which was determined to look the wrong way. Heather thought she wouldn't trust him with sweeping up, let alone healing. He just looked too funny to be taken seriously. And his accent was nothing she had ever heard before. Where could he be from? Far away, she was sure. Beyond even Nick Hollow, Emma had said.

"Yes, yes," Doctor Zeiger said, pushing some in the crowd away and bending to look at Smalls' feet. "Out of mine ways, you rabble-crowders. Let's having a looks at you crazy-tough fighter-kicker with your foots so discouraged by the cutting of the bird-blades."

"Is he going to be okay?" Heather asked Emma.

"I don't know. Let the doctor work," she said, polite but firm.

Heather moved back then, helping to relieve the crush of rabbits gathered around. She found Picket, who was staring off, away from the crowd. With most of the crowd focused on Smalls, few had noticed that Lord Rake and Helmer were having an animated conversation in harsh whispers.

"Picket, what are you—" Heather began, but he held up a hand.

Heather turned and saw the angry hand gestures, the strained faces. It was clear that Lord Rake was giving Helmer a piece of his mind. Helmer mostly listened, with some angry objections here and there. It was difficult to hear, but Heather moved forward to stand beside Picket, away from the worried onlookers near Smalls.

"It's reckless!" Lord Rake said. "You nearly did it again!"

"I had no idea," Helmer argued, "I would never—"

"You're needed, Helmer," Lord Rake growled. "How can we do this without you? You know what we're up against. You have to be safe! Remember the Green—"

"I know," Helmer barked. "You don't have to remind me of that! I'm trying to prepare myself."

"More like get yourself killed—and others!"

"I didn't intend for that. You know I would never—"

"Well, if you weren't so blind to anything good!"

"I deserve exile," Helmer said, looking down. "I deserve worse."

"Well, you're stuck with us, Helmer," Lord Rake said. "Even if it seems like it's worse for everyone."

"I won't stop practicing," Helmer said. "I can't change. It's who I am now."

"Don't forget who you were once," Lord Rake said, marching away, "and might be again!"

Lord Rake stormed past, too angry to even notice them, and pushed his way to the front of the crowd where Uncle Wilfred knelt beside Smalls.

"I'm fine," Smalls was saying, shooing everyone away. Lord Rake and Uncle Wilfred stayed.

"Doc?" Lord Rake asked, looking up at Doctor Zeiger.

"He is being correct," Doctor Zeiger said. "He'll being fine as a fiddle-diddle in the nick of no time flat. He is cutting a bad cut on one of foots, and other is nothing too bads."

"How soon can I be on the move?" Smalls asked.

"Not less than three and one-half days and you'll be well enough to moving everything of your feets," Doctor Zeiger said.

"Good. Thanks, Doctor," Smalls said, pushing himself up. Heather watched as Uncle Wilfred balanced Smalls, helped him rise, and offered his shoulder to aid him. She was struck by how much he cared for Smalls. Then Uncle Wilfred's face turned dark, menacing.

She looked to find what Uncle Wilfred had seen to cause him to turn so quickly from compassion to fury. It was Helmer, who had, in his brooding, sullen way, come near to see how Smalls was.

"Get away," Uncle Wilfred said coldly. Helmer, his eye twitching slightly, walked away.

"No," Smalls said. He looked after the black rabbit. Helmer stopped but didn't turn around. A small divide opened between them, with a wall of rabbits on either side.

Then Smalls, his fist over his heart, said to Helmer, "My place beside you, my blood for yours, till the Green Ember rises, or the end of the world."

No one moved. No one spoke. Heather watched as Helmer's head dipped, his hand went to his face, and he walked off quickly, disappearing behind Heyward's perfect shrubs.

Uncle Wilfred's face was contorted with emotions Heather could not read. He helped Smalls away and they disappeared inside the mysterious doorway, back inside the many levels of hewn stone corridors and a thousand mysteries. The stone corridors and strange doors held innumerable secrets, but not so many, Heather thought, as those who walked inside them.

She stared, not knowing what to think. Then she heard Emma. She was talking to Doctor Zeiger. "I will check on him; don't worry, Doctor."

"Listen, Emmarabbit, can you cover my shifts next four, five days?" Doctor Zeiger was saying. "They wanting Doctor Zeiger mineself to coming to Blackstone Citadel. Some kind of flu going on, and though there's probably nothing whatever-clever I can doing, they wants us doctor anyway, and the Lord of Rake wants mineself to going."

"Silly, isn't it?" Emma said. "Do they want you to fall ill as well?"

"Like I tells you always, mine Emmarabbit, we have job to heal body, we have job to heal mind. Job to heal mind often biggest job. Mind disordered much as body, or more."

"Yes, Doctor," Emma said, smiling.

"And don't not forget my other sayings," Doctor Zeiger said.

"Like 'Put on your britches and then make your stitches'?" she asked.

"Well, yes, yes," he said, "you must remember to have your own self in order best as you can doctoring self before you can doing anything to help safe-make the other ones of the folk-rabbits if you are hoping to be helping happy-maker."

"I understand."

"But this is one I'm meant, 'Don't discarding the apple for the worm. Discarding the worm for the apple.'"

"I think I understand. Oh, and Doctor Z," she said, noticing Picket, "do you want to examine another foot?"

"Of course," Doctor Zeiger said in mock enthusiasm. "I waked up this morning from dreams about feets, sniffed big-time major breeze of life and hoped with all my hopes that this day might be filled with stinky feets to examine. It's a dream coming truth."

Emma explained what had happened to Picket and her initial diagnosis of his foot. After a few minutes, Doctor Zeiger confirmed her diagnosis and, whispering so that

Picket could not hear, said, "You'll need all mine sayings on this one. He needs worm cut out in worst kind of ways. Mind is disordered more than foot, but I'm expect you know for this sure to know. Foot will healing soon. Mind and heart, take longer. I would prescribe much Maggie, and hold the Helmer."

Heather frowned. She understood the "hold the Helmer" part, sort of. But what did he mean by "much Maggie"?

Chapter Twenty-Three

CALLING AND COMMUNITY

Before she turned in for the night, Heather stood before the painting of what she was convinced was her old home in what had been the Great Wood. A heaviness fell on her. Images of Father, Mother, and Jacks filled her mind. She imagined them all together, living in the hollow in the painting. Looking at the painter's initials, F. S.— Finbar Smalls—she thought of Smalls, then of Emma, of the whole upside-down world and its million broken hearts. She wasn't sure exactly what they meant by the Mended Wood, but she began to long for it. She began to believe, somehow, that she always had been longing for it. She turned for her bed and saw that Picket's eyes were already shut. She blew out the candles, rolled into her bed, and was asleep at once.

*   *   *

The next day after breakfast they ascended the stairway to light. Picket appeared quicker, better. At least, his foot seemed better. He was getting more agile with the crutches.

As for his mood, he would say almost nothing. They were astonished as the morning light filled King Whitson's Garden. They walked around, silently enjoying the sun-soaked air, alive with color, a beauty they seemed to inhabit. Picket finally sat beneath the statue of Captain Blackstar, silent and ponderous. Heather watched him for a little while, then walked back to enjoy the flowers and trees and soak in the glow of the broken light blanketing the garden.

As for Heather, this interlude in light refreshed her heart the way the restful day and night had refreshed her body. Well, mostly restful. She thought back to the mad events of early yesterday and wondered if anything would ever feel normal again.

They heard noise of work from inside the nearby octagonal building of wood and windows. Lighthall. She wondered what was in there.

"Gort told me no one's allowed in there yet," Picket said, walking up and motioning to the building. "That access to Lighthall is forbidden." He said it with a hint of accusation.

"That's true, Shuffler," Emma said. "I don't know about saying it's 'forbidden,' like it's the secret tomb of Lander's Dragons. That's a bit dramatic. But no one's allowed in for now, except for the artisans."

"That's what forbidden is," Picket said, adopting Kyle's smirk as he sat down on a bench.

"You know you have a choice about how you see things, Picket," Emma said, frowning at him.

"What are they doing?" Heather asked.

"What artisans do," Emma said. "Making lovely things, I suppose."

"Why can't you answer our questions, Emma?" Heather asked.

"I want to, Heather. I really do," she said. "But the law of initiates is very important for the security of this community and that of the citadels. There has to be a period of trial. If we blab everything to every new arrival, we are setting ourselves up for betrayal."

"So they think we're traitors," Picket said.

Emma didn't answer immediately. She looked down, her eyebrows scrunched. "I don't think you're traitors," she said. "I call you my friends, and I trust you, even after such a short time. But this community has had to learn the hard way to be cautious with our trust. Perhaps that will be clearer soon."

Heather nodded, but Picket was still scowling. Heather squinted at Lighthall, trying to see the multicolored glass. There were breaks in the color where ordinary plain glass was featured. It looked like a long hallway leading farther in. She thought she saw a short white rabbit pass in front of a clear pane of glass. *It makes sense,* she thought. *If it's Smalls, perhaps he's just following in his father's footsteps.* She wondered how Smalls had come to be adopted by her uncle and what exactly had happened in the Great Wood. She wanted all the answers but had gotten used to being in the dark. Somehow this garden put her at ease and helped her be patient for the unraveling of the story she was somehow a part of, even if only in a small way.

They were silent for a little while, and Heather finally joined Picket on the bench.

"I could stay in here forever," Heather said, sighing loud and long.

"But I've more to show you," Emma said, reaching for Heather's hand and pulling her up. "C'mon, Shuffler," she said to Picket as she made her way down the brick walkway. They followed her. Picket slowed to gaze up at Captain Blackstar again before shuffling beneath the stone archway to the door.

They passed through the guarded door and into the long torchlit corridor. After a little while, this opened into the large circular hallway with the three doors. Hallway Round was busy, but no one was staying there except for the guards. These guards were at their posts by the large barrel beneath the double-diamond banner, and a few others were milling around, going from one room to another. A few passing rabbits stared hard at them, shaking their heads. This unnerved Heather. Why would some be so unfriendly to them? Who were they to draw attention?

She studied the barrel in the room's center. The guards each looked away as she looked at them. They seemed uneasy.

The door straight ahead was opened, and a bustling rabbit with stacked baskets of bread emerged. She looked a moment away from spilling them but somehow managed to keep them all steady. Behind her, the noise of the room she had just left spilled into the hallway. It sounded lively in there.

"Does that lead outside?" Heather asked. "To more workers?"

"No and yes," Emma said. "Come and see."

The door guard bowed slightly to Emma and opened the door, and Emma went through. He eyed Heather and Picket warily. But they followed Emma in, a great wall of sound meeting them as they entered.

It was a massive room, a deep cavern with high walls. The ceiling was a rough dome that appeared to go up forever. Heather and Picket gaped at the dizzying size of it. The hall seemed as wide as the field beside their home in Nick Hollow where they had spent endless hours playing Starseek. The walls were the same neatly carved rock they had grown used to at Cloud Mountain. They were lined with hundreds of torches. High above, huge windows let in wide shafts of light.

Before them were hundreds of rabbits engaged in numerous crafts. Adding them to the fairly large numbers of rabbits they had seen outside yesterday, Heather realized there must be several hundreds living in and around Cloud Mountain.

Row upon row of every kind of work imaginable was being practiced in this mountain hall. There was even a smithy in the distant corner, its pounding hammers and gasping bellows part of the chorus of noises that filled the air. The smithy was loud, but the noise mingled with the general din of the place, which was alive with conversation, instruction, and work. There were book-binders, wheelwrights, fullers, bakers, carters, and many more. There was a station where a fletcher was testing a new-made arrow on a long bow. An eager guard in green stood by, his fingers twitching with excitement. Picket's eyes widened, and he hobbled in that direction, until Emma put her hand on his shoulder.

"Wait. Not yet. I want to show you something else." She had to lean toward Heather and Picket to be heard over the din. "We can come back and explore later."

Reluctantly, Picket turned to follow her. As he moved, still a little awkward on his crutches, his eyes took in the amazing things all around. Painters made portraits, a chandler and several apprentices tested new-made candles, a barber stitched a wound while a rabbit holding an aching tooth waited nearby. And there was much more to see. The outside of the hall had hollows where a certain number of shops and workspaces were settled, while the large room teemed with booths and other temporary structures. Everywhere they looked, energetic work was underway.

Emma led them down a wide lane of portable booths, to an open area where a group of rabbits had gathered. Lord Rake, in his finest white, stood by, smiling. The gathered rabbits were looking at the two who stood near him. One was a middle-age rabbit, about Uncle Wilfred's age, a doe with kind eyes, glasses, and a bright apron. She had flowers wreathed around her high, handsome ears. The other was nearer to Picket's and Heather's ages, young and happy. They stood face to face, the young rabbit with what must be her parents right behind her, smiling and a little teary-eyed.

"What is this?" Heather asked.

"It's a calling ceremony," Emma said. "You see, we—" but she was cut off by Lord Rake loudly clearing his throat for silence. Noise continued in the hall at large, but the area of silence grew to include the booths and shops nearest the gathered crowd.

"My friends," Lord Rake said, "welcome to the calling ceremony of Gloria Folds. Please, attend to Mrs. Clove Halmond," he said indicating the older rabbit. The gathered rabbits cheered, and when the cheer faded, it spread the silence further throughout the hall.

"Pacer, please give the horn." Pacer, Lord Rake's cold lieutenant, walked over and handed the older rabbit a horn. She drew it to her lips and blew an earsplitting call. This caused the entire hall to stop work. Though many could not see, the hall was laid out such that most could hear. Then Mrs. Halmond spoke.

"Hear me, friends. I am delighted to present my apprentice, Miss Gloria Folds." More cheers. Gloria was beaming. "I have come to love this young lady and am delighted to welcome her into my work. She has shown great promise in the gardens, one of the brightest students I've had since I became garden mistress of our community." Gloria bowed, and Mrs. Halmond returned the bow, smiling wide.

"We are honored," Gloria's father said, "that you have a place for her. You are a credit to our community and a true herald."

"We are so proud of you, Gloria," her mother said to her, though loud enough for all to hear. "We couldn't be prouder. You have worked hard, been filled with kindness, and we're glad to see you go to a work you love—a work that serves so many." Gloria and her parents embraced.

"This is the important part," Emma whispered to Heather, and many others were whispering and smiling at each other.

They turned again so that Garden Mistress Halmond was facing Gloria. They were both smiling, but Mrs. Halmond's face grew suddenly more composed, serious. There was a sudden silence in the hall. Mrs. Halmond took a step forward and placed her right fist over her heart.

"I accept you," she said clearly, with solemn joy.

"I am accepted," Gloria said, attempting to mime Mrs. Halmond's tone.

"I bind you, with all honor, to release you better still."

"I am bound," Gloria said, "by honor and fealty, to serve you."

They bowed to each other, and Lord Rake began the applause that soon enough sounded like a thunderstorm in the hall. Gloria and Mrs. Halmond embraced, and there were cheers and well-wishes called as they left the hall, heading for the gardens on the village green.

Emma smiled at Heather.

"You're so happy," Heather said. "Everyone's so happy."

"It reminds each of us of our own calling ceremony," Emma said. "It reminds us that we belong."

They followed Emma toward the door. On their way, they passed a potter's station, where an old fat-faced rabbit was teaching three young rabbits the craft. The apprentices all appeared to be about Picket's age.

"Hello, Miss Emma," the potter said, setting his wheel spinning with his foot pedal and grabbing a glob of clay.

"Hello, Master Eefaw," Emma replied.

"New friends?"

"Yessir," she said, putting her arm around Heather. "This is Heather. That's Picket."

"Hello, this Heather and that Picket," he said, adding water to his wheel. "I'm Eefaw Potter. Quite a ceremony, yes?" They nodded. "Have you come to see the options for yourself?" He swept his hand dramatically over the room, slopping some clay onto his irritated students. He didn't notice.

"I suppose so," Heather said, trying not to laugh.

"I'm just showing them around, for now," Emma said. "They just got here."

"Well, be easy, friends," Eefaw said. "It's not that big of a deal. When you do choose and are chosen, it'll only be a career for life."

Heather and Picket looked at each other.

"I'm only kidding," Eefaw said, closing his eyes and wheezing. He waved his hand at them dismissively, which sent a glop of goopy clay sailing over their heads. "You have lots of time, and nothing is final. Still," he said, looking up and putting his hand to his chin thoughtfully, caking his short beard in clay, "most rabbits stick with what they choose first. So, it's very important to choose your work wisely.

That is, if they can take you on." He resumed his molding of the clay, which spun up and down his fingers on the wet turning wheel.

"Did you choose pottery from the start, Master Eefaw?" Emma asked as the clay took shape beneath his steady hands.

"Well, no," he said, again putting his hand to his chin and lifting his eyes to the heights, while his fresh clay began to spin out of control. "Come to think of it, I believe it was my fourth choice. My dad didn't live to pass on his own work." His foot kept pumping and the wheel kept spinning. The wet, malformed clay slid to the edge of the wheel, threatening to fly off in a thousand directions, soaking them all in the muddy substance. His students were alarmed but looked unsure of whether they should try to intervene. One very clean, very white rabbit with a bright pink bow edged close to the wheel, but just as the clay seemed certain to be flung away, Eefaw swept his arm out and said, "But I like it quite a lot," slinging mud all over the white rabbit while almost effortlessly snagging the clay from the wheel's edge. He whistled as he resumed working the clay, bearing his thumbs down in the middle, almost magically reforming the adventurous clay into a beautiful bowl. His exasperated students shook their heads and scowled. Noticing them for the first time in a while, Master Eefaw scolded them. "What have I told you loafers about staying clean?"

"I think Heather might be well-suited for the tale-spinners," Emma said, nudging her friend.

Heather felt panic rise, and she looked away. *Why am I so afraid of what I love to do?*

"She is a good storyteller," Picket said, frowning at her.

"Telling stories to littles is not the same as a calling," Heather said, blushing.

"I can think of few higher callings," Master Eefaw said, raising his eyebrows at Heather and motioning over to the storyguild.

Heather stared at the place, a large hollow where a tall rabbit appeared to be reading from a paper as students sat listening. She longed to go in and listen, but she was afraid. And she was embarrassed to be afraid. "We haven't decided what to pursue," she said.

"You have time," he said, smiling, his beard caked in clay. His students stood behind him, cross-armed and furious.

"Nice to meet you," Heather said as Emma shooed them away.

"One more thing!" Master Eefaw shouted to them as they drew open the door to leave. "This is a place where rabbits make and are made. You are what you do. Choose wisely, young Picket. Choose wisely, brave Heather. Understand?"

"Yessir," Heather said, nodding.

"The community needs you!" he shouted, throwing his arms out to indicate the entire vast hall of busy rabbits at work. Wet clay flew everywhere.

Chapter Twenty-Four

A SHAME

The three friends came through the door into the round hallway, barely containing their laughter. Once out of the massive hall, and out of danger of being hit with muddy clay, the laughter burst out of them like a long-awaited sneeze.

Picket, hobbling through the door, tripped and slid across the room, coming to a halt beside the large wooden barrel in the center of the room. When he looked up, he saw the tip of a spear.

"Back up!" a fierce rabbit in guards' green said, no hint of humor in his expression. Picket's face, which had only a second before been full of joy, now turned sour.

"All right, all right!" he said, hobbling to his feet with Heather and Emma's help. "You don't have to be so harsh."

"Yes, I do," the guard said. "There are traitors among us."

"Come away, Picket," Heather said. Then she turned on the guard. "I've never seen such rudeness!" she said.

"It's his job," Emma said quietly, with an apologetic look back at the guard.

"It's his job to be rude?" Picket asked as they moved back into the long hallway. The wounded, angry look that had slowly begun to evaporate in the laughter of a few moments before was returning.

"It's his job," Emma said kindly, "to protect us all."

"Well, somehow I think there are bigger threats to Cloud Mountain than a stumbling cripple," Picket whispered harshly. They paused inside the long corridor.

"The barrel," Emma said, whispering. "It's blastpowder."

"Blastpowder?" Heather asked.

"Yes," Emma explained. "It's there for our defense. The guards may set fire to the blastpowder if the mountain is under siege. It would blow up the hallways and the stairway, blocking the way to the village and the great hall. It's really volatile. They think it could possibly explode if the barrel is knocked over. That's why there are three guards around it day and night. Plus, some folks don't trust outsiders. Especially …"

"Especially what?" Heather said.

"Well, some here don't like your uncle very much, and so they don't trust you. But that guard was just doing his job."

Heather shook her head. She was sorry about the blastpowder, but she didn't understand why anyone wouldn't love Uncle Wilfred. She realized for the first time that it might be costing Emma something, perhaps a lot, to be such a good friend to them.

"Thank you," she said to Emma, smiling gratefully and taking Emma's hands. "Picket," she said, turning to him, "we should really apologize to the guard. He was only doing his job."

"No," was all Picket would say as he hobbled down the hallway toward King Whitson's Garden.

"Picket!" Emma called after him. "You don't know the way."

"I know the way, Emma. I'm not completely helpless."

"I know that, Picket," Emma said. "Anyway, there's something I want to show you."

"Forget it," he said bitterly.

"Don't go," Heather said. But he went on, saying no more. He grunted and grumbled as he disappeared into the long hallway that led back to King's Garden.

After he was gone, Heather shook her head.

"He'll be all right, dear Heather," Emma said, putting her arm around her friend.

"I hope so," Heather said, swallowing a sob. "It's like I've lost him too. I've lost all my family."

"Well, sister," Emma said, taking Heather's face gently in her hands, "you've got me now. And Picket'll come 'round. Trust me. This place has a way of undoing the worst sort of enchantments. Believe me, I should know."

"What do you mean?"

"Well, when I came here I was very little, but at some point I grew frustrated with my … well, my situation."

"About your parents?" Heather asked.

"Yes. That exactly," Emma said, her eyes moving to the third door in the round room. "But I had some help."

"Lord Rake?"

"Well, yes and no," Emma said. "He was what I was mainly angry about. I got it into my head that my parents had wanted to keep me but that he had somehow stolen me, instead of rescuing me. I wondered if they were good rabbits who wished for something else for me."

"They weren't good?" Heather asked.

"I suppose so, but I don't know," Emma said. "But that's not the point. I had no reason to doubt Lord Rake, and he was a good guardian to me. He had saved my life; this much I knew. Even if I knew—and still know—little else. Secrets stay hidden here for a long time."

"What changed your mind?" Heather asked.

Emma looked back at the third door. "Maggie O'Sage."

"Who is that?"

"Follow me," Emma said, dragging Heather back into Hallway Round and toward the unguarded third door. She put her finger to her lips, and Heather was silent. Emma opened the door, and Heather followed her in.

* * *

Picket was getting good at fuming. As he clopped on his crutches down the long hallway toward King's Garden, he let all the feelings of resentment, anger, and bitterness wash over him like a waterfall of self-pity. It was actually quite pleasant, in an ugly way. He was sick and tired of being treated like a useless, pathetic, bawling infant. Of course, when he thought about babies, he remembered Jacks. The sudden surge of sadness only joined the chorus of miseries all singing the song of how badly he had it and how unfair everything was. First, the humiliating failures at Nick Hollow, where he gave away their position to the wolves, causing them to be chased and nearly killed over and over. Then, the unbearable aloofness of Smalls, who deigned to order him around and had the gall to actually pick him up and rescue him at Decker's Landing, when he could have easily done it himself.

For the moment, Picket fought away the voice of conscience giving a different version of events in his mind, and he stubbornly focused on how unjust it had all been. Images of Smalls talking down to him, giving him orders, and rescuing Heather were all ingredients in a steaming, frothing kettle of fury that was ready to boil over.

He came to the doorway leading back to the sunlit King's Garden, teeth gritted. He knocked loudly, but there was no answer. He knocked again. Still nothing. So he tried the door himself, but it would not open. He was furious. He just wanted to get to his room and lie down on his bed and try to forget everything.

"Open this door!" he shouted. There was no reply.

Finally he raised one of his carefully fashioned crutches and smashed it against the wooden door. The door held firm, but the crutch shattered, showering the torchlit hallway with splintered shards.

The door opened then, and, in no time at all, Picket was taken to the ground and a sword was at his throat. Behind him, a spear was leveled at his head. Squinting up, he saw that the spear belonged to the guard who had threatened him beside the blastpowder barrel. The guard must have heard the noise and rushed down the corridor. Now Picket's anger turned to deeper embarrassment. How could things get any worse?

He looked through the doorway and saw Smalls looking in at him. "What have you done this time, lad?"

Chapter Twenty-Five

THE THIRD DOOR

Picket hobbled down the tall stone stairway from King Whitson's Garden in a furious silence. He was very low.

"I'm sorry, Picket," Smalls said, following behind him. They were headed back toward Picket and Heather's room. Both of them were on crutches, though Smalls had two and Picket now had only one. "I forgot how much it irritates you for me to call you 'lad.' I'll try to remember next time. In my defense, it's what I call many of my younger friends."

Picket said nothing, just hung his head and labored down the endless steps in the stone stairway. Above them the chains hung, apparently useless. *Like me.*

Smalls had helped Picket get out of the trouble he'd made for himself when he lost his temper, shattering one of his crutches on the door. Though one of the guards was resistant to Smalls, when Lord Rake came and Smalls spoke to him, they were allowed to go without any more questions.

Picket was deeply embarrassed. They passed by a pair of hunched whisperers who gave them cold looks. This happened often, and Picket didn't know why. Maybe they knew all about his failures. Maybe they were ashamed to be in his presence. Right now, he didn't care.

Smalls shook his head sadly. "Those guards back there at the door," he explained gently, "they're trained to protect the community. They have rules here that might seem a little strange." Picket made no answer, so Smalls went on. "You have to remember that most of the rabbits here escaped the afterterrors that followed the fall of the king. They are on edge, so when someone tries to break a door down, they have to act."

"But, I wasn't trying to ..." Picket began, but he fell silent again with an exasperated sigh.

"Just hang in there, la—um, pal," Smalls said, correcting himself. "It's not the end of the world."

"Too bad," Picket muttered.

They reached the bottom of the stairway. Picket resumed his use of the single crutch, lunging forward as fast as he could, though he was out of breath. He was exhausted, embarrassed, in pain, and eager to be rid of Smalls.

They continued down the corridor and hung a left. After a few more minutes of awkward silence, they arrived in front of Picket and Heather's room.

"This it?" Smalls asked.

Picket nodded.

"Is Heather around?"

Picket shook his head no, then opened the door and went inside.

Just before he closed the door, Smalls stuck his foot in and stopped it. "Ouch!" he cried, realizing he'd stuck an injured foot in. "Dumb instincts," he said, rubbing his foot. Picket said nothing, but he winced when he saw Smalls' foot get jammed.

"Listen, Picket," Smalls said. "I'm going to say this to you, because you hate me anyway and so it doesn't matter if you get even more angry at me." Picket tried to shut the door again, but Smalls wouldn't allow it. Instead, he shuffled into the room and stood in front of the paintings at the foot of the bed. "Listen, lad. And you *are* acting like a very little lad. You're not the only one bad things have happened to. You're not the only one who's lost someone they love."

Picket, who tried to harden his heart against Smalls, looked past him to the paintings on the wall. His eyes found the meadow painting of what they believed was their old home in the Great Wood. He saw the artist's signature at the bottom, "F. S." *Finbar Smalls*. A celebrated artist who was now lost. Picket lowered his eyes, and tears started to form.

Smalls went on. "You have got to pull yourself together and stop moping around, feeling sorry for yourself. I know, Picket. I know what you're going through. I know it so well." He turned his back on Picket and faced the wall of paintings. Seeing the large painting of the meadow in the Great Wood, Smalls reached out and touched it gently. Picket thought he heard a sniff.

After a few moments, Smalls lowered his hand, lowered his head. With his back still to Picket, he said softly, "We can't always save them. And we just have to do our part." Without looking at Picket, he quickly crossed the room and left, closing the door behind him.

Picket sat in the silent room, looking at the meadow painting and feeling like the lowest creature in the world.

* * *

Heather was amazed at what was behind the third door. Each door in Hallway Round had been a surprise. The first led to the garden and fields, the village green, and more. The second led to the massive stone hall where so many worked. And this third door, after a steep stone stairway leading down seven flights, revealed a long mossy porch, overlooking what must be the whole world. At least Heather believed the lookout would reveal miles and miles if it weren't for the mist. In the garden and village green above, the mist was thin and wispy. Here it hung heavy and thick, like a slowly shifting wall only a few yards from the porch. It was the thick belt of cloud she had seen from the boat near Decker's Landing. Dense, impenetrable fog. If the fog wall were gone, this would, she imagined, be a breathtaking view.

Unlike behind the other two doors, where hundreds worked and played, this ledge of stone, moss, and mist was occupied by only three rabbits. Two were painting on the near side of the porch, closer to the door. On the far side, up a small flight of steps, a single rabbit—an older lady—sat working vigorously at her sewing.

At first Heather thought it might be Lady Glen, but a closer look showed many differences. Where Lady Glen was firm and intimidating, this lady appeared softer, almost worn out. She was more like a mysterious cottage than a regal tower. From time to time she looked up longingly at the mist; then, when her attention was required, she attended to her sewing. She never stopped. Her hands seemed to be part of the needle, the thread. She worked as if by magic. Heather had been sewing for a few years, and her mother had always sewed. But neither could sew half as fast as this lady. There were baskets on both sides of her chair, full of clothing.

Emma motioned for Heather to follow her, and they walked toward the lady. As they passed the artists' stations, Heather saw that each painted a stunning vista, an incredible distant view of a wide green woodland, with rivers and waterfalls, fields and flowers. A magical sight.

Heather was astonished. She saw how they peered into the fog, squinting, then placed paint on canvas, bringing the work to life. She shook her head as they walked past, and Emma nodded, smiling.

They walked slowly up to the lady, who smiled at them in turn. Emma curtsied, and Heather did the same.

"Good afternoon, ma'am," Emma said.

"Hello, Emma," the lady said kindly. "Please. Won't you have a seat and tell me who your friend is?"

The two girls bowed and sat down. "Ma'am," Emma began, "may I introduce Heather O'Nick? Heather, this is Maggie O'Sage, the wisest lady in the world."

"I'm very pleased to meet you," Heather said.

"And I, you, my dear," Maggie said. "And Emma, as I've told you and your esteemed guardian many times, you may dispense with the absurd 'O'Sage' business. They believe they honor me by making me out to be so wise. You may call me Maggie, or Mrs. Weaver."

"Yes, Mrs. Weaver," Heather said.

"So, you are from Nick Hollow?" Mrs. Weaver said. "I have been there a few times, before the last war. It was quite lovely then."

"Yes, ma'am," Heather said. "It was."

"So, you are new to this community, along with your bitter little brother," Mrs. Weaver said. "And Emma has brought you to me so that I might give you the high-minded purpose of this place and these rabbits. Am I correct?"

Emma smiled, and both girls nodded.

"Well, I suppose someone has to explain things around here, and the poets and tale-spinners are, of course, never called upon. Only this mad old lady who sews all day and stares off into mist. Surely she's the best for the job." She laughed, and the girls, seeing she was amused, smiled.

"I'm pretty sure I would rather hear it from you, ma'am," Heather said.

"So you shall," Mrs. Weaver said. "What do you know so far?"

"If I may, ma'am," Emma said. "Heather knows very little. She's only had a little bit of a story about King Jupiter, and she knows nothing of the fall. Only, she knows there's been a fall, and that the Great Wood is ruled by wicked masters. She hasn't had her initiation yet and is bound by the law of initiates. She doesn't know about—well, about very much."

"It's an awful tale, Heather," Mrs. Weaver said sadly, her eyes going once again to the wall of mist. "If this mist were gone, you'd need fewer words. For beyond it lies the saddest sight in all of Natalia. Sometimes, very rarely, the mist will clear—for only a moment—and you can see the horrible ruins of the Great Wood. But we can talk more of the fall another time. You must already understand those things pretty well, and more can be added. But what of the Mended Wood, yes?"

"Yes," Heather said, her words rushing out. "I don't understand it all. Rabbits work and play, keeping hedges straight and rooms clean. They make soup so good you could scream and paint scenes that aren't there!" she finished, pointing to the two painters at work on the other side of the porch.

"I understand, dear," Mrs. Weaver said, patting her arm.

"Why?" Heather asked. "I want to know why."

"And I will tell you," Mrs. Weaver said, looking kindly into Heather's eyes. "Since the awful day King Jupiter fell and the Great Wood was lost to tyranny, our world has been wounded to its heart. No greater peril has existed for us since Whitson Mariner's trekkers first came to this place. There are secret citadels, though only a few, which have kept alive a hope of invading and retaking the Great Wood. I wish them well, and part of my sewing and mending goes to support them. But there's another kind of mending that must be done. This place is full of farmers, artists, carpenters, midwives, cooks, poets, healers, singers, smiths, weavers—workers of all kinds. We're all doing our part."

"But what good will all that do?" Heather asked. "Shouldn't everyone fight for the Great Wood—for King Jupiter's cause?"

"Sure we should," Mrs. Weaver said. "In a sense. Some must bear arms and that is their calling. But this," she motioned back to the mountain behind her, "this is a place dedicated to the reasons *why* some must fight. Here we anticipate the Mended Wood, the Great Wood healed. Those painters are seeing what is not yet but we hope will be. They are really seeing, but it's a different kind of sight. They anticipate the Mended Wood. So do all in this community, in our various ways.

"We sing about it. We paint it. We make crutches and soups and have gardens and weddings and babies. This is a place out of time. A window into the past and the future world. We are heralds, you see, my dear, saying what will surely come. And we prepare with all our might, to be ready when once again we are free."

Chapter Twenty-Six

BOUND

They stayed with Maggie Weaver until lunch, then went down to the Savory Den. It was packed today, but even so, Heather was certain everyone didn't eat down there. There wasn't nearly enough room. After a short, frustrated search for Picket, they gave up and decided to go ahead and eat.

"So," Emma said, "what'd you think of her?"

"She was amazing," Heather said. "One of the most incredible rabbits I've ever met. I didn't want to leave."

"I knew you wanted to stay on," Emma said, "but that's just it. Everyone wants to. So there's a kind of unwritten rule that she politely doesn't let anyone stay for too long. An hour, maybe half that again. So many want her advice that she tries not to let anyone take all her time."

"So, when she said, 'Oh, my children, could you take this basket to Master Shelling?' that was our cue to go?"

"Exactly," Emma said, smiling. "She's subtle, but effective. Time with her is like gold around here."

"And her sewing is unreal!" Heather said. "It's like she's always doing two jobs."

"Lord Rake says she's the wisest rabbit he knows. And I think he's known everyone ever. He goes to her for advice every week, at least. She takes no apprentices, eats little, and gets more sewing done than the next best three. She's a wonder."

"Now I understand what Doctor Zeiger said to you. 'A lot of Maggie; hold the Helmer.'"

"Yes," Emma said, frowning. "Helmer is a plague, and Mrs. Weaver is a cure. It was my number one plan for getting Picket well again. His foot will heal, and pretty fast, I think. It's the other stuff I'm worried about. I'm so frustrated he wouldn't come."

"I'm sorry, Emma. Thanks for caring about us. I feel like it's costing you," Heather said, glancing around and seeing, once again, scowls and frowns.

"Maybe we should look for him again after lunch," Emma said, brushing off her concern.

"I agree. I don't like him being alone," Heather said. "I'm getting the feeling that we're not exactly welcome in this place."

* * *

Picket wasn't alone. He had eaten lunch early and made his way back up the steps, through King Whitson's Garden, into Hallway Round, past the blastpowder barrel and its wary guards, and into the sunlit air of the village green. His foot felt better, but he knew it was still a little ways from being healed.

222

For the first time in days, he knew precisely what he wanted to do. There was one thing and one thing only he was interested in. He wanted to fight anyone who had anything to do with what happened to his family.

"Good morning, Picket," Heyward said as Picket passed the stone tables that lay alongside the endless neat rows of hedges. "You seem to be moving better today than yesterday."

"Thanks," Picket said, not stopping. He didn't want to get sidetracked by any crazy talk about how straight these hedgerows were. He had a crazy thing to do himself.

"You are without your female companions today?" Heyward said, matching Picket's stride, walking along beside him.

Picket sighed. "Yes," he said. "I am free of my jailers at the moment." Then he added, "Or I was," under his breath.

"That reminds me of my hedges," Heyward said. Picket had a feeling that everything reminded him of his hedges. "Sometimes I feel like I am imprisoned by the hedges." He tucked his enormous shears beneath his left arm, and with his right hand he stroked his chin. "Other times, I feel I am the jailer. I keep them in line. I restrict their movements. It's really some deep, deep—"

Heyward became suddenly speechless when he recognized where his little walk with Picket was taking him. Right to the large maple and right in front of Helmer the Black, who was lying in the shade.

Picket looked over at Heyward, whose wide, suspicious eyes said everything his mouth didn't.

"I'm sure you have some clipping to do, Heyward," Picket said. "I won't tie you up."

Heyward nodded and was about to speak when they heard a gravelly voice mumble, "I think we *should* tie him up. Just for fun."

"I'll see you later," Heyward said, and he turned and walked quickly away.

Picket stood beneath the mostly barren boughs of the massive maple, staring at the reclining rabbit. Picket saw that there were still a few tied-off traps in the trees above. More insane games of life or death. He noticed too the black shield with its awful emblem, the red diamond symbol that so nearly matched the one worn by Redeye Garlackson, who had tried to kill him and his sister and had done who-knew-what to the rest of his family. He noticed too the impressive sword, also black, with a solitary emerald inset on the hilt.

Now that he was closer, he saw that there were flecks of grey in Helmer's fur. Picket had thought him younger. But now that he could really see him well, with sunlight streaming in, he looked haggard, unwell. Helmer didn't move or speak. He lay on his back, fiddling with a short knife.

"I'd like you to train me," Picket said. "I need to learn how to fight."

"That's the guards' business," Helmer said dismissively. He tossed the knife into the air, letting it spin and spin until it came down again, and he caught it by its handle. "Go cry to Lord Rake."

"I don't want to."

"Well, I don't care," Helmer said. "He's in charge of all military personnel on this mountain, and I wouldn't train a ladybug without his permission. And I never talk to anyone, let alone train them. And I'm struggling to see the difference between you and a ladybug."

"So you would do it if he approved?" Picket asked. "I thought you hated Lord Rake."

"No," Helmer said flatly. "I wouldn't."

"You wouldn't help me get revenge on those who ruined my family?" Picket said in a growl, his temper rising.

Helmer threw and caught the blade several times, as if he had no interest in the young rabbit. Finally, he said, "That's right. I wouldn't. As much as I'm moved by your need for revenge—and that is definitely my main interest in life—I'm sorry, little one; I can't be bothered with you."

Picket seethed. All the hurts and helplessness, all the blundering and misery in his heart rose like a slow-building storm. "Listen to me," he said. His voice was a surprise, even to himself. Somehow he kept it even but packed it with all the menace he could muster. "I'm sick of being told what to do. I'm tired of being the helpless crybaby who needs his diaper changed. I want to do something about what's been done to me and mine. And the way I see it, being the best soldier in this army is my only way of ever doing something about that. The way I see it, you're the rabbit to train me. If you won't, I'll never leave you in peace."

"Oh, you'll leave me, lad," Helmer said. "The second I want you out of my sight."

"I think you're underestimating me."

"I have no estimation of you at all, child." Helmer yawned. "You're nothing."

Picket felt these words like blows, but he held his ground. He was silent for a while. Then he said, "What happened to you?"

"None of your concern," Helmer said.

"I guess you don't mind that your name's a disgrace?" Picket said.

"Same as yours," Helmer said.

Picket didn't exactly understand what he meant. Did Helmer know of all the blunders and mistakes he'd made in the last few days? "You disgust—" Picket began, but Helmer cut him off.

"Enough," he said. "Now, I know you're pathetic, lad. So I let you dish out your rotten fruit here a little. But I'm full of it now. Get out of here."

"But—" Picket began again.

"Not one. More. Word," Helmer said, and there was silence for a moment.

Then Picket erupted. "You coward!"

Helmer half-rose and his arm shot out. The knife moved quickly. Picket thought for a moment that Helmer had thrown it at him, but it sailed over his head, slicing through a taut rope, and sunk in the tree. A massive wooden bird, released by the snapped cord, bore down on Picket.

Picket acted before he could decide anything. He lunged, but he had forgotten about his bad foot. He buckled, unable to escape. At the last moment, a strong kick from Helmer sent the swooping menace past him. Helmer sliced the cord with another knife, and the wooden bird fell to earth. Picket clutched at his foot, pain racing up his leg. He would have escaped, had his foot held up. Of course that only reminded him of how he'd hurt his foot to begin with. It was always something. Another layer of bitter resentment lay over him like a cloak.

Picket's fury outstripped his pain. When Helmer passed him, walking leisurely back beneath the tree, he lunged for the black rabbit, this time launching from his good foot. But Helmer was too quick. Picket was knocked back to the ground, groaning from new pains.

By the time Picket recovered enough to try to slink off, he looked up to see his sister, along with Emma and Lord Rake, walking quickly his way. Heather looked worried and angry.

"Perfect," Picket said. "Pile it on." His shame and embarrassment knew no end.

"What is happening here?" Lord Rake asked as he reached the perimeter of the maple. Helmer was lying down again. Picket struggled to his feet. There was a gash in the earth where the wooden bird had skidded to a halt. "Helmer? What have you done now?"

Helmer didn't respond. Lord Rake advanced on him. But Picket spoke up. "He was showing me a few things."

"Picket?" Heather asked, eyebrows arching and mouth tight.

"Yes," Picket said. "He was kind enough to show me some maneuvers. I want to be in the guard, so he was helping me."

Lord Rake's frown said he didn't believe this for a second. Emma was trying to get Picket to let her examine his foot. "You'll need to rest it, Picket," she said, shaking her head.

"What really—?" Heather began, but Picket looked at her, his face pleading for her to be quiet and let him escape with a shred of dignity. "Well, let's go," she said.

While they made to leave, Lord Rake peered down at Helmer. Picket thought another confrontation was imminent. He tried to block it out, leaning on Heather as they walked slowly away. His embarrassment and resentment tumbled around inside him, but it was no longer a seething anger. He felt bent up, broken, and worthless. Tears came hot and heavy, sliding down his face as he fought to keep from sobbing. He had never felt so low in all his life.

Then, out of the awkward silence he heard a gravelly voice call out.

"I accept you."

"What?" Emma, Heather, and Lord Rake all said together. Picket turned and saw that Helmer stood just behind an astonished Lord Rake. Helmer's fist was over his heart.

He said it again. "I accept you."

"Now, wait a minute—" Lord Rake began, but Picket's raised voice silenced him for a moment.

"I am accepted," Picket said, tears standing in his eyes. He had stopped crying. His fist was over his heart.

"I bind you, with all honor, to release you better after," Helmer said.

"I am bound," Picket said, pausing to recall the words he had marked at the calling ceremony of Gloria Folds. "By honor and fealty, to serve you."

They bowed to each other. Helmer walked away, back to the partial shade of his maple tree. Picket, leaning on Heather, turned and walked the other way. Heather was too astonished to speak, and it was Emma's turn to brood.

"Tomorrow morning, ladybug," Helmer shouted back to him.

Picket grinned.

Chapter Twenty-Seven

QUESTIONABLE PAST

Lord Rake caught up with Picket and Heather in front of the statues of Whitson and Blackstar. Emma stood by impatiently as her guardian explained things, her arms crossed and her foot tapping. Lord Rake had spoken to Helmer and had reluctantly agreed to permit the arrangement, albeit on a trial basis.

"Here is how this will happen," Lord Rake said, a touch of anger in his voice. "Every morning, you will report to Maggie O'Sage. Then you work with Helmer during the day. Then, every evening, you're to sit with Maggie again. After that, you'll have an initiate's lesson in Lighthall," he said, pointing to the eight-sided room, which just now was erupting in colored blasts of light, "with your sister. These are the terms of your apprenticeship."

"I agree," Picket said quickly, almost as if to cut off any other terms. He made to walk away.

"Picket," Lord Rake said, stopping him and looking into the young rabbit's eyes. "I want you to be careful. Please? Will you do that?"

"As careful as someone training for war can be," Picket said, bowing quickly.

Lord Rake would have to accept it. He seemed to, with a persistent look of concern. He nodded to Picket and then turned to leave them. Over his shoulder he said, "I'll see you tomorrow night, at Lighthall, after supper. If you're still alive." He disappeared down the brick path back toward the hallway.

Emma's frown looked to be permanent, and, waving to Heather, she followed after her guardian. As Heather and Picket descended the long stairway, Picket moving a little gingerly on his bad foot, they could hear Emma's raised voice trailing behind her. She was clearly furious. But what about Heather? She was silent.

* * *

Heather wasn't sure how to feel. She was concerned about Picket. She wanted him to be well and to do good. She wanted what she believed her parents would want for him. She was still concerned about him, but her concern had simply shifted. She had been worried about him brooding and moping around, a sullen shadow of himself, doing nothing. Now, she worried about what he *was* doing, what he might become under the influence of the reckless rabbit with the mysterious past. But she was glad that he'd agreed to see Mrs. Maggie Weaver. So she was concerned, but with a ray of hope poking through the dark cloud of her fears.

* * *

The next morning at breakfast, Picket was full of nervous energy.

"I'm so glad you're meeting her, Picket," Heather said.

Picket murmured something and chomped his food. "I don't want to be late," he managed to say in between bites of honey-drenched bread.

"I think Mrs. Weaver will do wonders for you," she said.

He frowned. It was probably a mistake to say that, she thought. Best to let it happen naturally. Hopefully there would be enough Maggie O'Sage to offset the damage Helmer might do.

"What should I call her, Maggie O'Sage or Mrs. Weaver? I'm confused," Picket said. "What's the story with names here, anyway?"

Heather looked around for Uncle Wilfred, Lord Rake, or anyone older and wiser than she. But no such luck. "I'm not sure, Picket. I think last names used to only be used by lords and ladies, like Rake. But these days, rabbits use either their calling as a last name, like Eefaw Potter, or their home, like us with O'Nick. Of Nick Hollow."

"I know that. But we never used that name before. And Father isn't even from Nick Hollow, really," Picket said.

"I don't know," she said. "Maybe it's just something they do more here. Go on now. Won't you be late?"

He stuffed another large slice of bread in his pocket

and quickly hobbled from the room. A small wave was all Heather got in farewell. She looked down at her plate. She was still working on her first plateful, while Picket had polished off three.

"Picket O'Bottomless-Pit," she murmured to herself. She closed her eyes and thought of Picket, their parents, and little Jacks. She prayed they would all be safe and together again. Somehow.

Kyle appeared in the Savory Den. Noticing Heather, he waved. Then he and a small parcel of his gang came and sat all around her.

"Good morning, Kyle," she said. "Good morning, bucks."

"Good morning to you, Heather," Kyle said, and his gang nodded to her, all grinning in a mischievous, slightly clueless way. "Have you heard the rumors?" Kyle asked.

"Nope," Heather said, feigning disinterest. Inside, she was eager for answers, even from this apparently unreliable rabbit. "But I did hear some interesting things when I had breakfast with Jupiter's heir after returning from an all-night tour through the marvels of the lost land of Terralain. A fascinating conversation. He had a few prophecies about young rabbits who lie."

"Very funny," Kyle said. "Say hi for me next time you see him."

Heather laughed. "I'll do that."

"You know, Heather, you could have really had breakfast with Jupiter's heir this morning and not known it was really him," Kyle said, his shoulder raised.

"I had breakfast with my brother," Heather said, shaking her head.

"You never know," Kyle began. "Bilton Chandler told me he knew something bad about your brother. And now he's apprenticed to Helmer the Blackhearted?"

"Okay, you rogue, enough of that. I won't hear you speak ill of my perfect, polite, and posh little brother," she said. "What's the news this morning? I'm sure you have something juicy to share."

"I do," he said, smiling wide.

"Okay, what is it?"

"Only that the secret citadels are in turmoil, nearly all of them." Kyle looked side to side, then resumed, touching his nose. "The word is, they are sick of waiting. Some of them want to attack Morbin now and go down in an awful, inevitable defeat. You know, your real death-and-glory party. Others are sown full of traitors—which, beg your pardon, should interest you—who are in the pay of the Lords of Prey. They are causing all kinds of turmoil. The word is that the lords and captains are all meeting here over the next week to decide what to do."

"What'll happen?" Heather asked, unable to pretend she wasn't interested.

"It could be the end of the resistance," Kyle said flatly. "Which in a short time would mean the end of this place." He appeared oddly unfazed by this.

"But we've only just gotten here," Heather said. "And no matter what you say, I like it here."

"Sure, it's okay," Kyle said. "Just a little too strict for me."

"Anything is too strict for you, Kyle."

"True enough," he said, shrugging. "But listen, Heather. I like you. You've been kind to me, so I want to level with you." He looked at his gang. "Take a hike," he said. His followers dispersed.

"Okay?" Heather asked, a little confused.

"Listen," Kyle went on, looking back and forth. "I know I'm breaking the law of initiates, but I don't care. I don't know about Terralain," he said, uneasy, "and I'm not sure about Jupiter's heir. I've heard stories about how wonderful Terralain is since I was little, and every dreamy poet you meet thinks it's real. I want to believe in Terralain—more than you know. Jupiter's heir is a real rabbit, though no one I've talked to knows for sure who he is. The fallen king had about ten sons, and most of them are fighting for the title of heir in the Great Wood. But no one knows who, or where, the true heir is. So, rumors fly."

"Jupiter's sons are in the Great Wood?"

"Most of them, sure, or what's left of it. The oldest, Prince Winslow, is the nominal governor of the wood. Some of the citadels want to go over to his cause, believing he can lead a real revolt. Others think he's so close to the Lords of Prey that he's compromised. They believe he's too tight with Morbin himself. Morbin's the king of the Lords of Prey and the one who killed King Jupiter."

"Oh my," Heather said, engrossed. "Winslow is allied

with his father's murderer?"

"It's all politics in these great families," Kyle said, swatting at the air dismissively. "All the highborns are the same. Greedy, entitled, and looking to lord over others."

"I wouldn't know," she said, frowning.

"Listen, Heather. I'm leveling with you because I like you," he looked around again and lowered his voice. "There are important rabbits who don't approve of you being here, and things could go very badly here real soon. The Whitson Stone is already lost, or so it's believed, and if the Green Ember doesn't show up, then the fight will go on between the citadels and the king's sons."

Emma entered the room, saw Heather huddled with Kyle, and stomped toward them, a stern look on her face.

"What?" Heather asked. "I don't understand. Who doesn't approve of us?"

Kyle looked back at Emma and rose to leave. Heather grabbed his arm. "Wait, Kyle. Don't go. What's the Green Ember?"

"It's the—"

"What's going on?" Emma asked, cutting Kyle off.

"I was just leaving," Kyle said. With a pensive shrug and a look of regret, he left.

"What was that liar saying?" Emma asked as Kyle disappeared through the stone door.

Heather wasn't sure what to say. She felt she needed time to sort out her questions. "Oh, nothing much."

"Well, I've got to eat and run," Emma said, stuffing

some bread in her mouth. "I'm needed at the hospital. I'll see you later?"

"Yes, sure."

"Are you sure you're okay, Heather?" Emma asked through her chewing.

"Just a lot on my mind, that's all."

"Don't believe anything Kyle says. I once overhead him telling Captain Pacer that he knew what happened to Prince Bleston's Waywards. And sometimes when he talks about Terralain, you feel like he's speaking from his heart. But he's not. He's a liar! I know from experience, dear. Trust me. Don't let him worry you."

"All right," she said absently.

"I've got to go," Emma said, hustling away. "We'll talk later!"

*   *   *

Heather sat at the table, alone. She felt lost, like she didn't even have enough information to know whether or not to constantly worry. No one had told her where to go or what to do today. Strangers had so often shot her the unkindest looks. What did that mean? And who could Kyle have meant when he said important rabbits didn't want them there? She was frustrated. When would answers come?

The thought of visiting the storyguild made her panic. Her other interest, healing, was another matter. She was interested in starting at once, but Emma had told her they weren't taking anyone else on for another few months. That would be after Doctor Zeiger got back and had finished the first season of the current apprentices, which included Emma. That left her caught in between. How odd that sullen Picket had found a place here when she had not. She couldn't even talk to Mrs. Weaver right now, because she knew Picket was with her. She wasn't about to sit around and brood about what Kyle had said, though she felt a nagging worry creep into her mind and settle. She trusted Emma but felt like Kyle might be telling the truth.

There was only one thing to do. She would wander around and explore and try to find some answers ahead of initiation tonight. She might even be able to find Kyle again, though he was pretty good at disappearing.

In a few minutes, she was heading up the long stone stairway, not certain where to start. Lord Rake had said they would have their initiates' lesson in Lighthall. She was glad, but she wondered why they would be allowed in now. Gort had said no one was allowed yet. Was it completed? Were they making an exception for them? If so, why them? They were nobody special. There was nothing about their family to deserve any special honor. Or was there? Why was Lord Rake so concerned about Picket being with Helmer?

So much was possible. Everything felt shrouded in a mystery as heavy as the fog covering the mountaintop. She could imagine beyond it, like the painters on Mrs. Weaver's porch, but she didn't know what was truly there. She believed it might be only a barren wasteland.

She took the last steps two at a time and sprang into King Whitson's Garden. She immediately felt bad, for her noisy entrance had apparently disrupted the quiet contemplation of an older couple. They were both a greying brown color. They had been sitting on a bench, hands clasped, their heads together, but sat back quickly with a look of mild alarm when she thundered in.

"I'm so sorry," she whispered, sliding to a stop.

"Never mind, dear," the lady said. "It was time we got to work anyway." They rose slowly and, hand in hand, made their way down the brick path toward Hallway Round. She wondered where they would be headed—the great hall, the village green, or the mossy, fog-drenched porch? *Everyone has somewhere to go but me. But I'm going to find some answers today.*

Now she had all of King Whitson's Garden to herself. She was amazed that no one else was there. Maybe it was like Mrs. Weaver, a precious commodity that no one felt right about keeping for themselves for very long. She wandered around, looking at flowers and plants, smiling and trying to allow the serenity of the place to calm her nerves and ease her worries. She fingered the split in her ear. She had thought of tying a bow there or seeing if a doctor could sew it together again. But something in her wanted to let it alone. It was a mark of their journey and who she was becoming. Smalls had said it didn't diminish her beauty. She sometimes wore a bow, but not one to cover that ear. Pretty, yes. *But I'll be who I am and remember where I've been.*

Thoughts of the storyguild haunted her. Emma had said there was a place for her, that she'd spoken to the master and reserved her a spot. All she had to do was go to the great hall and find their section, walk in, and take her place.

She tried to distract herself by peering into the windows of Lighthall. But there was nothing to see in that hallway, just a wall of beautiful multicolored glass. The real mystery was farther in, where nothing could be seen, but plenty heard. There was the consistent sound of cutting, hammering, and low talk.

Then, just as she had given up and planned to head for the village green, she saw a white form pass before one of the low windows.

Smalls.

What was he up to in there? She knew he must be sad about his father, and maybe being in a place where artists were at work reminded Smalls of him. She didn't want to disturb him, but she wanted to have a look.

She crept along the path. When the path ended, she waded into the mulch and plants, directly behind a wooden panel on the outside of Lighthall. She was only a few feet from the door.

She heard voices. Was she eavesdropping again? She had done it on the boat, had listened to Uncle Wilfred and Smalls for a few minutes, until Picket had woken up. But that had just happened naturally. This was deliberate. Was it wrong? Of course it was.

Just as she made up her mind to leave, the voices grew

closer, clearer. Now she froze, afraid of being seen or heard.

"I have to go out for some supplies," an older voice said. "I'll be back soon."

"All right, Master Glazier," came another voice. A familiar voice. Smalls. "I'll stay here for a little while. Thanks."

"You're welcome anytime," the older rabbit said. "And please, call me Luthe. It pleases me that you feel close to your father here." There was a short silence.

"Very few—" Smalls began.

"I know it," Luthe Glazier said. "You don't need to tell me. I understand."

Heather heard footsteps, a door opening, then closing. Thankfully, he hadn't left by the door near her. She sighed and stood up slowly. Then she heard more footsteps and saw a shape through the broken foliage walking down the path toward her. She ducked low again, hiding behind the cover of a large bush. She was too afraid to look up and see who it was.

She heard the door open and someone go in. By the time she looked again, the door was closing. She moved toward the path but heard an urgent voice.

"It's bad, Smalls." It was Uncle Wilfred. "Pacer says the wolf patrols get closer every day. Their garrison down at Decker's Landing is growing. They seem to know something's up here."

"And Harbone?" Smalls asked.

"Harbone Citadel won't last much longer, I'm afraid."

"Why not?" Smalls said, irritation plain from his tone.

"Can't they hold it together just a little while longer? A few more months?"

"That's just it," Uncle Wilfred said. "They don't think it will be only a little while. They think it's more likely we'll all be betrayed, discovered, and ... well, you know what happens after that."

"You must plead with them," Smalls said.

"I have," he said, frustrated. "But they ... they ..." he was having a hard time going on. "They don't trust me."

There was a long silence.

"Wretches," Smalls said bitterly. Heather stood frozen, eager to hear what it was that was happening outside these walls. But now she was overcome by guilt. She wanted to get away. She searched for a way to escape silently.

"But you know it must be hard for them," Uncle Wilfred said. "I look just like him."

Just like who? thought Heather. She knew of only one rabbit who looked like her Uncle Wilfred. A dread settled over her, holding her motionless.

Finally she shook free, remembering her determination to get away. Now she wanted to go and go quickly. She was afraid of what she might hear. She stepped carefully out of her hiding spot and tiptoed down the path.

"It's not fair," Smalls said.

"I would do the same, if I was them. How can anyone trust me or anyone in my family?" Uncle Wilfred said.

That was the last Heather heard as she ran along the path and down the stone stairway.

Her mind raced as she ran back to her room. Why would Uncle Wilfred believe no one should trust anyone in her family? A sickening dread came over her, along with a flurry of questions she could not answer. Why had Father fled so far away from everyone? Who was the Lady Glen? Was Father a traitor, conspiring with her? Was Mother in on everything? Why had Father wept so much—and he never wept—when he told her and Picket of King Jupiter's betrayal? Did he have something to regret?

She had always wanted to be like her parents. She had wanted answers, wanted the truth. Now, however, she wasn't sure about any of those things.

Chapter Twenty-Eight

A Bad Good Day

Picket arrived on the village green after half an hour with Maggie Weaver. He was still thinking about what she had said to him—the very few words she had said. But he must move on. He had to be prepared for what Helmer might throw at him. And he realized that Helmer might actually throw things at him.

Picket wasn't exactly sure why he had asked Helmer to train him. He just knew, immediately knew, when he saw the insane fight with the swinging wooden birds that this was his rabbit. Picket wanted nothing more than to be the best warrior he could be, so that he would be ready the next time he met up with Redeye Garlackson or anyone who was on the wicked wolf's side.

Today, he got a reluctant wave from Heyward as he passed the neat hedgerows. Picket noticed with some relief that Heyward was a lot less chatty when Helmer loomed.

He took in a deep breath and tried to focus. Helmer lay beneath the tree, wearing his usual black pants and a matching shirt, but today he wore a grey jacket with the same red diamond symbol on the breast. It was unsettling walking up to such an unpredictable rabbit. Picket wasn't sure if he would jump up and attack him or start snoring.

As he neared the tree, Picket thought of attacking the black rabbit himself in a mad flurry. Somehow he thought this might actually impress Helmer. At the last moment he decided against it. He might be killed doing such a thing.

"Good morning, Ladybug," Helmer said, his voice a guttural rasp, as though the air he used to speak was passing through a rusty old gate.

"Good morning ... Wasp?" Picket said.

"Ha," Helmer chuckled. "I like that. But you will call me Master, child."

"Yes, Masterchild," Picket said.

"Well, obviously you have a deep, soul-level need for humility," Helmer said, levering up onto his elbow. "You will receive that momentarily. But if you're as courageous on the battlefield as you are full of ... well, bristling insanity here, you might do some serious damage before our certain and inevitable defeat."

"Certain defeat?" Picket asked. "Bristling what?"

"Lesson one!" Helmer shouted as he kicked his legs up and landed hard on the ground, upright and at the ready. "You listening, Ladybug? Because your apprenticeship starts now."

"Yes, Master Helmer," Picket said, taking a few steps back.

"How many weapons do I have?" Helmer asked. Picket

took a quick inventory, though he thought Helmer might be concealing some.

"Two. Your knife and the sword," Picket said.

Helmer responded with an immediate attack. He hit Picket, kicked him, took off his jacket and struck him with it over and over, then threw rocks at him. Picket scrambled around, trying to dodge rocks, block blows, and escape the whirlwind of whipping coat.

After a few minutes, Picket was sucking air and begging for mercy. Helmer hadn't done him serious harm but had just made enough contact in his blows to make Picket feel them. And Picket did. Wheezing, he clutched at various hurts all around. Suddenly his sore foot didn't seem so bad. In fact, he had gotten around on it okay in his mad dash to escape the onslaught.

"This wasp stings, yes?" Helmer asked.

"Yes, Master Helmer!"

"Will you have a sword with you every time you are in a fight, Ladybug?"

"No, Master Helmer."

"Lesson number one," Helmer said, kicking a spray of loose dirt into Picket's face, causing the young rabbit to fall over, digging at his eyes.

"I can't see!"

"Lesson. Number. One," Helmer said evenly. "Everything is a weapon."

* * *

Heather looked out over the mossy porch into the heavy fog that blocked out the whole world. She was frustrated but felt like this was where she belonged. There on the porch, waiting to speak to Mrs. Weaver, she was unable to see far enough to satisfy her desire. She wanted to know what was beyond the fog, both on the mountain and in her heart. She wanted to know. She wanted to see the past, the future, even the present with far more clarity than she had right now.

After she had sprinted away from King Whitson's Garden and the overheard rumors, the stray pieces of her family's painful secrets, she had run to her room. She had tried to think, tried to reason out answers to the riddles surrounding her.

Giving up, she had run to Hallway Round and then to this porch, hoping to speak with Maggie Weaver, the Sage of Cloud Mountain. But all she had done for an hour was wait. Wait, and peer off into a cloud barrier that summed up all her frustrations. She glanced at the artists, painting their imaginary scenes of beauty, and wanted to spit at them. She didn't, but she felt like she might scream. Maybe then someone would pay attention to her and give her some answers.

She sat on the mossy stone, leaning against the grey mountainside, and wept quietly. She worried and wondered and, finally, dozed off.

* * *

"Are you all right, dear?" It was Maggie Weaver, bending over her and touching her face tenderly. "You were calling for your father."

Heather came awake, saw that she was still on the porch and that Mrs. Weaver's kindly face was before her. "I'm sorry," she said, not really thinking.

"Don't be sorry, girl," Mrs. Weaver said. "Just come along and let's talk a moment."

Heather rubbed her eyes, still wet, and followed behind the hunching form of Mrs. Weaver. They sat down.

"I'm sorry," Heather said again.

"For what?"

"I'm not sure," Heather said. "I think ..." She hesitated. "I want answers, but I'm afraid of what those answers might be."

"This is from wisdom, child," Mrs. Weaver said. "Growing up is terribly wonderful. But often it's also wonderfully terrible. Ha, a riddle of words amounting to nothing. A stuttering cleverism that falls as short as my feeble steps. But this is true. A teacher could become rich if he ever perfected the art of helping mature students unlearn many awful things. Enjoy your innocence, my dear. Even if it only lasts the day."

* * *

Picket limped through Hallway Round, hurting in a dozen places. Hobbling through the door, he made his way past the bending, intent painters, up the stairs to the level where Mrs. Weaver always sat on the far side. His vision was still spotty from the dirt kicked in his eyes, and one eye was all but swollen shut from a rock that had struck him dead-on. He was near the steps when he realized that Mrs. Weaver was with someone. He turned quickly to try to slink back and wait his turn, but he heard her say, "Come along, Picket."

Picket turned again, wincing at the pain, and made his way slowly up to where Heather—he now saw it was her—sat alongside the sewing sage.

* * *

When Heather saw Picket, her hurt turned to fury. "What has that villain done to you?" she shouted, springing to her feet and sprinting to his side. "It's outrageous!"

"Heather, it's—" Picket began, but Heather was just warming up.

"I'll show him! He should know better than to do this!" She crossed quickly to her brother and examined his swollen eye and then the rest of him.

"Heather, listen to me—"

"I can't believe Lord Rake allowed this!" Heather said. "After all you've been through—"

"Heather, seriously, if you'll—" Picket tried, but Heather wasn't done.

"He'll get what's coming to him, if it's the last thing I do. I'll—"

"Heather," Mrs. Weaver said with some authority.

"Yes ma'am?" Heather said, a little stunned by Mrs. Weaver's tone.

"Be quiet," she said firmly, but with a smile. "And sit down, girl."

"Yes ma'am," Heather said, a little puzzled and put out. She sat down, seething like cold potatoes in a hot pan.

"Picket, son," Mrs. Weaver said, turning slowly to him, "how was your day?"

Picket looked up at her through his swollen eye. He looked over at Heather, then back at Mrs. Weaver. He smiled wide. "It was wonderful."

"Good," Mrs. Weaver said. "I'm eager to hear all about it."

Heather's jaw hung open.

"Heather, please be a good young lady and latch that trap of yours. I'm not a doctor, and looking down your throat, as nice as it is, isn't on my list of things I prefer to do today."

Heather shut her mouth.

"It was a perfect day," Picket said, still grinning. *Was that blood on his teeth?*

"Good, my boy," Mrs. Weaver said. "I thought it might be. Let it settle on you, Picket. For the rest of today will be hard."

Chapter Twenty-Nine

DARKNESS IN LIGHTHALL

Every time Heather tried to speak, Mrs. Weaver gave her a discouraging look. While Picket gushed about being pelted with stones, hit in the face, whipped with a jacket, and insulted with names like "Ladybug," Mrs. Weaver just sat there nodding.

"It was fantastic," Picket said, for what felt to Heather like the fifteenth time.

"It sounds lovely," Mrs. Weaver said. "I especially enjoyed the part where he kicked dirt in your eyes."

"If only," Heather blurted out, "he could have killed you! Then we'd throw a party!" She was angry and tired of holding it in.

Mrs. Weaver shook her head. "Picket," she said, "will you excuse us, my boy? Perhaps ask lovely Emma to take a look at your eye and your foot, and, well, your everything." She laughed, and Picket did too. "You'll need to be ready for more of the same tomorrow."

Heather's eyes bulged, but Mrs. Weaver gave her an authoritative gesture to be silent.

"Thank you, Mrs. Weaver," Picket said, getting to his feet again. "Thank you so much." He smiled apologetically at Heather and limped off.

When he was gone, Mrs. Weaver smiled up at Heather. "You must let him be who he is, Heather. And you must let him become what he will become."

"Like Helmer?" she said, astonished.

"No, dear," she said, "like Picket."

* * *

When Heather finally made it down to dinner an hour later, she found Emma, Picket, and Heyward all sitting down to eat.

"We waited for you," Picket said, his mouth full.

"Thanks," she said, a little smirk showing. "You're here laughing up a storm with a gang of friends, smiling like you found lost treasure, and I'm stomping around getting lectures about correcting my attitude." She threw her hands up. "Did someone throw the world in reverse today?"

Everyone laughed, including Picket. Picket laughed! This showed her that she had been wrong, somehow, and that Mrs. Weaver was right. Heather felt a spark in her heart as she saw a small glimmer of the old Picket. Maybe even the new Picket. *Maggie O'Sage*, she thought. *How well she has earned that name.*

Heather went to get some soup, a delicious-smelling mix of parsley, potatoes, and broccoli. She was still angry at

Helmer and mistrustful of his motives and tactics. But she had other things to worry about now, and she knew at least some answers would come in a few hours at the initiation.

She sat down to eat with her friends, thankful to have them. She laughed with them as Picket told them about calling Helmer "Masterchild" and "Wasp" and all about his day of training. Emma had early apprenticeship tales of Doctor Zeiger's strange language and confusing orders. Heyward talked of a new method for calculating the straight edge and how it would only take him six months to build and how he'd saved half the coins to buy the supplies. Everyone laughed, and, after a moment, Heyward joined them. Heather relaxed. For the moment, she almost forgot about her absent father's honor, her brother's crazy mentor, her own crippling fear of doing what she felt inspired to do, the deadly dangerous world, and all the horrible mysteries surrounding her like an evil army in the dark.

Almost. Her smile was real, but a labyrinth lay behind it.

* * *

It was dark. Heather and Picket walked through King Whitson's Garden and up to the front door of Lighthall. Picket was still limping a little. The garden was as lovely at nightfall as it was in the daylight. The moonlight added a glow to everything, making the garden all blues and blacks with a silver glint. Heather was heavy-hearted, while Picket was smiling. She hadn't felt like she should burden Picket with what she had overheard earlier, especially on a day when he was happy. The only day he had been at all happy since their adventure began.

Heather knocked. After a few moments, Lord Rake opened the door and beckoned the two to come in.

They came through a dim, narrow hallway that ended in light. Heather walked, head down, behind Picket. She bumped into her brother.

"Picket," she said, annoyed, looking up at him. As she raised her head, she saw what had caused him to stop. The room was lovely, both serious and arresting. It was round, wood-walled, but set off by stunning multicolored glass scenes of incredible height.

Heather gaped, walked forward, and slowly spun around, trying to take it all in. She imagined it must be all breathtaking bursts of light in the daytime. Here in the moonlight, the scenes were duller, more subdued, but still beautiful.

She walked around silently, reverently. Here was a place for contemplation, for humility. She read a thousand calls to awe in that room, before she knew anything about why it existed. She gazed at the high ceiling, the carefully carved wooden walls, and the bright gigantic windows of colored glass.

She walked to the middle of the room, where Lord Rake stood alongside Uncle Wilfred. She spun again slowly and tried to take it all in. The colored windows were pictures, clear and fine. There were scenes of war, of armies colliding, of single combat. There were characters, most notably a tall brown rabbit with a crown glittering in the sunlight and a burnished blade in his hands. Heather noticed that these windows were tales, and each told a story of some event. There were eight on display.

A huge cloth covered two others, glazier's supplies neatly stacked on the floor beneath the tenth. Was it incomplete? Heather was already thinking of it as *the Room of Ten Tales*. Ten windows. But each window had several scenes, so each was a complex story.

"It's King Jupiter, isn't it?" she asked, pointing to a window made up mostly of red. It featured a beaten wolf and the heroic rabbit descending on him with his death-dealing sword as the red sun set behind them.

"Yes," Uncle Wilfred said, his voice a little hoarse. "It's the king."

"Garlacks?" Picket asked, as they looked at the wolf. Uncle Wilfred nodded.

"I understand you came across his son, Redeye?" Lord Rake said. They nodded. "He is a deadly ally of Morbin Blackhawk. That must have been frightening."

"It was," Heather said, glancing around at the many windows all around the room. She caught Picket's eye, and he looked down. The old gloom was settling over him again. *Is that all it takes?* she thought. *One mention of that awful day by Seven Mounds in Nick Hollow and he's back to brooding?*

The several scenes included in the eight visible windows each featured a central image in the round, with related images above and below. The shape of each mural was the same, tall rectangles with a bulging circle in the center, bursting past the rectangle's confines. King Jupiter's triumph over Garlacks made the final scene. It was featured in the center, large and plain, the two combatants and a red sunset. But the images above and below were of other heroic rabbits, of other allies, of fights with wolves, and one of what looked like rabbits signing a document at a table. Heather, with a shock, noticed a grey rabbit at the table, beside the king.

"Who is the grey rabbit?" she asked, trembling.

"That's part of what you're here to learn, my dear," Lord Rake said.

Uncle Wilfred tried to smile, but he looked down. She looked from window to window, noticing the grey rabbit in many scenes. The eighth window's central image featured the grey rabbit with the king, side by side, looking out over a vast land. At their feet were broken swords and spears, shattered bows and cast-off shields. Before them were plowed fields, children at play, works of art, and rabbits working.

"It's a vision of peace," Lord Rake said, smiling regretfully at the image. "It's one we've tried to recapture here in this community."

"It's a lie," Uncle Wilfred said, sadly. Lord Rake said nothing, but only hung his head.

"What happened?" Heather said, unable to keep the questions inside any longer. "Please, just tell us what happened."

Uncle Wilfred looked up at the image of the grey rabbit with King Jupiter, shook his head sadly, and then turned to face Heather and Picket. "Our family betrayed the king."

Chapter Thirty

THE GREEN EMBER

"Part of the purpose of initiation is to tell the whole story and help you see your place in it," Lord Rake said, motioning for the young rabbits to sit in the center of the room on two stools. "I will move rather quickly tonight, in view of your eagerness to hear how your own family came into this tale. If you have heard some of this before, please bear with us." They nodded.

"Lord Rake will tell you of the first eight windows," Uncle Wilfred said, "and I, sharing your blood, will tell you the tale of the ninth." They nodded, swallowing hard, and looked up at Lord Rake.

"King Walter Good had the Whitson Stone, as had all his fathers before him. This ruby, which signaled the right to rule, was passed from father to son and heir for hundreds of years. King Good was Lord of the Thirty Warrens and the father of King Jupiter Goodson," Lord Rake said, motioning toward the first window. The window center was edged in black, and in the center stood two figures, an old rabbit, King Good, and his son, Prince Jupiter. "King Walter Good, in the twentieth year of his reign, privately named his third son, Jupiter, to be his eventual heir. The oldest son, Bleston, was furious. He believed the crown was his inheritance. A gloomy resentment settled on him, along with a resolve to revenge himself against Jupiter, whom he named Upstart. He was stronger than Jupiter then, it must be said. He was a brave warrior, and none could best him in battle. But he had his wicked grandfather's way, and King Good could not allow this to be his legacy. He hated the idea of a swift return to the cruel lordship of the Thirty Warrens. So he denied the throne to his eldest son."

Lord Rake motioned to the top of the window, where a muscular rabbit in warrior's garb huddled with several others. "Bleston bitterly contemplated a revolt against young Jupiter, even while their father lived. Jupiter was troubled terribly by the strife. After hot words were said and no peaceable solution managed, Prince Bleston left the First Warren with a large company of malcontents.

"King Walter Good was saddened by this tumult and promised to make the succession clear, as had been the custom in the past. He called a great gathering of all the nobility in the wood, along with allies from far and wide. When all were gathered, he took off his crown. The king's crown had been worn by his father and father's fathers for many generations, the line unbroken back to Whitson Mariner himself, even though it had waned and become corrupt over time. The crown was all of gold, its points waving like so many flames. It's a lovely crown, as you can see." Lord

Rake motioned toward the crown, more clearly visible in the second window, atop King Jupiter's head. So bright and beautiful was the crown, it appeared the king's head was wreathed in flames. The wreathed points of gold were the flames. At the front of the crown, along the base, there were many gems. Most of these were a fiery orange.

Then she saw it.

The center stone was an emerald. A large bright stone. Heather's mouth fell open.

"I think you begin to understand," Lord Rake said. "The stones along the bottom serve as sort of embers for the fiery crown, and the center stone, larger than the other embers, is an emerald. It is the Green Ember. It is the ancient symbol of succession, going back to the kings of Golden Coast.

"At the assembly, King Walter announced that when he had picked his successor (and they did not all know that he had done this), he would honor the old ways and remove the Green Ember, bestowing it upon his heir. This the heir would keep safe, a down payment of the stewardship of authority he would one day fully own. The crowd began to whisper, asking if he would do this now. He smiled and asked Chancellor Perkin to come forward. Chancellor Perkin—father of Perkin One-Eye, if you've heard those legends—came forward and, with a special knife, removed the emerald. He handed it, bowing, to the king. King Good raised his hands, and the room was silent. 'My son, my life, my heir, my glory: Jupiter Goodson, rise and come forward. Receive this token of your calling.' They all cheered, for Jupiter was well-known and well-loved in the wood, and they had feared the stern and selfish nature of Prince Bleston."

"So he became king then?" Heather asked.

"No. He only received the symbol that he would one day become king," Lord Rake answered. "He kept the Green Ember for another five years. Then, when his father was killed, he was crowned, and the Green Ember was restored to the crown of fire at his coronation." He pointed at the second window again. The scene was august. King Jupiter stood in the center, crowned with the wreathing flames of gold and dazzling in golden armor, with his solemn soldiers behind him.

"So he ruled and reigned with great power and goodness. There is more to tell," he said, walking past the windows and vaguely motioning to the scenes, "when we are able. For now, let us say that King Jupiter was great. He was everything his own father imagined a king could be, and more. He won great wars, like this one in the Red Valley against Garlacks," he said, pointing to the fifth window. "That was a brutal struggle. I remember it well. Garlacks could not believe what was happening to him. He was very proud. To be defeated by a rabbit in single combat was the ultimate shame. His son, Redeye Garlackson, is full of resentment and bent on revenge. He serves Morbin Blackhawk, but his true and deepest desire is to blot out King Jupiter's line and memory from the earth. How they were thwarted! What a victory the Red Valley saw."

"It was magnificent," Uncle Wilfred said, "among our happiest days. That is when we all began to believe that anything was possible with this heroic king on the throne."

"He won many other wars," Lord Rake continued, "with the help of his incredible band of warriors, like Lord Perkin One-Eye. He had Harlen Seer, Stam, Pickwand, Fesslehorn, and Gome the Agile. Never before, and not since, has there been one to compare with him. We believed him indestructible."

He paused and shook his head sadly. "We were wrong." Now he was at the eighth window, and he hung his head.

Heather studied the scene. The center showed King Jupiter and the grey rabbit, the very familiar-looking grey rabbit—even from behind—as they surveyed the open horizon with shattered instruments of war at their feet. Peace. Liberty. Rest. The window was a scene that would inspire any who saw it. Unless they knew more, she suspected.

Uncle Wilfred stood before them, trying to smile. "There's no use delaying, children," he said. He pointed at the grey rabbit. "This is Garten Longtreader." He almost spat the name. "He was King Jupiter's chief ambassador. Together, they brought peace to the known world. Before the Lords of Prey came, their policy ruled. King Jupiter held the world together, and Garten Longtreader was his thread. For years he traveled far and wide, spreading King Jupiter's peace. The Longtreaders were all employed in this service, and Garten was our captain." Uncle Wilfred shook his head and closed his eyes, as if he might drive the reality from his mind.

"It truly was marvelous work," Lord Rake said into the silence. "Until the turning."

"This is my brother," Uncle Wilfred said, indicating the image of the grey rabbit, Garten Longtreader.

"No!" Picket shouted, tears streaming. "Father would never do that. He wouldn't betray the king; I know it! He couldn't have!"

"Now, now, son," Lord Rake said. "Let your uncle finish."

"Picket, no," Uncle Wilfred said quickly, frowning. "Your father never did. No, son. Not your dad. Garten is our oldest brother. Your father and I were his lieutenants."

Heather sobbed, relieved to learn that her father wasn't the betrayer pictured in the eighth window. "So our father is innocent?" Heather asked.

"No," Uncle Wilfred said, "no more than I am. He and I both feel—and deserve to feel—tremendous guilt over what happened."

"Too much guilt," Lord Rake said.

"Never!" Uncle Wilfred roared. "We should have known; we should have found out. There were clues we should have followed. We could have saved the king."

"No one who knows the truth can doubt your loyalty, or that of their father," Lord Rake said. "It's only those who don't know the full story who still doubt."

"And that's almost everyone," Uncle Wilfred said. "I'm so sorry, children. Heather, Picket, I beg you to forgive me. Our family name is hated. Longtreader is a curse word. Because of my inaction and misplaced faith we have lost our family reputation. We have lost our king. We have lost all."

The children wept and clung to each other. Heather thought of Nick Hollow and the wonderful ignorance of her life. She longed to go back, to forget all she was learning. She wanted to close her eyes to the truth, to walk away and spend her life forgetting.

Uncle Wilfred pulled the cover off the ninth window.

Chapter Thirty-One

JUPITER'S CROSSING

The scene was awful. The center circle of the ninth window showed a clearing between two woods, an open crossing between the two places of cover. The field was full of hideous birds—hawks, eagles, owls, and falcons. In the center an enormous black hawk loomed over the form of a brown rabbit, a crown of flames on the ground beside him.

"For me, this is the worst of it, my dears," Uncle Wilfred said. "I was there, but my brother, the villain Garten, did not kill me. He betrayed the king, delivered him up to Morbin himself, and stained our family forever."

"What happened?" Picket asked, almost inaudibly.

"I won't say all here," Uncle Wilfred said, "but such was King Jupiter's trust in my brother and your uncle, Garten Longtreader, that he met Garten at the crossing without any cause for alarm. I was with the king, but as we drew near I was sent on an errand to Lookout Point, a fort in the trees overlooking what we now call Jupiter's Crossing. I was roughed up, gagged, and tied to a post. I could see it all. I watched as the king was set upon, almost totally without aid, by wolves, evil rabbits in Garten's employ, and the Lords of Prey. Redeye Garlackson was there. Morbin Blackhawk, their king, was there. I heard every word that passed between them. Morbin was sneering, proud. He looked eager to humble the king. I don't think he meant to kill him, but he had a plan of even more wickedness devised to bring about his evil ends. But the king provoked Morbin.

"'You are betrayed, Jupiter,' Morbin said in his triumphant, spiteful rasp.

"'Yes,' the king said, 'but it will not hold. All will be well.'

"'Well? Well?' he sneered. 'You are captive, O great and mighty king. You will die,' Morbin said.

"'Yes, I will. But already an answer to this treachery and murder forms in the mouth of the Great Wood.'

"'Then I will burn the wood,' Morbin sneered.

"'Even if you burn the Great Wood down, Morbin Bird, among the smoldering embers they will find that one is green. This is the seed of a new world. It will yield in time a Mended Wood, greater even than what I have seen.'

"'A happy fantasy,' Morbin said, cackling.

"'Yes,' the king said. 'I am my father's true son, and my son is true. Let your talons strike; let the sky blacken with your cursed foul army. You cannot kill an idea. You cannot murder a dream. You will fail, Morbin, because—' But he was allowed to say no more. Morbin did his foulest deed," Uncle Wilfred spoke through tears. "And so ended the reign of King Jupiter the Great." Uncle Wilfred could say no more.

Lord Rake picked up the telling. "And so ended the golden age of the Great Wood and the Hundred Warrens. Morbin did burn the Great Wood. The afterterrors, as you have some idea, were a true horror. Wolves, led by Redeye Garlackson, were let loose to kill, ruin, wreck, and ravage. Birds of prey, led by Morbin's lieutenant, Gern, were death from on high. It was awful. Most of the army, by Garten Longtreader's design, was far away on what turned out to be a clever and cruel diversion. There was really no one there to oppose the rampaging force of blood and fire that overwhelmed the Great Wood, even to the First Warren itself.

"The king's family fled; everyone fled. I was, to my enduring sadness, away with the army. By the time I got back, all was a ruin. That's when we did all we could to save who and what we could, formed the secret citadels, and went into hiding. I persuaded as many artisans and farmers as I could to come here. The one place I knew about that Garten Longtreader didn't. But that's another story.

"I agree with Wilfred that they had meant to keep the king, to manipulate him for their ends. But when provoked, Morbin did his awful work, and Jupiter's Crossing has been a hallowed, horrifying place ever since. It is the site of our evilest hour, our greatest pain. Jupiter's Crossing is sacred, terrible, and …" He hesitated.

Uncle Wilfred spoke again. "Jupiter's Crossing is the end of the world."

Heather felt anger stir inside her. *Unfair!* The word

blasted through her mind. *Unfair!* She hated the work of Morbin, hated him. Hated all the Lords of Prey. She resented Garten Longtreader, betrayer of the king, ruiner of their family. Father and Mother had fled far to Nick Hollow to escape the name of Longtreader. Selfish as it was, she felt most angered by the unfairness of having never seen King Jupiter in his day, in his glory. She felt like she had all the bad and none of the good the world had to offer. She felt profoundly betrayed, and yet still guilty. *Longtreader.* Her own blood. Her name. Betrayers. Traitors.

"I'm sorry, children," Uncle Wilfred said. "I wish I could have stopped it. If I could go back—ah, I have imagined it a thousand times!—and rescue the king. Oh, there would have been a war, yes. The most difficult one yet, against the coming of the Lords of Prey. But King Jupiter would have prevailed. Without him, and with his lords and captains away with the army, the rest were easy to scatter."

"And all was lost in the Great Wood," Lord Rake said. "It's true. High costs all around," he said. And Heather saw for a moment what the afterterrors must have meant for Lord Rake's own family.

"Many horrors. The ruin of our family being only one," Uncle Wilfred said. "A small thing, yes. But to us, it's like a sentence of death."

Heather and Picket cried, not knowing what else to do. They felt the crush of this news, the weight of a hated name. "So we are Longtreaders," Heather said. "And we betrayed King Jupiter the Great."

"Our name is a ruin," Uncle Wilfred said, embracing them. "I'm so sorry."

"You might take another," Lord Rake said, "if you believe it is so spoiled."

"Never," Uncle Wilfred said. "My life's work has been and will continue to be the restoration of the name of Longtreader to its former place. A name synonymous with Kingsbuck."

"I have never gone by the name Longtreader," Picket said, trying to control his tears, "but from now on I will never go by another." He seemed to somehow relish this news, as if it confirmed the place he had suspected he ought to occupy in the world. All the joy this day had held was gone, and the bitter, gloomy Picket returned, still more shattered.

"How can we show ourselves around here?" Heather asked, suddenly panicked. "Do others know who we are?"

"Many do," Lord Rake said. "You have no doubt had some scornful looks, some disapproving stares, especially when with your uncle. I'm very sorry to say that everyone associated with Garten is suspicious to most. This is especially so in the citadels, but it's also true here."

"I'm sorry, Uncle," Heather said. "It's not fair."

"I believe it is fair," Uncle Wilfred said. "I deserve the scorn. You two and Smalls don't, however."

"None of you do," Lord Rake said. "Don't be fools. We're all on the same side. And we all have the same goal: the Mended Wood that King Jupiter foresaw."

Uncle Wilfred and Picket nodded somberly. Heather looked up at the ninth window. The center image was of Jupiter's Crossing, alive with birds of prey, wolves, and other creatures. The captured king was in the center. The image above showed a great black hawk with a golden face—Morbin, she supposed—beside the grey rabbit, Garten Longtreader. They looked down on the body of the king, Garten bending to pick up the fallen crown. The wreathed flames of the crown glinted in the sunlight; the jewels shone brightly. But she noticed something amiss.

The Green Ember was missing.

The bottom image of the window was a burning wood; homes were destroyed and rabbits fled in terror as birds swooped in and wolves attacked. She winced, recalling her own awful experience and imagining it multiplied across thousands of homes.

"What's behind the cloth of the last window?" she asked.

"It is unfinished," Lord Rake said.

"Unfinished?"

"For the present," he said.

Chapter Thirty-Two

THE RISING

Heather woke to noise outside her door. Picket's bed lay empty. She cautiously crept along the wall, listening. Shouts, angry and insistent.

She cracked the door and peeked down the long stone hallway. She saw Pacer, Lord Rake's lieutenant, arguing with Gort, the cook, and some other rabbits dressed in livery she did not know. She shook her head and closed the door.

It had been a week since their initiation, and tensions were high. Everyone in leadership was on edge. Emma had warned her that things were coming to a boil. Cloud Mountain was hosting a conference of most of the lords of the various secret citadels. They had brought along their top captains and plenty of soldiers. The place was teeming with unfamiliar, unfriendly faces. She expected to learn any day that they were all going to have to flee the mountain and find their own way in the world. Or maybe just she and Picket would go. Being a Longtreader was hard, even dangerous, at present.

She had stayed in her room, sometimes going to read in the libraries. She often saw Picket there, on an assignment from Helmer, of course. He studied old books of war tactics and personal combat and pored endlessly over maps. Picket said that Helmer wanted him to know how to get anywhere and do anything. Heather thought about mentioning what low expectations Helmer had, but she held her tongue. Her brother was, as Mrs. Weaver said, who he was. She would have to deal with that.

But she hated the suspicious looks of the lords and captains of the citadels. She seethed at the whispers, the cold and angry distance. Emma told her not to pay attention, but she couldn't ignore it. Picket grew more sullen and determined with each judgmental look. He had been doing double the ordinary training sessions with Helmer, and each night he came back exhausted. He continued to meet with Mrs. Weaver, but he said little to Heather about it. His foot was fully healed, and despite the bruises from his training, he was physically healthier than ever.

Heather's unease grew daily. Since the arrival of the citadel leaders, the whole community had changed. Where it had at first felt so warm and inviting, it now felt like a bubbling stew of uncertainty and anger. Maybe the assembly tomorrow would help.

Lord Rake had called an assembly of the entire community in the master hall in the morning. It would mark the anniversary of the fall of King Jupiter. That was all she knew. That was tomorrow. She had no idea what to do today. Since their night in Lighthall, where they learned their family's story, she had sulked in her room. She was ashamed to admit it, but that was the truth. She had tried to distract herself with reading and actually had learned quite a bit more about King Jupiter and the Great Wood, but she knew she would have to act soon. The storyguild was there, waiting for her to come in and shock them all by how powerfully dumb her stories were. They could laugh at her and then ridicule her for her traitor's blood. She shook her head. *I'm not ready for that. Not strong enough yet.* The voices of consolation came, telling her she was right. There was no rush. *Later*, they said. *Later, when you're ready. Too much uncertainty in life now.* She dressed and headed for the Savory Den.

When she arrived she noticed that there were more soldiers than usual nearby and that many of them were unfamiliar to her. *They must be from the citadels.* Some scowled at her. Most ignored her.

"Heather!"

She turned to see Uncle Wilfred. He had been in the corner and was just now leaving. "Hello, Uncle Wilfred," she said.

More scowls.

"I'm sorry we haven't had time for more lessons, or anything, this week," he said, putting his arm around her. "It's been a tough week. I'm sorry. You have needed me, and I haven't been there for you or Picket."

"It's all right," she said, loving the comfort of his embrace. "We're doing okay. Anyway, you have bigger things to tackle at present."

"Yes, I'm sorry I do," he said. "Things are a little, well, uncertain."

"I'm picking up on that."

"It's getting," he bent to whisper, "so tense that we may need to make a plan to get you both out of here. It hasn't come to that, but I just want to warn you that it may. I'm so sorry."

"I understand," Heather said.

"I wish I could tell you that everything will be all right, Heather dear. But you know I can't be sure of that."

"I know."

"Well, do keep your chin up," he said. "We all have hope of the Green Ember rising and the dawn of the Mended Wood."

"Yes," she nodded. She didn't want to discourage him. She put on a brave face.

"Of course," he said, exhaling, "then things will only just have started."

"I don't know if this helps, Uncle," she said, unable to avoid looking over at the leering soldiers, "but I'm proud of you."

"It means the world to me, dear," he said, a tired smile forming on his lips. "I'll take encouragement anywhere I can get it, but most especially from my bright, beautiful niece."

"All this suspicion is a heavy load, I'm sure, especially for you." She raised her voice so that those nearby could hear. "All these rabbits all on the same side filled with resentment and mistrust. It's frustrating."

"It is," he said.

"It will not be so in the Mended Wood," she said.

"In the Mended Wood," he repeated, his hand over his heart. "Heather, there's more to you than what's easy to see."

They hugged and he hurried off. As she turned to find some food and a seat, she noticed that the leering guards had looked away. She sat down at an unoccupied table.

As she ate, Kyle came in. She hadn't seen him for days.

"Hi, Heather," he said. He looked exhausted. His usually carefree attitude was replaced by tired eyes and uneasy glances all around.

"Hello, Kyle," she said. "Are you okay? You look so—"

"Awful?" he said, bringing his smile out again. "I know. I should be."

"Been doing tireless noble deeds?" she asked, eyebrows raised.

"Not very often," he said. "Listen, Heather. If someone really changes, do you think they can be trusted again? Even if they've done bad things in the past?"

"I think so," she said. "Kyle, what's wrong?" She was worried, but she tried to joke with him. "Have you found the hidden heir to the throne?"

"What if it was me?" he said, his eyes earnest and worried. "What if I was the true heir? There would be things I'd have to do, things I would be asked to do, that I didn't always want to do."

"Kyle, you're worrying me," she said. "What's wrong?"

"I'm noble, but I have to act like I'm not. My father would want me to—"

He stopped short when a stocky rabbit, new to the room, came over and planted himself in front of Heather. His tunic bore a red moon crossed with spears, a little ruby in the middle. She noticed several others who wore tunics bearing the same sign.

"Hey, girl," he said. "Longtreader girl. I just want you to know that your family is full of traitors, and I don't care what Lord Rake or anyone else says; we should throw everyone named Longtreader into the darkest, farthest prison."

"That's uncalled for," Kyle said, standing. The whole room was silent.

"Sit down, you brat," the stranger said. "You should be jailed for conspiring with the enemy."

Heather was shocked. It was one thing to get dirty looks and another to be embarrassed in front of everyone. "I'm not ... that's not ..." she began, but her voice died away.

"Just you know, we've got our eyes on you," he said, pointing a chubby finger in her face. "This time the Halfwind Citadel stands ready to intervene to stop your treachery. We won't be caught standing idle. Not this time. "

"You fat villain," Kyle shouted, and he lunged at the stranger. Kyle surprised him and knocked him over, but it took only a few seconds for the strong rabbit to get on top of Kyle, strike him a few hard blows, then regain his feet. Kyle writhed on the ground, holding his hand to his mouth.

"All right, all right, Captain Frye," Gort said, jumping in the middle. "I ask you, sir, to please leave the youngster alone," he said, holding up his hands for calm. "We only eat here. We don't want any trouble."

"You prepared a table for trouble when you welcomed Longtreaders," Frye spat. "We were just leaving." With a menacing glare at first Heather, then Kyle and Gort, he left quickly with several bucks following him out.

Heather went to Kyle's side. She helped him to his feet and then a seat. "I'm so sorry, Kyle."

"I had him right where I wanted him, but the sun got in my eyes," Kyle said.

Gort sighed and stomped back into the kitchen.

"Well, we are in a cave, so it must have been very surprising," she said, smiling.

He smiled back and accepted a cloth to dab his wounds. "I can't believe no one stepped in to help," he said.

"Thank you for trying," she said. "It means a lot."

"Like I said, Heather, I like you. I just hope we can always be friends, no matter what."

"Why did you ask if someone can be trusted again after they change?"

"Because I have to believe it can happen."

"I have no doubt you can be the rabbit you aim to be, Kyle."

"I wish I was so sure."

"What's the latest rumor?" she asked.

"It's grim," he said. "All horribly grim."

Chapter Thirty-Three

FIGHTS AND FACTS

Beneath Helmer's maple tree, Picket went through his sword exercises. He sliced, blocked, attacked, dove, spun, jumped, slid, fell down, shot up, and did it all again. Over and over.

"Too predictable!" Helmer shouted from the comfort of a shady spot a few yards away. He seemed to only partially pay attention. But Picket had learned that Helmer had an unbelievable ability to perceive his surroundings, no matter how disengaged he appeared to be. "Mix it up, Ladybug!"

"Yes, Master Helmer!" Picket shouted and threw himself into the routine with renewed vigor.

Picket was not the rabbit he had been a week before. He was leaner, stronger, quicker, and tougher than ever. He could handle a sword reasonably well and was less inclined to whiney backchat.

"Impressive! That's better," Helmer mumbled.

Picket stopped, shocked to hear praise, albeit mumbled, from his tempestuous tutor. He was rewarded for stopping with a small rock hurled his way. "You stop when I say so!"

Picket dodged the rock and resumed his routine.

In a few minutes, Helmer stopped him. "Okay, that's good. Now, up in the tree."

"The tree?" Picket said, nervously eyeing the limbs above.

"Yes, Ladybug. Do you have a problem with that?" Helmer said. "Do you think all combat happens on the ground? We're fighting birds, among other things, Master Softhead! So we're going to work on maintaining balance at a height. Which mostly means you're going to walk on thin high limbs while I throw rocks at you."

"Um, well," Picket started. He looked up. The tree seemed to wobble before him. He thought he might faint. "No, sir ... no problem." He walked slowly toward the tree, reaching up to find a grip and climb. All his training so far had been on the ground. He was not ready for this.

His vision blurred, and he fell to his knees. Panic swelled inside him until he was convinced the only thing he could do was run away.

"Afraid of heights?" Helmer asked. "Perfect. You really are a mixed-up lad. You come here full of defiance and anger, and then you show up and you're a horrible, hobbled mess. You spend a week with me, and now you're such an efficient student it's scaring me and I begin to think you might someday be some kind of decent soldier. And now this. You've got a doe's fear of heights."

"I can conquer it, sir," Picket said, his voice cracking.

"Yeah, you sound like it's got *you* pretty well conquered."

"I'm willing to work and overcome anything, sir. Including this," Picket choked out.

"Okay, okay," Helmer said, smiling ruefully. "We'll tackle this fear of high places tomorrow. If tomorrow ever comes. I'm too tired to hold your hand and sing lullabies to you tonight."

Picket hung his head. No matter how hard he worked, no matter how sure he was that he'd built a fortress around his heart, there was always a breach. It felt like ages ago that he was afraid to climb the old maple in Nick Hollow to find the starstick. But he was still that same kid, afraid of every bird, afraid of every height.

"Don't worry," Helmer said. "It's just another enemy to be taken down in the end."

Picket looked up and half-smiled. Sometimes, he thought, Helmer seemed almost like a real rabbit. "Yes, sir."

"Don't just stand there like baby with no head! Get the woods!"

They practiced for another half-hour with wooden swords, Picket always showing improvement, always learning, and always receiving hundreds of painful raps from his phenomenal master's sword. *One day*, Picket thought, *I will be like him. Untouchable with a blade. Then let Redeye try me again.*

After this final exercise, they were finished for the day. Picket gathered his few things—which included his own straight steel sword, a gift from Uncle Wilfred—and prepared to leave.

"One last thing, Picket, before you go," Helmer said.

"Yes, Master?" he said, spinning around and coming to attention.

"Relax, son," Helmer said. Picket changed his rigid position only enough so that it could be seen to be somewhat different. "Well, son, you're no slouch, and that's saying something."

"Thank you, sir."

"Listen, Picket, I want you to be aware that things around here are changing. I don't know what the next weeks, or days, may bring. But Rake believes we may soon have trouble from the enemy. That is, if the various citadel lords don't cause a war inside this, um, sanctuary of peace and understanding first." He laughed one of his hard-edged laughs.

"Master Helmer, I will be ready when trouble comes to do my part in our victory over the enemy."

"Picket, I like you, kid, but you aren't serious, are you?"

"Very serious, sir."

Helmer paced a few steps away, then turned back to Picket. "Two things. One, you aren't fighting—not anytime soon, anyway. And two, we won't win."

Picket blanched. "What do you mean?" His stony would-be-soldier face was giving way. Something of the vulnerable child showed through.

"I mean that we *can't* win. The odds are too great. We don't have the organization, or the leadership, or the numbers. If we were all united—and we're far from it—we would have the same chance as a worm on Morbin's dinner plate. But we don't even have that."

"Begging your pardon, Master," Picket said, emotion touching his words, "but I can't agree. We have to win. We have to keep fighting, and clawing, and surviving, and going on till we empty the forest of every Redeye Garlackson, every Morbin Blackhawk, every last bird of prey filling the sky. We have to!"

Helmer shook his head. "What we have to do, Picket, is face facts."

Picket shook his head. "I have to find my family," he whispered, tears starting. "I can't give up on them."

Helmer's face contorted, seemed to soften for a moment, then resumed its stern indifference. He exhaled slowly, then spoke. "Listen, son. In real life bad things happen all the time. You miss your only chance to do something great; you don't measure up when it counts; your mother gets sick and dies; the flood destroys your home, and that's it—it's gone." He was getting louder, more emphatic. "The rabbit dies in the war, and he's gone, just gone! And you can't bring him back. You can't bring any of them back." He paused, turned away, then spun back and faced Picket. "The fact is, I served King Jupiter, and I loved him. But this ain't a bedtime story, lad. The king was killed. We lost. It's over. No happy ending here. 'The Mended Wood' is a child's motto to keep alive the pathetic hopes of rabbits who just need to face facts. It's all over. There is no more Great Wood, no glory coming. The glory is behind us. It's the sad end of a happy tale. That's real life. They don't like you being a little bitter? I say it keeps you alive. Let it settle in, lad, because it's reality you're dealing with, and the more of them that do the same, the better. We've lost, and we're losing, and we're going to keep losing till we lose it all. They are going to find this place sometime, probably soon, and we'll all be forced to flee. Or it will be worse. Rabbits like me and you will die vainly trying to defend the last little corner of light in the world." He looked out over the village green, at the many rabbits working and talking and eating and laughing. "I've been a soldier all my life, Picket. I've been with many at the end. We're alone here, and the stories are all wrong. Nothing ends well. We're going to lose, Picket. The stories are all wrong."

Chapter Thirty-Four

Traitors' Table

Next morning, Picket and Heather walked to breakfast early. They hoped to avoid the long lines expected ahead of the assembly. Picket was sullen but wouldn't talk to Heather about it. She suspected that something had happened with Helmer. She guessed the old nut had gotten to Picket. She resented Helmer and feared what he was making of her brother.

"What's it like with Mrs. Weaver now, Picket?" Heather asked, sliding past a gang of angry-eyed soldiers. A change of subject might help.

"It's fine," he said, putting himself between Heather and the next knot of soldiers in the hallway.

"'Fine'? Is that all you can say?" she asked. "'Fine'? What does she say? What do you say? What are some of the words spoken from your mouths? Can you give me a little something more than 'fine'?"

"Fine," he said. "I mean, sure. Sure, I can." He thought for a minute. "Well, I come away with far fewer bruises than in my time with Helmer."

"I'll bruise you," she said, slapping at his shoulder. "If you won't talk, maybe I can get her to tell me. I'm sure she has the best of advice."

"It's not really like that, Heather. She does often say, 'Remember who you are, Picket Longtreader,' but she usually just listens to me," he said, and his tone caught her off guard. It was a little embarrassed, but also defiant.

"She does? Really?" Heather thought this was mad, like a waterfall letting a teardrop put out a fire. "But she's so wise. I'd think she would be filling your head with her advice all the time till your thick head leaked sagacity."

"Nope."

"So, is it any help?" Heather asked.

"I love it."

"Good, Picket. Hey, that's wonderful," she said, unable to keep a hint of doubt out of her tone. "I'm glad."

"You sound genuinely thrilled," he said. "And by 'thrilled' I mean 'completely unconvinced.'"

They made it into the very crowded Savory Den and got in line for food. Most of the population of Cloud Mountain ate in their own homes, or even in the great hall. The Savory Den was ordinarily a place for visitors, but with the Citadel Congress meeting, there were plenty of these. Most were tough-looking soldiers, and many gave them suspicious looks.

Emma came in and joined them in line. "Hello, Longtreaders," she said. She liked to use their true name, and she didn't mind saying it loudly. Most everyone knew who they were by now, so she had decided she wasn't going to slink around about it.

"Hello, Emma," Heather said, hugging her friend. Picket waved and smirked.

"Hey, Shuffler," she said, punching Picket's shoulder. "How's the foot?"

"Fine," he said, "but my shoulder's killing me. I keep running into fists this morning. Too bad there are no doctors around."

"Well, try to pretend to be tough," she said. "If you can."

"Honestly, you guys are so mean to each other," Heather said, waving a disapproving finger at them.

"A truce?" Emma said. "What do you say, Shuffler?"

"Sure," he said. "For one hour."

"Agreed."

"Good," Picket said. "My shoulder needs a break."

Heyward joined them, with a neat, short bow to both Emma and Heather. "Good morning, ladies." He slapped Picket's shoulder. "Hello there, soldier."

They all said, "Good morning," though Picket was wincing.

They got their food at last, a vegetable pie with a golden- brown crust they could barely wait to devour. Heather saw Gort's head poking in and out of the kitchen, taking in the eager looks from the hungry patrons and the satisfied smiles where rabbits sat eating. She gave him a big smile when she caught his eye. His face lit up, and he disappeared back inside the kitchen, yelling at his staff, "Stay after it, you amateurs! This is your chance to impress some citadel lord and escape there to cook for soldiers in a war zone. It'll be much safer for you, especially if you don't stop adding so much salt!" She heard a crash and apologetic rumblings.

They sat at a crowded table, half occupied by some young friends—a few rabbits their age who weren't afraid to be seen with them—and half by soldiers from one of the citadels. The soldiers in for the Citadel Congress had crests and heraldry telling where they were from, but Heather hadn't figured it all out yet. These had badges on their shoulders or crests on their tunics featuring a shield split in two. The left side displayed a large green diamond surrounded by a circle of nine small red diamonds. The right side showed only a single black star. She thought of the Black Star of Kingston. She wondered if these soldiers were from Kingston Citadel.

At the head of the other end of the long table sat a tall rabbit with grey and black fur. Clearly, he was a lord. His chest bore the same crest, large and beautifully sewn. He also wore a gold chain with a bright medallion, like Lord Rake's. His shoulder bore a black star patch. Heather caught him looking at her and Picket, his eyebrows creased. Then he smiled warmly, surprising her. She smiled back. *I guess they aren't all against us.*

"How are my dear friends from Nick Hollow this morning?" Heyward asked. He was one who was still a little wary of using the name Longtreader.

"Fine," Picket said, smirking at his sister. "Fine, fine, fine."

"How are you, Heyward?" Heather asked. "And how goes the hedging?"

"It's a disaster up there," he said, pitching his voice low. "All these guests here, tensions high, and clumsy, crooked hedges everywhere to simply add to the discomfiture of the community. I'm embarrassed."

"Well, talk to us about embarrassment," Picket said, patting Heyward on the back, "when your uncle betrays the king and ruins everything ever."

"It's very similar," Heyward said, nodding seriously. "Only you two can understand me."

Heather heard a harsh voice from behind say, "Traitors eat with traitors." They turned to see the stocky rabbit from Halfwind Citadel, Captain Frye, smirking.

"I eat where I like, Captain Frye," the black rabbit lord said. "And I doubt Lord Ramnor would like you insulting another citadel's lord. And as long as we're dishing out maxims to live by, how about this one: 'Cowards taunt children.'"

"They aren't children anymore, Lord Victor," Frye said, his bulging eyes now turned on the Longtreaders with scorn. "They're nearly full-grown—at least the girl is. And even the boy's old enough to pass along information to Morbin's side. I've seen him with my own eyes, out at night, sneaking around. Going, no doubt, to a meet up with the enemy wolves and to pass on our secrets. They'd love to attack while all the lords and captains are here."

"You lie!" Picket shouted, rising to his feet. The room went quiet.

"Now, Frye," Lord Victor said. He stood and raised his hands for calm. "This isn't the place—"

"Well, I've already lodged a complaint with Lord Rake, and Lord Ramnor knows," Frye said, his face like a simmering kettle. "But Rake doesn't believe the buck's capable of treason. Imagine that, a Longtreader incapable of treason."

A few rabbits laughed, mostly the rabbits of Frye's company. But the rest were quiet, looking back and forth between Picket Longtreader and Captain Frye.

"I would never do that!" Picket shouted. "I'd do anything for the cause. Any of us would." Picket moved toward Frye, his jaw set, hand reaching for his sword. But several of Lord Victor's soldiers held him back.

"You know what, bucky?" Frye said, smiling sickly and coming closer. "The last rabbit who said that to me was named Garten Longtreader." He let this hang in the air a moment, then pointed at Picket's chest. "And he looked an awful lot like you."

"An awful lot," one of his fellows said. Then more said the same. Then still more kept repeating it.

"An awful lot."

"An awful lot. Longtreaders: an awful lot."

The saying went round and round the room, "The Longtreaders are an awful lot," until finally Lord Victor shouted, "Silence!"

The room quieted. There were many different kinds of faces staring at Heather and Picket. Angry faces. Sad faces. Uncertain, tense, and wounded faces. Heather wanted to get out. She clenched Picket's arm.

"Let's go, Picket," she said and they made for the door, along with Heyward. Emma came as well, seething with rage. Heather saw that Lord Victor was following, along with several of his soldiers.

Heather was furious. Before they reached the doorway, she turned, pointed at Captain Frye, and said, "You're wrong, sir. You can't refight Jupiter's Crossing in a dining hall against children. I know you're angry and hurt. We are too. We want this war to end just like you do. Our parents and baby brother are either dead or Morbin's prisoners right now."

Frye shook his head, let go a chuckling "Hurrumph."

Someone said, "So they say," and a few murmured similarly.

"Of course," she said, shaking her head. "We're the problem. If we were gone, everything would be fine." She left.

Chapter Thirty-Five

RUMORS OF TRIAL

Heather didn't know where to go.

"Let's find your uncle," Emma said.

"She's right," Lord Victor said. "Your uncle's a wise rabbit, valiant and patient. He's endured this sort of thing for many years."

This only made Heather feel worse. He'd been treated like this for years? What kind of life was that? A life lived in constant sacrifice for rabbits who distrusted and despised you. What an awful lot. Thinking those words made her remember the room repeating "Longtreaders: an awful lot." She was sick.

Emma came beside her, taking her hand and helping her to stay steady.

Picket, furious and fed up, turned to head back down the corridor to the Savory Den. Several of Lord Victor's rabbits stood before him, gently restraining him.

"No, son," Lord Victor said. "You'll gain nothing by fighting a rabbit who was in wars before you were born."

"I'd feel better," Picket said.

"You'd feel dead."

"I don't care anymore," Picket said. But he slowly relaxed, and the rabbit soldiers stepped back.

At a subtle signal from Lord Victor, his rabbits stayed between Picket and the path toward the Savory Den but withdrew and stood apart, talking together.

"Are you all right, Heather?" Lord Victor asked.

"I'm okay," she said. "I just want to go ..." She wanted to say "home," but she didn't know where that was.

"I know, Heather dear," Emma said. "Come to my room for a rest. Help me with her, Shuffler," she said to Picket. Lord Victor nodded, seeing that Emma had employed Picket, distracting him from his revenge, and had everything under control.

"Please, Heyward," Emma said. "Go and find Wilfred Longtreader and ask him to come to Lord Rake's quarters."

"My pleasure, Emma," Heyward said, and with a sad glance at Heather, he ran off down the corridor.

"If you will excuse me," Lord Blackstar said, his face weary and sad. "I know it feels like the end of everything here, but it's not. Not quite yet."

"Thank you, Lord Victor," Emma said.

He nodded, placing his fist over his heart. "My place beside you, my blood for yours; till the Green Ember rises, or the end of the world." He left, and his soldiers followed.

"Let's go," Emma said. They helped Heather along for a little while, and soon she was walking on her own.

"I think I'm fine now," she said.

"I was like that for weeks when I came here, and my troubles were nothing like yours. You both are very brave," Emma said.

"Emma, dear, your problems were like ours—are like ours," Heather said. "You lost your parents to Morbin; you lost everything. We still have each other, and we have you."

"Well, we've all got each other, it's true," Emma said. "And I'm sticking with you through whatever comes."

"Till the Green Ember rises, or the end of the world," Picket said, almost as if to himself. His brows furrowed and his head sagged.

* * *

They were in Lord Rake's quarters, which were less spacious and grand than they had expected. There were three rooms: Emma's; a common room, where Lord Rake slept; and a large conference room, where, Emma explained, Lord Rake met with the council and others. Emma was fixing tea while Heather and Picket ate a modest breakfast of bread and cheese, since their breakfast had been cut short.

"It's not Gort's work, but it is, technically, food," Emma said.

"It's fine; thank you so much, Emma," Heather said. "Where would we be without you?"

"I just have to run to Mrs. Blake's for some honey. I don't want Shuffler here to go without his much-needed sweet stuff," Emma said. "I'll be back in a few minutes."

"Thank you," Picket said.

Emma left, and the two of them were alone. They could think of nothing to say to each other. Heather had always been the one to pick them up, to encourage when things were gloomy. But she didn't have it in her, so she absently chewed her food, giving in, for the moment, to the slow, insistent despair.

After a few minutes, they heard quiet footsteps and, believing it was Emma, said nothing. But soon they could tell it wasn't their friend. They heard loud male voices, and they were arguing. The thick stone between rooms muffled the sound some, but the Longtreaders could tell that Lord Rake was arguing with someone, a few someones, in his conference room.

"I won't turn them over," Lord Rake was saying. "Listen, we have bigger problems than a trial for Wilfred Longtreader right now, Ramnor."

Picket advanced and put a finger over his mouth, motioning for Heather to be silent. Heather frowned but didn't know what else to do. *So this is how Emma stays so informed,* she thought.

"We do; I know, Rake," Lord Ramnor said. "But I can barely keep my own citadel together over this issue. Most of my captains want a trial. And other citadels are far worse. I mean, it was all I could do to convince Blackstone Citadel to come at all. They were convinced it was a trap. Ronan doesn't even want to be in the same room with Wilfred, or any Longtreader. And now these other two are here. It's just too much."

"We have to unite," Lord Rake said. "We can't possibly leave valuable, valiant, entirely committed rabbits out. Or, worst of all, put them on trial."

"But I've spoken to Wilfred. He's agreed to a trial. He thinks it might help clear his name or get us all beyond this issue. So we *can* unite."

"It's out of the question."

"I have no great love for Wilfred." This was another voice, raspy and even. Master Helmer, Picket knew at once. "But he's no traitor. He's a fool, to be sure, and an idealistic one at that. But I won't stand by and let him, or my apprentice and his sister, be put in prison. That'll happen when I'm no longer able to lift a sword."

"It shouldn't come to that," Lord Ramnor said.

"I hope not," Lord Rake said.

"So you're training the Longtreader lad, Captain Helmer?" Lord Ramnor asked. "That's wonderful. Really, just perfect," he said, sounding as if he believed it was the farthest thing from perfect.

"It's more complicated than that, Ramnor," Lord Rake said. "Far more complicated."

"What do you mean?" Lord Ramnor said, intrigued. "You don't mean he's—"

"I just mean there is no possibility that we will allow Wilfred Longtreader, or those he calls his kin, to be taken away and locked up. It is simply out of the question."

Lord Ramnor replied without anger. "If the citadels are agreed, it doesn't matter what you and the council here decide. We have the power of force, you know. Your guards aren't able to withstand us all."

"I really do hope it never comes to that," Lord Rake said. He sounded exhausted. "I can't understand how we have managed to become so divided with such a clear common enemy."

"King Jupiter wove a peace with the thread of Garten Longtreader," Helmer said. "Now Longtreader's work is unraveling that peace. And he is equally brilliant in this."

"Garten," Lord Rake said. "*Not* Wilfred. Garten Longtreader is at work undoing our peace—not our Wilfred."

"Of course," Helmer said.

"Well, I had to try to work out a deal," Lord Ramnor said, "but I can see it's a nonstarter. I'm very sorry about all this."

"Me too," Lord Rake said.

"So, Captain Helmer," Lord Ramnor said, "how is the young Longtreader? I thought you gave up training bird bait years ago. Why him? Does he have all the warlike cunning of a diplomat?" He laughed.

Picket's face darkened.

There was a longish pause, and Picket imagined Helmer's face to be made up with scorn. Then he spoke. "The lad's a natural thinking fighter. He can do fast, accurate calculations with ease. His mind is incredible, and applying his gifts to war has been a ... well, a pleasure. He's one of the best students I've ever had. But he's got weaknesses. Plenty of them, actually. But three primary weaknesses."

"And they are?" Lord Rake asked.

"He's afraid of heights," Helmer said, and Picket hung his head. "And he's paralyzed by fear of any and all birds. It's a crippling lack. But with time—time it appears I don't have—I think we could address these weaknesses. He's learning quickly. If he ever learns to master these, he could become a truly exceptional warrior."

"What's the third weakness, Captain Helmer?" Lord Ramnor said.

"He believes we can win."

Chapter Thirty-Six

A Voice in the Hall

An hour later, Picket and Heather were packed into the large hall along with most of the Cloud Mountain community and many more. Picket was quiet. Heather hadn't been able to get much out of him since they left Lord Rake's quarters. Uncle Wilfred had come to check on them and stayed on with them since.

There were four in their group. Smalls stood on one side, with Heather to his right. Uncle Wilfred stood on the other side, with Picket on his left. They were near the back. Behind them, as if separate from the Cloud Mountain community, stood most of the lords, captains, and soldiers who had come from the secret citadels. Most of them looked angry. They appeared to resent this assembly and were making it clear by standing apart. There was a large gap between the last of the Cloud Mountain rabbits and the citadel warriors. Heather believed they wished to get this over with and get back to what they thought of as real work.

"Heather," Smalls said, "I need to ask you something."

"Anything," Heather said. She had seen little of Smalls over the past week, but every time she had seen him he looked more tired, more discouraged. She was angry at herself for focusing so much on her own troubles that she had ignored his. "What can I do for you, friend?"

"We *are* friends," he said. "And I need friends now, as you do. Our Wilfred is not popular around here, and that means neither are we. It's unjust."

"It's awful."

"Finding friends has been hard," Smalls went on, carefully, she thought. "But I've been talking to Kyle lately."

"Kyle?" Heather asked, surprised.

"Yes. And I see this surprises you. This is why I thought it was important to ask you. Are you and he friends?"

She thought for a moment, remembering how he stood up to Captain Frye and received a bloody lip for his trouble. "Yes," she said. "Yes, we are friends."

"Do you trust him?" Smalls asked.

That was a harder question, but she wanted to believe that Kyle was trustworthy. She thought he was becoming trustworthy. What finally tipped the scales in Kyle's favor was loyalty. So many were against them, out to do them harm. Kyle had demonstrated that he was a loyal friend.

"Yes," she said. "I do trust him."

Smalls face tightened, then relaxed. He nodded. "Thank you, Heather. Many hard choices lie on that."

This made Heather suddenly fearful, and she felt a need to qualify her approval of Kyle with a warning, but Lord

Rake was coming to the stage. A hush fell over the assembly. She looked behind, and her eyes locked with Captain Frye. He smiled a grim, contemptuous smile. She noticed that many others were watching them as well. They were easy pickings if the lords wanted to take them prisoner.

Smalls seemed aware of this. He subtly eyed all possible exits.

"My friends!" Lord Rake said, his voice booming in the massive hall. "Fellow heralds of the Mended Wood, we gather today in a moment of crisis. Not our first, and not our last. We meet today to conspire against gloom. To say that what we see is not all that can and will be seen!"

Rabbits began to stir. Heather felt her pulse rising. Uncle Wilfred smiled.

Lord Rake continued, his voice strong. "We are not what we appear to be, not what we will be, not where we will be. We are heralds of the Mended Wood. We see and speak of that reality while strong rabbits stand prepared to receive and give harm on our behalf. Much of our work here is to support the citadels. We supply food, clothing, and much more to these brave fighting rabbits who stand ready every day to go to war on our behalf. My dear friends, I give you the lords, captains, and soldiers of the secret citadels."

As a mass, everyone turned to the back, to face them. Then the crowd erupted in wild, exuberant applause and cheers. Those toward the back surged on the visitors. They shook hands, bowed respectfully, and in their many ways thanked and paid tribute to the warriors. There was a mingling for nearly five minutes, and then Lord Rake tapped a staff on the floor of the platform.

Rabbits began to reform the crowd into something like the shape it had before. But Heather noticed that it was harder to see now where the Cloud Mountain community and the citadel rabbits were divided. She saw that many of the soldiers now wore wreaths of flowers and held other gifts. They seemed pleased, but embarrassed. She still stood beside Picket, and Uncle Wilfred was beside him on the other side. But she couldn't see Smalls. She wondered if he was nearby or if he'd simply slipped out.

"My dear friends," Lord Rake spoke again, "I will not keep you long. I ask you to quiet down, as much as you can, and listen for a moment to one of Cloud Mountain's most lovely treasures. Maggie O'Sage." He went to the steps and helped her up. She walked slowly, using a cane. When she reached the center of the platform, the room was silent.

Heather stood on tiptoes and dodged back and forth to see over the shoulder of the tall, swaying rabbit in front of her. She wanted to see Mrs. Weaver.

"Hello, my friends and fellow heralds of the Mended Wood. I speak to you today because Lord Rake has asked me to, believing it will serve you to hear my story. I have been here for seven years, in this seed of the new world, in this little community of anticipation, in this shadow of the Mended Wood. Though I am not noble born or anything more than a commoner at work on her sewing, I have some-how come to be seen as wise. Some of you have come to me for advice, and I have given you the best I could. This puzzles me still, but I have come to a kind of acceptance of it. I'm so honored to have a place among you and to serve you however I can, whether by sewing or sayings.

"You find me on the mossy porch, looking into the mist, beyond which lies the ruins of the Great Wood. Why? Am I insane? Many have asked, but few have received an answer. Now, I will tell you.

"When our king was betrayed and murdered, my husband, Mr. Edward Weaver, was taken prisoner in the after-terrors. He gave himself so that I could get away. I honored his sacrifice, did just as he said, and escaped. Almost every day I am thankful to him but also regretful that I did not stay with him to the end. But that is not important now. Mr. Weaver was a good husband, a fine weaver, and a rabbit deeply loyal to the fallen king. I do not know if he is alive or—" and here she stopped and looked down.

The hall was silent. She coughed and then went on. "Though I sometimes hope he is alive, other times I hope that he has been spared the terrors of captivity by those monsters of the sky. One of the worst things about this world is that we so often don't even know which terrible thing to hope for.

"I know you mean well when you honor me with the title of Maggie O'Sage, but this is why I insist on Maggie Weaver. That is who I am. Mr. Weaver is my other half. If he is gone, then I am half-dead. So, while you mean well, it's disrespectful to Mr. Weaver to give me another name, and I won't allow it. I am Maggie Weaver, and I never will be anything else.

"I stand on the porch, overlooking the Great Wood, believing that perhaps one day the mist will clear, and Edward will be there. The Mended Wood is not a place to me only; it is him. It is all our loved ones, as they are or in the place they longed for and loved.

"I am anything but a general—though as a girl my mother did call me a general nuisance. But I shall be so bold as to marshal you to action, to call on your best efforts, to command you—dare I say—to be vigilant and faithful and unified in the cause of King Jupiter."

Cheers filled the hall, but Mrs. Weaver did not move; she only bowed her head. In a few moments, she raised her hand and silence resumed. She went on. "I call on you to be faithful to King Jupiter and to be faithful to his true heir."

The hall erupted in a shout, almost unified, of "Yes!"

"We must stay together," she said.

"Yes!" they shouted again, this time together.

"We must end senseless division," she said.

The hall shouted, "Yes!" Heather shouted with all her breath, noticing that loud calls of "Yes!" were pouring out from behind her as well.

"We must come together to fight our common foe—in our art, in our arms, with our farms, and our hearts!"

"Yes!" the booming reply came again. Then silence descended like a blanket, though the energy in the hall was bubbling beneath a shallow surface of respectful quiet.

Chapter Thirty-Seven

THE TENTH WINDOW

Heather filed out with all the others, everyone finding their way back to their jobs, families, pains, and pleasures. She walked with Picket and Uncle Wilfred out into the sunlit air of the village green. The song had gone on for a while, lamenting verses, offset by the hopeful refrain "It will not be so in the Mended Wood." She thought of all the times she had heard rabbits in this community counter a despairing word with this phrase. She had thought it was only a word of encouragement. She hadn't realized they were singing to each other a song of hope.

She knew she loved this community, that they had become her own. Not taking the Longtreader controversy into account, she knew this was a place her parents would have loved. Her father, who was a scholar, would have found a wonderful home among the books and the other scholars who remained. She wished they would have come, or could have come. She knew now why they had no place to go, within either the citadels or Cloud Mountain. She understood now why they had gone so far away. She was saddened by the weight of this reality. What joys she could have grown up with, were it not for their family name. Her parents, and Baby Jacks, would be safe, were it not for that title: Longtreader.

"Uncle Wilfred," she said, "was Uncle Garten a bad rabbit?"

Uncle Wilfred sighed. "I don't know," he said. "Sometimes I think we're all bad, when we focus on our own place."

"Is that what he did?"

"I think so," Uncle Wilfred said. "He began to think less about the grand cause and more about his place in it. He thought less of how he worked to serve King Jupiter and more about what he accomplished."

"It's heavy," Picket said. "I hate the weight of it."

"Me too," Uncle Wilfred said. "Don't stop hating it. It's a useful fuel for hard work."

"How long?" Heather asked. "How long until it's different?"

Uncle Wilfred sighed, then smiled. "I ask myself that question every day. I don't know the answer."

"Why won't King Jupiter's heir come out of hiding?" Heather asked. "Why won't he show up, show the Green Ember, get himself crowned, and start the war?"

"Did King Jupiter even give the Green Ember to his heir?" Picket asked. "Did he have time, before he died?"

"Yes, Picket," Uncle Wilfred said. "He did."

"So why not fight now?" Heather asked, though it

terrified her to think of it. It seemed, as Mrs. Weaver had said, the best terrible option.

"I wish it were that simple," Uncle Wilfred said. "But you have had a chance this week to get a glimpse of how fractured our side is. The citadel lords aren't united on whether or not they would even support the heir—though they all say they would. But many talk of creating a new protectorate, where a strong lord leads our side until the heir is ready. Others think we should unite behind Jupiter's oldest son, Winslow. But most of us believe he's as good as a traitor himself, since he's accepted a token governorship of what's left of the Great Wood under Morbin's rule. A petty king paying tribute to keep up appearances."

"Isn't it better to do something than nothing?" Heather asked. "Won't the enemy act if we don't?"

"Very wisely said, Heather," Uncle Wilfred said. "That is why the lords are here. Everyone knows we need to do something soon. Before the enemy acts."

They sat quietly for a while. Then Picket and Uncle Wilfred got into a discussion on Randalgam's *History of War*.

Heather looked down into the village and saw a white rabbit making his way toward the near side of the village green. Smalls. He looked troubled, his head down.

"What's wrong with Smalls?" she asked.

"I don't know," Uncle Wilfred said, his face full of concern. "He hasn't been very talkative lately."

* * *

315

Picket buried his head. He had never given Smalls anything but trouble. Seeing the small white rabbit still filled him with resentment and embarrassment.

"I'll go and talk to him," Heather said.

"Good," Uncle Wilfred said. "He needs friends these days. As do we all."

This made Picket even more uncomfortable. He felt ashamed. Smalls deserved better.

* * *

Heather joined Smalls as he returned to Hallway Round. She sensed his heavy mood, so for a little while neither of them spoke.

Just before he passed through the door, Smalls stopped. He looked at Heather, then over her shoulder to where Uncle Wilfred stood talking with Picket. Heather followed his gaze and saw Uncle Wilfred place his fist over his heart and nod his head. Smalls nodded, put his fist over his own heart, then turned and kept walking. He spoke as they entered the doorway.

"Heather, I'm going away for a while."

"Where?" she said, surprised.

"I'm going to try to find my mother. I have heard a rumor about where I can find her. I think she's in danger."

"I didn't know your mother was still alive," Heather said. "Where is she?"

"She's in a place called Exile Glen," he said, whispering

so that no others could hear. They had reached the long corridor that stretched from Hallway Round and its three doorways down to King Whitson's Garden.

"But you're not going alone, are you?" she asked. "Surely Uncle Wilfred is going with you."

"I won't be alone the whole time," he said. "But Wilfred's staying here."

"I hope you know what you're doing," she said.

"Me too," he said, and doubt was plain in his face. But he mastered it, and a resolute expression replaced it. "Please say goodbye for me," he said. "To Wilfred, Picket, and our other friends. Wilfred may be angry that I've gone. But tell him my mother needs me, and I'll come back with all those who are with her, if I can."

"I will," she said, tears starting in her eyes.

They were in King Whitson's Garden now. He stopped. "I have a last errand before I leave. So, goodbye, Heather Longtreader. I hope we will meet again in happier days."

She hugged him. "Thank you, Smalls. Thanks for saving us at Nick Hollow and for being our friend." She remembered a blessing her mother used to say. "Farewell, wherever you go off to. May you find friends aplenty and of foes find few."

He nodded, smiled, then turned up the path, making his way toward the door into Lighthall.

Heather nodded. "Goodbye." But when he reached the door, she remembered Kyle. She wanted to warn him not to take her too seriously when she said that she trusted him. She felt a sudden urge to beg him to stay, so she ran after him, pulling open the door. Heather hurried through the hallway, heard talking, but was in no mood to eavesdrop this time. She ran into Lighthall, sliding to a stop as Master Luthe and Smalls embraced. They saw her but kept on talking.

"So, Master Luthe," Smalls said, "I'm leaving. I wanted to thank you for what you've done. And what you will do."

"It's my honor," Luthe Glazier replied.

"You have done well, and Father would be very pleased with your art," Smalls said.

"Thank you," Luthe Glazier answered.

"I love your work and am eager to see what you do next," Smalls said.

"All my time is spent on the vision of the tenth window," said Luthe.

There was a pause; then Smalls spoke. "Mine too."

Heather was confused. She looked from the two rabbits to all the window images, all the stories of the fallen king. Then she saw Master Luthe's workstation, where glass and instruments lay on benches. A massive cloth was piled in the corner, and the tenth window, partially finished, was uncovered. Her eyes fell on the massive center circle, a half-completed vision of the Mended Wood. In the topmost panel, above the half-done middle image, she saw the picture of a very familiar looking white rabbit. He was short, but glorious, wearing a crown wreathed in flames, a bright emerald in its center.

When Heather looked down, Master Luthe was there. Alone.

"Where's Smalls?" she asked.

Master Luthe turned. "He's gone, Miss Longtreader."

Chapter Thirty-Eight

BREACH

Heather didn't know what to do, so she stayed in Lighthall a little while. Master Luthe wouldn't say where Smalls had gone and advised her strongly against following him. She knelt on the floor and watched as he carefully inlaid a small pane of colored glass, sealed it in place, then began work on the next. Slowly, the middle image of the Mended Wood began to take better shape. As she watched, her fears about her family, about the whole wounded world, ebbed.

Master Luthe's touch was tender, his eye keen, and his work splendid. As awful as the ninth window was, with its terrifying rendering of the burning of the Great Wood and the horrors of the afterterrors, the tenth was picturing a great reversal. She was seeing the other side of the tragedy, the world that lived, for now, only in the hopeful hearts of those who, though not seeing, saw. She gazed and was glad. And the topmost picture pleased her most.

There stood King Jupiter Smalls, the Green Ember blazing on his crown of wreathed flames. He looked noble, strong, and glad. He looked like himself, she realized. It was an image of what he would be when his day came. She longed for that day.

She had been wrong when she assumed Finbar Smalls was his father. His father was King Jupiter.

Finally, she left Lighthall, finding a bench in King's Garden. She sat and thought through her journey, everything she could remember that Smalls had said or Uncle Wilfred had said about Smalls. She shook her head. Everything made sense now. Or, almost everything.

Then a seed of worry sprouted in her mind. She needed to find Uncle Wilfred and tell him that Smalls was gone.

She rose and walked quickly through the corridor, into Hallway Round, and outside onto the village green. She found Uncle Wilfred and Picket going through some exercises together with wooden swords, both laughing.

"Hello, my dear," Uncle Wilfred said, just blocking a sneaky stab from Picket. Then he saw her face, and he motioned for Picket to wait. "What is it, Heather?"

"I know," she said. "I know everything."

He nodded.

* * *

Picket was pleased. He had been encouraged by the assembly, heartened to carry on his work. He wanted to keep believing, no matter what Master Helmer said. He enjoyed practicing swords with Uncle Wilfred, the few chances he got. He was getting better, and he liked that his uncle saw it. Uncle Wilfred was a lot quicker with praise than Helmer and much slower to anger and scorn. Picket had just jabbed at Uncle Wilfred and almost made contact. He saw Heather out of the corner of his eye but kept up the attack. He hoped he could score a point while she was watching.

But Uncle Wilfred signaled a stop, and Heather said, "I know. I know everything."

Uncle Wilfred nodded.

"You know what?" Picket said.

Before Heather could answer, screams of terror filled the air. Picket looked past Heather and saw rabbits running, grabbing children, and fleeing for the village. Scattered soldiers made for Hallway Round. Uncle Wilfred tossed aside his wooden sword and refastened his belt and scabbard. Picket did the same, his nervous fingers failing to secure the belt for several tries before finally fastening on his sword. Now the fleeing rabbits were running past them, toward the village.

"Wolves!" they were screaming. "Wolves inside!"

Uncle Wilfred spoke fast. "I want you both to go to the caves past the village. Hide out there."

"I'm coming with you!" Picket said.

"You can't, Picket. Not yet," he said. "Now, Heather. Where is Smalls?"

"He left! Went to help his mother. To a place he called Exile Glen," she said.

"With?"

"I don't know," she said, fear and confusion filling her. "He said he wasn't going alone."

"Okay. Stay in the caves," he said. "If I make it back, I'll find you there. But I'm sure you understand that I have to find Smalls."

She nodded.

"What's going on?" Picket shouted.

"Stay with your sister," Uncle Wilfred yelled. "Do your duty. I'm trusting you!"

"Kyle!" Heather shouted. "He might be going with Kyle!"

Uncle Wilfred stopped and spun around. "Did he say that?"

"No, but I think it's likely."

Uncle Wilfred looked furious. "Who could have told him he could trust that rogue?" he said, and then he tore off toward the danger, drawing his sword.

Heather gasped and put her hand to her mouth.

"I don't understand, Heather," Picket asked. "What is going on?"

"Picket," she said, panicked, "I think I may have helped betray Jupiter's heir."

"What?"

"I'll explain as soon as I can!" she shouted, and she ran toward the danger, toward Hallway Round and the wolves inside the mountain. "We have to get to Smalls' quarters. There may be something important there. We can't let it fall into the wrong hands."

They ran, dodging rabbits in flight, and made it to the

door. It was open, and screams poured out of it like water from a spout. They heard the fierce, horrifying growls of wolves, the sound of snapping jaws and scraping steel and stone.

They hesitated a moment in front of the door. Picket, his sword bared, looked at Heather. "Is it worth it?" he shouted above the terrifying din.

"It might mean everything!" she called back.

He nodded, then leapt into the doorway. Heather followed, trying to think faster than the fear that threatened to overwhelm her.

Hallway Round was a nightmare of confusion. Soldiers stood by the blastpowder kegs, ready to destroy the stairway, blocking entrance. But rabbits were everywhere. Wolves attacked in fury all over. One wolf snapped at a knot of rabbit soldiers, who fought back hard. Picket could see they were overmatched. Across the round, two farmers and two soldiers were desperately resisting the advance of a hulking charcoal wolf armed with a shield and a long many-spiked javelin. His stabs were death. Dead and wounded rabbits lined the floor. Uncle Wilfred had already made it through.

Heather tried to focus, ignoring the fear. It was a long way to Smalls' quarters.

"It won't get any better," Picket said. "We have to go!" he shouted, running for the corridor. Passing by an intense fight, he joined several soldiers as they pushed back a snapping, furious wolf.

There was a sharp horn blast, and the wolves all perked up. They howled, growled, and made a furious advance, one

coming inches from catching Picket's head in its jaws. Then they all fell back quickly, heading for the way out.

The stunned rabbit soldiers slumped, breathed heavily, then cautiously chased after the wolves. Many of the soldiers were from different citadels, and they fought hard and bravely side by side. Picket and Heather followed the vanguard of the bravest who charged after the retreating wolves. They reached King's Garden, tried not to notice the destruction and violence that had occurred there moments before, and ran down the great stone stairs, taking them by fours and barely staying upright.

They reached the bottom and shot off through the stone corridors, colliding with terrified rabbits, bloody wounded rabbits, jumpy sword-swinging rabbits with looks of terror on their faces. After a few winding turns, they made it to the hallway where Smalls' room was. As they got closer, they saw that the door was open.

Picket ran ahead, his sword at the ready. He didn't stop when he reached the door. He dodged inside with a cry. A startled rabbit cried out in surprise, spun around, and dropped the wooden box he had been holding.

"Kyle!" Heather shouted. The room had been ransacked, and he was alone. "What are you doing?"

"Heather," he said, shrugging nervously, "I was looking for something, to keep it safe during the attack."

Heather crossed the room and picked up the box Kyle had dropped. "You liar!" she shouted. She opened the box but found only papers inside.

"What did you do?" she pleaded with him. "Kyle, where is he?"

"I did wrong, Heather," he said, shivering and shaking, rubbing his hands together. "I made a deal, and he's gone. He's finished. I'm sorry!"

Heather screamed. Picket bounced back and forth on the balls of his feet. He was confused, but he had decided to back Heather up, whatever came.

"Where is he now, Kyle?" she said, her voice strained. "Where is Jupiter Smalls, son of the betrayed and murdered king, keeper of the Green Ember and rightful heir to the throne?" She was screaming at him.

Picket was stunned. *Jupiter Smalls? Jupiter Smalls!*

Kyle slumped before Heather's withering stare and sat

in a crumpled mess in the corner. "He is betrayed," he said. "By me."

"Where?" she shouted. "Where is the Green Ember? Where is Smalls?"

"He must have it. I advised him to leave it here. I had hoped I could get it after he was gone so it wouldn't go to Morbin."

"Morbin?" Heather asked. "You've betrayed him to Morbin Blackhawk?" She was furious, and she slapped him.

Picket came behind her, his sword poised.

"Yes," Kyle said, withering. "Indirectly. I regret it now, but I had orders from my father."

"Talk, Kyle," she said. "And make it quick, please! If there's anything of good left in you."

"I will, Heather. I never meant to hurt you. I always thought of you as a true friend. In fact, I had hoped you would understand my reasons."

"I don't care about you, or your reasons," Heather shouted. "I just need to know what happened!"

"Okay, okay," Kyle said. "I have been sneaking out at night, meeting secretly with the captain of the wolf garrison down at Decker's Landing. I made a deal with them. They aren't enough to overwhelm this place, so I devised a plan to get Smalls away and to get this place distracted by a wolf raid while I made off with the Green Ember."

"What about Smalls?" Heather asked.

"He's headed for a bigger trap."

"Where?" Heather asked, seething.

Kyle hung his head.

"Where?" she screamed in his face.

"Jupiter's Crossing," he said. "At Jupiter's Crossing."

Chapter Thirty-Nine

SUNDERING

There was no sign of the Green Ember in the room. Heather made certain. Kyle was right; Smalls must have it with him.

"We can't wait, Picket," Heather said, turning to her brother. "We have to act fast. All the best soldiers will be in pursuit of the wolves, leaving this place empty. No one here will listen to us. We have to get to Uncle Wilfred and Lord Rake."

"But they'll be far away," Picket said. "They'll be in the vanguard of the pursuit. We have to get to Smalls!"

Heather stomped, paced back and forth. They must make the best worst choice. "We don't have time to figure out the right course. We have to act. We go find Lord Rake and Uncle Wilfred. Maybe they can get a small force together. Maybe they can make Jupiter's Crossing in time to save Smalls."

"Okay," Picket said. Heather nodded. Picket went on. "You do that. But I'm going to find Smalls. You're faster than me, and I've studied the maps; I know the terrain. You find help, and I'll try to get to Smalls."

"No," Heather said. "We can't separate again! I can't lose you."

"I know, Heather," Picket said. "I don't want to separate either, but this is beyond us and our own problems. We are Longtreaders. King Jupiter's heir is about to be murdered at Jupiter's Crossing. We have no choice. We have our duty."

There was a short pause. Then Heather said, "You're right."

"What about him?" Picket asked, motioning with his sword toward the hapless crumpled rabbit in the corner.

"We can't do anything about him," she said, and she ran for the door.

Picket looked at Kyle, then at his sword. He took a few steps toward him.

"Come on, Picket!" Heather said.

Picket shook his head and ran after his sister.

In the Savory Den, the wounded were being cared for. Emma was there, binding a vicious bite wound while deep scrapes bled through another wrap. The Longtreaders ran to her and made a hasty explanation. They said little about Smalls.

"Okay, go!" Emma shouted. "But come and help me, Heather, please, when you've given your message!"

Heather nodded and said, "I will if I can." Then she ran off again, just behind Picket.

They reached the mouth of the cave and ran out into sunlight. It was a mass of confusing sounds and sights. They were instantly overwhelmed by the noise of desperate cries for help, barked orders, muffled sobs, and a din of crackling, clanging, wild upheaval. They saw the mist, as usual, blanketing the nearby forest. There were soldiers running and doctors caring for the wounded. Smoke issued from small fires, and the whole scene seemed a blur of mad motion. There were soldiers charging into the woods, but in every direction. No one seemed in charge.

"Longtreaders!" they heard someone shout. Heather despaired. "Lay hands on those traitors!" It was Captain Frye, and he was wounded. He broke free from Doctor Zeiger, who was bandaging his bloody arm, and ran at Heather and Picket. "Hold them," he shouted. But chaos reigned and he was unable to get anyone to follow his command. "I'll deal with you myself," he said, painfully drawing his sword with his good arm. "Stay and be held accountable for this treason."

"It wasn't us, Captain Frye!" Heather shouted. But the old rabbit was coming fast, surprisingly fast for his heavy frame and injury.

Picket knew he was a deadly swordsman, good arm or not. Picket stepped in front of Heather just as Frye lunged, blocked his stroke, and kicked dirt into the sputtering captain's face.

Captain Frye cried out, and Picket spun on him, kicking him to the ground. He landed hard, crying out and grasping his mauled arm. Picket loomed over him, sword poised at the captain's throat.

"Stop!" Heather shouted. "He's on our side, Picket!" Picket looked at his torn and bleeding arm. Wounds received from the wolf attack. This angry old rabbit had run toward the danger while most ran away.

"You're right," Picket said wearily. "He's wrong about us, but who can blame him?"

Captain Frye gasped and clutched his bleeding arm as Doctor Zeiger appeared at his side. The captain looked up at Picket, confusion and worry showing.

Heather peered all around. "Did anyone see which way Wilfred Longtreader or Lord Rake went?"

Only Doctor Zeiger answered. "I not have seen them, Longtreaders. I having come out just few minutes of go. Mine sorry. Why need so bad find Lord Rakes and the Wilfred?"

"We need to warn them of something worse, Doc. This was only a distraction from the real treachery. Jupiter's heir is in terrible peril!" Heather said. "Picket, do you know your way?"

"I do," he said.

"Then go! You have to try to stop him before he gets there. Everything depends on it."

"I know," Picket said. "I love you, Heather."

"I love you, Picket."

Picket spun and ran off into the woods, displacing a great swath of fog as he disappeared. Heather shook her head.

"Wilfred, Helmer, and Lord Rake all went southeast, Missy," she heard. She wiped her eyes and saw Captain Frye sitting up and gasping. Doctor Zeiger was wrapping his damaged arm again, shaking his head and wincing.

"You'll help me, a Longtreader?" she said.

"We met a large pack of the snappers here and eventually sent them running. But we've paid for it." He looked at his arm and the fallen forms of motionless rabbits nearby. "The retreat sounded, and Wilfred and Captain Helmer led the pursuit."

"Which way is southeast?" she asked. She couldn't even tell where she was in the fog and smoke and clattering confusion.

Captain Frye pointed, then put his fist over his heart. She returned the gesture.

"Captain, there's a rabbit inside Uncle Wilfred's room. He's the one you saw sneaking out at night, not Picket. They do look alike. He's the rabbit you, well, tussled with in the Savory Den. His name is Kyle and he's your traitor."

Captain Frye nodded. "I'll take care of it."

Heather ran hard, breaking through the mist as if unaware that battle, blood, and wolves waited beyond.

Chapter Forty

RUN TO DEATH

Heather was running faster than she ever had, heedless of her own safety. Through thickets and clearings she ran, past boulders and groves, down the mountainside to the wolf pursuit. She was afraid of meeting with a desperate wolf on the run. She was afraid of being struck down by a confused, frightened soldier from her own side. She was afraid she would lose her footing and be injured or plummet over a cliff. But she ran on, pounding the ground, flying through the air in great galloping leaps. Time was the greatest enemy now and had for allies a thousand other perils. Could she make it to any rabbits she knew? If she did, would they listen to her? If they did listen to her, could they do anything in time to help?

Picket would soon be miles away. His path to Jupiter's Crossing lay on the other side of Cloud Mountain, down paths she didn't know and neither of them had ever seen. She knew he had studied the maps. But could she be sure he knew enough to find his way?

Something told her he would. As Helmer had said, Picket had a keen mind for figuring out distances, speeds, and the shortest route. He was always good at that in their old game of Starseek, and now he would need it to catch up to Smalls. If his greatest weakness was fear of heights, his greatest strength was calculation. But he was going in a different direction.

She was on somewhat familiar terrain, had traveled this way before. The pursuit of the fleeing wolves was back toward Decker's Landing.

It felt so long ago.

She crossed a wide ditch with an earth-spraying leap and landed smoothly on the other side, resuming the pursuit. She was headed downhill, and the speeds she reached were exhilarating. She was, in a strange way, almost happy. She had forgotten what wild joy filled her when she ran, how alive she felt. She powered on.

In a few minutes she came to her first sign of trouble. She saw the displaced nature that was a clear sign of a struggle and caught sight of a wounded rabbit. She slid to a stop and ran to him.

"Are you okay?"

"I'll make it," the rabbit soldier said through gritted teeth. Heather doubted this. He was very weak. She had to make a quick decision. The fate of the king's heir rested partly with her. But how could she leave a wounded soldier to die?

She ran to his side and rolled him over where he could rest his head against a tree and sit up. His side was slashed by a blade, and his shoulder was torn from a vicious bite. She saw his tunic, a blood-red moon crossed with spears.

He was from Halfwind Citadel, perhaps a soldier serving under Captain Frye.

She tore at his tunic and bandaged his shoulder. She wished Emma were here. But she did her best, and it seemed to help.

She called out as loud as she could, "Help! Wounded! Here!" Then she looked back at the soldier. His eyes were losing focus. "Stay with me," she said, shaking his face gently. He awoke and looked at her. "What's your name?" she asked.

"Jo Shanks," he said, and he coughed.

"Okay, Jo. You have to hang on, all right? Help is coming. My name's Heather, and I've stopped the bleeding. You'll be okay; just sit tight."

"Why are you helping me?" he asked. "You're a Longtreader. The wolves ... You betrayed us."

"No, sir," she said, bending to kiss his cheek. "Never. But I must leave you now, Jo, and I'm sorry for that. But be strong. Today we strike a blow against our foes."

He smiled a half-confused smile. She cried out for help once more, then took off in her mad, heedless dash down the mountain.

In a few minutes, she heard noises. Bad noises. She slowed and headed for the sounds she feared. She crept through stony ground, the rocky floor of a series of stony outcroppings. She stepped over rocks the size of her head and bigger.

As she got closer, she could distinguish the sounds. A pack of the well-armed wolves was descending on a knot of rabbits. She saw Helmer at the head of them, shoulder to shoulder with Uncle Wilfred. They were outnumbered. There were seven wolves and only five rabbits. This was desperate.

She had reached the vanguard of the pursuit, and they, in their courageous charge, had outrun their fellows so far that they had become the quarry as the fleeing wolves turned to fight back.

"Hold your lines!" Helmer shouted, urging his fellows to stand together. "The pursuit is nearly here! Be bold and do your worst!"

She made a hasty plan and bolted up above the skirmish and located several large rocks. These she gathered together quickly. She could hear the wolves growling as they attacked, and the sounds of bitter struggle reached her ears. One and two at a time, with great exertion, she hurled the large rocks down the hill. The rocks crashed down, could collide with friend or foe. That was a risk she had to take. She wanted the sound of them.

She thrashed around in the wood, making as much noise as possible, stomping and shouting out, "There they are! Pursue the wolves, soldiers. Charge them, companies A and B! Attack!" She tried to sound as fierce as possible, pitching her voice low and adding all the menace she could. To this frantic ruse she lent her own life, charging down into the midst of the attack.

Most of the wolves were withdrawing, turning to flee based on the deceptive sound. Some were in the throes of

battle, and nothing could tear them away. She ran near the hottest part of the fray, on the hillside just above. Two wolves were poised over a wounded Helmer, though he gritted his teeth and lashed out with his knife. His sword was several yards away. All else was confusion, but she saw bloody contests all around. Her wild, careering rocks found two wolves, one stunning an attacker for long enough so that a rabbit was able to elude him. Another rebounded off the ground and found a snapping jaw, sending the springing wolf spinning, to land heavily on the earth, lifeless.

She focused on Helmer and sped his way. She launched from the hillside with tremendous force, planting her powerful feet directly against the head of the foremost wolf. He buckled, crashed wildly into his fellow attacker, and they crumpled to the ground in a tangle, with Heather landing awkwardly just beside them. One wolf didn't move, but the other shook his head, bared his teeth, and came for Heather. She made to dive away, but when she tried to lever up with her arm, it didn't work. Broken, she realized, as the drooling jaws opened to destroy her.

But Helmer was there. He lowered his shoulder and sprang against the wolf's deadly leap, knocking him out of the air. The wolf landed heavily and then quickly got to his feet. By now he was surrounded by fierce, furious rabbits. The rest of the wolf pack was dead or gone.

Heather turned away as he met his end, and Uncle Wilfred ran to her side.

"Are you okay?" he asked.

"I think so," Heather said, getting to her feet slowly. "I think my arm is broken," she added, trying to stretch it.

"Let me look at that," Uncle Wilfred said. "And what are you doing here? Why did you disobey me?"

"Make it quick," she said, pointing to the sling he was creating. "We have to move."

"You're not going anywhere," Uncle Wilfred said.

"Please listen! Smalls is going to Jupiter's Crossing," she said, panting. "It's a trap."

"No, no. That can't be," Uncle Wilfred said, finishing the makeshift sling. Heather's arm was now bundled against her body. But she could still run. "No, no!" he repeated.

"Smalls has a good head start," she said, "but Picket's trying to reach him. They're waiting for him there, wolves, birds of prey, who knows what. Kyle betrayed him with a story about Smalls' mother being in danger. I have no doubt he set it up by giving good intelligence to Smalls that proved to be true before that."

"No!" Uncle Wilfred said. "Not again."

"It's my fault," Heather said. "I told him I trusted Kyle."

"Now's not the time for blame," Helmer said. "It's time to act."

"They'll have a force there," Uncle Wilfred said. "We have to rally the captains, as many as we can."

"Rake's got the horn," Helmer said quickly.

"You go for Rake," Uncle Wilfred said. "I'll run for Jupiter's Crossing and pick up whoever I can along the way."

"Agreed," Helmer said. He clasped hands with Uncle Wilfred and ran off.

Uncle Wilfred turned to Heather. "And you'll go back to—"

"I can't leave Picket!" she shouted, "I'm coming with you."

"You'll go back and rally whoever else you can from Cloud Mountain," Uncle Wilfred said. Then he sprang away, running like he was on fire.

Heather adjusted her wrap, took a deep breath, and blocked out the alarming pain in her arm and the ragged burning of her lungs.

She charged back up the hillside.

Chapter Forty-One

RETURN TO JUPITER'S CROSSING

Picket knew the landscape from maps, but it was different to be on foot. He didn't recognize this tree, or that hillside. He lost his place in small ways many times, correcting course when he came to a large stream or a bigger landmark that he recognized. He kept up a steady pace, measuring his endurance against the long road he knew he had before him. He wouldn't stop. He hoped Smalls would, and so he hoped to overtake him before he reached Jupiter's Crossing.

If Smalls beat him to the crossing, he knew it would be too late. A terrifying image kept presenting itself to his mind. It always found him arriving just in time so that he could, like Uncle Wilfred with King Jupiter, see the horrible thing happening and be powerless to alter anything.

He bounded on. His feet dug into the earth, shattering clods and spinning rocks, as he threaded through brush and sped through clearings. His heart pounded. His body cried out against the pace, screaming at him to rest. But his mind argued back. *Don't stop. Never stop.*

He had reached the base of the mountain in what he believed had been good time and had made good progress across the foothills, stopping only to drink. He had eaten nothing since their breakfast of bread and cheese in Lord Rake's quarters that morning. Hunger gnawed at him, but he only drove on harder, refusing to consider rest.

He ducked beneath a branch, snapped past several more, and sped on through an overgrown patch of forest. The woods were silent. He heard his own breathing, felt his own pounding heart, knew the familiar grind of displaced earth beneath his feet. He felt alone in the world.

He hoped to reach Smalls before nightfall, but he was no scout. He wasn't able to read the ground. He could only pursue the quickest route he could calculate from Cloud Mountain to Jupiter's Crossing. He hoped he was fast enough to keep that hallowed ground from doubling its deadly reputation.

Most of what he knew, he'd learned from Uncle Wilfred. Jupiter's Crossing had been crossed for many lifetimes, though it had before only been called "the crossing." The place called Jupiter's Crossing meant the narrowest gap between forests and had been where rabbits would cross. They were easy targets for birds of prey. It had been deadly to try to cross there time out of mind, but King Jupiter made travel through safe. This was why Morbin Blackhawk had relished the irony of this location for King Jupiter's fall.

When the sun was halfway down the sky in its evening descent, Picket despaired. He believed he had only a few miles to go before he would reach the hallowed crossing. He was more and more convinced he would be too late. Weary, hungry, and hopeless, he went on.

The last few miles toward Jupiter's Crossing were hard, harrowing work. He jogged now, urging his weary body on. His thoughts were occupied with the many mysteries he was facing. Heather had called him Jupiter Smalls, the son and heir of King Jupiter Good. Smalls had the Green Ember. Picket thought back to Nick Hollow and the Lady of the Glen. Was that Jupiter's widow—Smalls' mother? So much that Uncle Wilfred had said now made sense. How ironic was it that all those who hated the Longtreaders, Uncle Wilfred especially, had no idea that the one he devoted his life to protecting was Jupiter's heir. They had kept Smalls' identity a secret, and he could see why. Now he, nephew to the traitor Garten Longtreader and marred with the scorn heaped on the Longtreader brothers, was the only one near enough to help the lonely, hunted prince. He was the only one who could save Jupiter Smalls.

He shivered.

He felt the weight of the task settle on him. It would crush him, he was sure. He was as much Uncle Garten as he was Uncle Wilfred, or Father. Hadn't he as much as betrayed Jacks? And had he not betrayed Smalls as well, with all his moping, moody foolishness? He would stumble, as he always had. He would show he was unequal to the task. There would be birds. He almost vomited at the thought. Terror seized him, so that he could barely put one foot in front of the next. At least he could stay on the ground, die on the ground like a rabbit and not up in a tree.

He carried on, trying to think of his father, mother, and Jacks. He thought of Heather, Emma, and Heyward, Helmer, Mrs. Weaver, Uncle Wilfred, and Smalls. He tried to be brave for them all. He could not save the world, but he could go down fighting. For Heather and the rest.

I will at least do that.

Then Picket saw what he had been looking for: a stream running north, the unmistakable sign that he was getting close. He slowed, suddenly conscious that there might be wolves, birds of prey, or any number of evil creatures in the area. They would likely leave this path unguarded, lest Smalls should become suspicious. It was almost certain that they could take Smalls in the forest along the way. But if they waited for him to come to the infamous clearing, they would greatly reduce the possibility of an escape. As the horrors of history had demonstrated, there was nowhere to hide at Jupiter's Crossing.

The sun was getting low, nearing the horizon of trees, when he had his first glimpse of the clearing. He followed the path now, darting through the trees and peering ahead, searching for some sign of Smalls.

Then he saw.

Jupiter Smalls lay on the field in the midst of Jupiter's Crossing, his arms bound behind him and his neck laid bare to the teeth of Redeye Garlackson.

Chapter Forty-Two

THE END

Picket was afraid. But seeing Jupiter's heir on the ground, seeing that monster poised above and hearing his laughing taunts, changed something in Picket. He was afraid, but a violent fury rose in him, drowning out his fear.

Redeye Garlackson spoke. "How now, young prince? Where is your keeper? Has your Longtreader betrayed you as well? I think so." He cackled, his gravel voice rattling out. "No one will come for you. My wolves have done their work. My spy has done his work. You, like your father, are doomed."

"You can never kill enough of us," Smalls said. Picket wasn't surprised to find his friend's voice even, steady. "Another will rise in my place and deal death to you, just as my father did to yours."

Picket inhaled. He felt for the grip of his sword hilt.

A harsh growl rose in the wolf's throat. "I'll snap your neck, Jupiter Smalls," he barked, "and feel nothing but delight."

Picket stepped out, ready for a wild run at the wolf, but froze when he heard another voice.

"Lord Morbin waits." This voice did not belong to any wolf. And it sounded familiar to Picket. Very familiar. He ducked back behind the tree, stealing glances at the shadowy scene. "The rest are prepped for Akolan, and Lord Morbin wants him added to their number. A crown jewel for his treasure. However," he said, and Picket saw him emerge from beneath the shadows of the trees across the clearing, "he said it didn't matter much to him whether this rabbit prince lived or died. Of course, you do have quite the score to settle with him. And the setting is just too delicious here. I think perhaps we should kill him." Picket saw who it was and knew why the voice was so familiar.

Garten Longtreader.

Picket gasped. He looked so much like Father. He tried to keep his breathing even and made ready to spring into a last, desperate attack. But when he looked again, the grey rabbit was rifling through Smalls' satchel. He stopped, smiled, and removed his hand. In his hand, fused with the last of the day's light, gleamed a large emerald.

Over his uncle's left shoulder Picket saw two massive birds leave their high perches and fly toward the center of Jupiter's Crossing, where Garten Longtreader was poised to order the murder of Jupiter's heir. One was a giant eagle and the other, a hawk. Not Morbin Blackhawk himself, Picket knew, but these two were like him—massive, terrible, and cruel.

Picket almost fainted. Paralyzed with fear, he found it nearly impossible to move. But move he must. He breathed deeply and thought of Master Helmer. *How I wish you were here with me, you mad old soldier.*

He fingered his sword hilt but left it sheathed. An old image of the Starseek game came to his mind, and he relaxed, remembering Heather and the family he loved, the cause they all believed in and for which he was laying down his life. And the Starseek game reminded him of another thing, of how his mind worked. Of what he was good at. He gave one last, hasty look at the scene, then whipped back behind the tree, his back plastered to the trunk. He closed his eyes and quickly mapped out his foolhardy attack.

One breath. He smacked the tree, drumming out the fear. Another breath. He remembered, with a welling fury, his family's ruined name, the attack on his home, his parents and Baby Jacks. One last breath. He thought of the cruel treachery revisiting the royal household here.

It must be now!

He ran from his cover and straight for the center of the field. Garten Longtreader examined the Green Ember with satisfaction, and Redeye Garlackson moved to kill Prince Jupiter Smalls.

Picket had covered half the field when he was spotted. Garlackson raised his head, a grim delight on his face. He seemed to recognize Picket. Garten may have too, for he stepped back quickly and tripped, spilling the emerald high in the air.

The birds didn't wait. They flew straight at Picket, the

foremost one—the eagle—swooping low with his talons poised.

Picket never stopped. He ran *faster*. The hawk circled behind, directly above Garlackson, behind and above the speeding eagle. Picket saw how it was. They would take him in turns.

When Picket was a few yards from the swooping eagle, he went as low as he could, shortening his strides and dropping low to the earth. The eagle smiled a terrible, knowing smile. The smile seemed to say he had seen small creatures try this desperate action a hundred times, that rabbits were always so very afraid and sank low, but it never helped.

They were nearly face to face now, the screeching eagle so close! The eagle dropped lower, and as he did, Picket sprang suddenly up, leaping hard and quick directly at the eagle. The eagle's face showed shock, confusion. He lashed out with his talons, but he had hesitated.

Picket raised his powerful feet and soared just past the grasping talons, kicking the eagle's head and landing heavily on the predator's back. From there, Picket sprang again, using the bird's firm back to launch higher into the air. The eagle was driven hard to ground and knocked senseless by the succeeding blows to his head and back and the unmoving earth.

Meanwhile, Picket flew.

He sailed through the air with terrific force right at the circling hawk. This bird, stunned by what he'd seen, extended his wings and tried to beat back a short, regrouping retreat.

THE END

It was too late. Picket spun forward in the air, feet over head. As the bird's wings extended, Picket planted his powerful feet directly in the hawk's middle. It was a devastating kick. The hawk was knocked back, breathless, to fall spiraling to earth. Picket's momentum had been arrested in midair.

Beneath him, Redeye Garlackson stood stunned. He swerved from Smalls to face this rabbit falling like a meteor from the sky.

Picket did fall. He fell fast. As he did, he drew his sword for the first time in one deft, lightning motion.

Garlackson turned and looked up just in time to see the flashing blade that ended his life. He lay dead on the ground as the red sun set.

Picket rose slowly to his full height, breathing hard. He stared at his sword and at the lifeless wolf.

A moment later, Picket sliced the ropes that held Smalls and helped him up. Garten Longtreader had fled, at first crawling, then running into the woods. The stunned hawk was nowhere to be seen.

"My brother," Smalls said, clasping Picket's hand.

Picket smiled. "My place beside you. My blood for yours. Till the Green Ember rises, or the end of the world."

Smalls nodded gravely. He bent to find his sword. It was lying right beside a bright green gem. Smalls slid on his satchel and returned the stone to its depths.

"We need to go," Smalls said, sheathing his sword. But as he did, the woods ahead came alive. A row of wolves appeared, nearly fifty strong, snarling furiously as they looked on their dead captain.

Picket shook his head. *Of course. Master Helmer said there are no happy endings.*

Smalls smiled sadly at Picket. "Let's make it a good end," he said.

"Yes, my lord," Picket said, bowing quickly. Somehow, he felt unstoppable. "Let's make them remember." They drew their blades and stood, side by side, shoulder to shoulder, at the center of Jupiter's Crossing.

The wolves charged, teeth bared and spears poised. Picket braced himself for the end. But before the attacking wolves got halfway to the rabbits they slowed, then stopped. Their expressions changed. They hesitated, eyes widening.

Picket heard a noise from behind. He turned. A host of furious rabbits crashed into the clearing. Uncle Wilfred was at their head, and beside him, Helmer. They were flanked by soldiers, captains, and lords from various citadels and from the Forest Guard. Lord Rake, Lord Victor Blackstar, Captain Frye, Heyward, and a hundred others charged in.

"For Jupiter's blood and Jupiter's heir!" Uncle Wilfred cried.

"For the Green Ember!" Lord Blackstar shouted. They drew even with Smalls and Picket, and all advanced together, putting the ragged band of wolves to flight.

Chapter Forty-Three

AFTER THE END

Picket dashed into the fray, side by side with Jupiter Smalls, slicing at the retreating wolves. They pursued for a few minutes, then Smalls stopped. Picket stayed with Smalls, grateful for a chance to rest. When had he last rested?

Lord Rake came up beside them and bowed quickly to Smalls. "Prince Jupiter," he said, handing him the horn. "I suggest, lord, that we call off the pursuit."

Prince Jupiter nodded, then sounded the horn clear and long. At once, soldiers came trickling back through the woods, and everyone worked their way back to Jupiter's Crossing. "You're right, Lord Rake," Prince Jupiter said once they had gained the clearing. "We all need rest, and we're too few if they are reinforced and turn on us."

"But what if they share our location? What about the security of Cloud Mountain?" Picket asked.

"It's likely they've already sent word as far as Morbin," Uncle Wilfred said, breathing hard as he jogged up. "There's little we can do about that now."

"Uncle Garten was here," Picket said.

"Then it's certain," Uncle Wilfred said with a scowl. "Morbin knows."

"We'll have preparations to make, my lord," Lord Rake said. "Up the mountain and elsewhere."

"The world has changed today," Prince Jupiter Smalls said, looking at Picket.

More and more had gathered now and were circling around them, chattering and slapping backs. Torches were lit and Jupiter's Crossing was illuminated. Uncle Wilfred, seeming to remember himself, raised his hands. The rabbits, breathing hard and smiling, grew quiet.

"My friends," he called. "Your prince—Jupiter Smalls!" He dropped to one knee and bowed his head.

Picket followed his uncle quickly, bending the knee and bowing his head. Everyone else did the same.

Picket looked up to see the prince with his arm extended toward him, motioning him over. "Stand with me, Picket," he said. "If you will."

"I will do nothing else," Picket said, rising and crossing to Smalls' side, "for as long as I live."

"Loyal rabbits all, please rise," Prince Jupiter said. They stood. "We have pressing matters still, so I'll say little for now. But I call you to remember, by your honor, and to faithfully repeat, that on this day, in the place of my family's greatest loss, the name Longtreader meant salvation." He pulled Uncle Wilfred to one side and wrapped his arm around his shoulder. "And for many years, I have been protected by the name Longtreader."

Picket beamed, tears standing out in his eyes. Heather found him, and they stood together beside the prince and their uncle. "Thank you all for your valiant work. We will need more in the years to come. The war is only starting now, but this, the first battle in our war for liberty, is won."

Cheers and shouts filled the air above Jupiter's Crossing.

* * *

There were fires all over, surrounded by tired, happy rabbits, leaning on swords and swapping stories. The company rested and shared what provisions they had. They cared for the wounded as best they could and saw to the care of the few who had fallen. All were exhausted.

Picket and Heather sat around one of many fires. Prince Jupiter had called a halt halfway back to Cloud Mountain. Picket took water and his share of the scant provisions. Heather blinked and rubbed at her eyes. Uncle Wilfred insisted on perfecting the sling he had hastily made for her earlier.

"But you're as bad off as I am," she said wearily.

"Not quite," he said, smiling through a painful bruise on his cheek, a swollen eye he could barely see out of, and an awful gash on his neck. "I've had worse."

Lord Victor Blackstar sat across from the Longtreaders at the fire, beside Helmer and a smiling, sometimes wincing, Captain Frye. Uncle Wilfred finished his adjustments to the field sling and turned to Lord Blackstar.

"Where's the prince, Lord Blackstar?" he asked.

"Prince Jupiter is at the central fire," Lord Victor Blackstar said, pointing. "He asks for the captains and lords at his signal. He has procured Lord Rake's horn."

"Well, my dears," Uncle Wilfred said to his niece and nephew, "I must attend to His Majesty. I'll be back. Captain Helmer will care for you," he said, saluting his old comrade-in-arms. The wall between them seemed to have crumbled, Heather noticed happily.

"My brother," Helmer said to Uncle Wilfred, "these two just reversed the most devastating loss imaginable today and turned it into an unthinkable victory. I'm starting to think they can take care of themselves."

"I suppose so," Uncle Wilfred said. "But I'm still their guardian, no matter what unheard of heroics they have performed." He trotted off, his relieved laughter filling the darkness as he disappeared into the shadow between fires.

Before the halt, Heather hadn't stopped running for hours. She had found Captain Frye and Lord Blackstar back at the mouth of the cave and convinced them to gather what strength they could and fly with all haste toward Jupiter's Crossing. They had come quickly down the mountain, then met up with Uncle Wilfred and Helmer's combined band of stragglers. They made a significant, and what proved to be a winning, force. They had taken a direct but little-known path and never stopped. They had seen, on their approach, Picket's incredible flight and fight, his mind-boggling rescue of Prince Jupiter Smalls from two birds of prey and a wolf.

Heather slumped onto her brother's shoulder. "My arm hurts, sure. But what's worse is being this tired. I can't keep my eyes open, Picket."

He laughed and put his arm around her and held her. "I'm proud of you," he said.

"Hey, that's what I'm meant to say," she said. She kissed his cheek, remembering, when she did, the soldier she had left in the woods. Jo. She hoped he had made it. There was always a cost in these horrible battles, she knew. But it might have been worse today. It might have been much worse.

There was a short horn blast.

"That's the prince's signal," Lord Blackstar said. "Come on, Helmer."

"Why me?" he asked. "I'm no lord."

"Come on, Lord Captain of the King's Army," Lord Blackstar said. "No more hiding who you really were. Well, really are."

Helmer smirked, rose slowly, and made to move toward the central fire. He stopped in front of Picket and held out his hand. Picket grasped it. They looked at each other for a moment. Helmer let go and walked outside the firelight. But he paused, turned, and said, "I guess ladybugs can fly, after all." He disappeared into the night.

Picket smiled.

"I've never heard of such a thing as what you did in all my life," Captain Frye said. "And I've seen wars, Longtreaders. Terrible wars. I saw King Jupiter cut down Garlacks. I saw Perkin One-Eye surprise the eagles of Dell Beck. But I've never seen, or heard of, anything like what I saw you do today. If I hadn't seen it, I would never have believed it."

"It was a wonder," Heather said.

Chapter Forty-Four

THE BEGINNING

Several days passed. They expected an attack, but it hadn't come yet. Intelligence reports were conflicted, but for now they increased security and prepared for war. The trades resumed, and life, albeit warily, went on. Heather made her way through Hallway Round and into the great hall. She waved at Eefaw Potter and smiled at the countless nods of courtesy, the wordless blessings, and the many who humbly said, "Thank you." Behind her, she heard gasps and grateful whispers of the name Longtreader. Her name. But she would not let herself be stopped by a grateful crowd today.

She walked past the chandlers and the barbers and paused a moment before the door of the storyguild. She drew a deep breath and walked in.

The master stopped in mid-sentence and looked up at Heather in surprise. The room fell silent, and the gathered tale-spinners looked at her with amazed expectation.

"My name is Heather Longtreader," she said. "And I have a story to tell."

* * *

Heather's tale was written down and copied, then copied again, and again. Soon it was being passed from Cloud Mountain families to the Halfwind Citadel's soldiers. From Halfwind it was copied and passed again to Harbone, Kingston, Blackstone, and every secret citadel. It spread far beyond. It reached even those cowering in the burned-out hollows of the Great Wood. The last paragraph of the story was set apart on its own page, written large across the middle.

The Green Ember burns; the seed of the New World smolders.
Healing is on the horizon, but a fire comes first.
Bear the flame.

* * *

Picket warmed his hands by the fire Helmer had made beneath his old maple tree on the village green. They had been practicing with wooden swords; their deadlier versions were sheathed on the grass nearby.

"You're improving," Helmer said.

"Thank you, Lord Captain," Picket said.

"I told you, Bucky, if you keep calling me that," Helmer said, tossing his knife up and down in his hand, "I'm going to make your life miserable."

"Since the battle, I've spent every day training with you," Picket said. "I don't know how it could get much worse."

Helmer smiled. "Oh, it can."

Picket laughed, then looked up to see Captain Frye hurrying toward them. He stood up. Helmer sat up.

"There's news," Captain Frye said, breathing hard. "We just received word from our network—reliable word—" He puffed, holding up a finger and catching his breath.

"What is it?" Helmer asked. "I thought we already knew that Morbin was regrouping."

"Not that," Captain Frye said. "They sent word about prisoners. They think they've discovered where they're being held. We believe, Picket, that your family might be among them."

Picket nodded and took up his sword, buckling it on his belt.

The End

The adventure continues in...

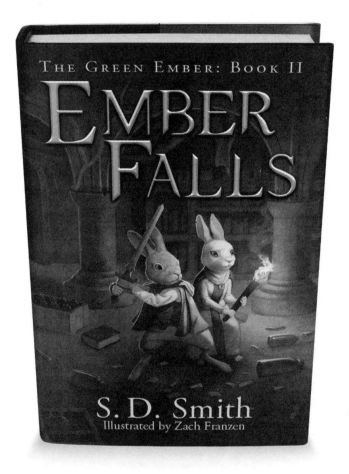

THE GREEN EMBER: BOOK II

EMBER FALLS

S. D. Smith

Illustrated by Zach Franzen

PROLOGUE

How am I going to die?" Prince Lander asked. "Will I be carried off by those monsters?"

"I don't know, Your Highness," Massie said. "But it's better to live as you will want to have lived, rather than spend your time worrying about the end. You are right here in your story. Don't skip ahead." Massie stood alongside the young prince on the prow of *Vanguard*, scouting the increasingly turbulent river for perils.

"Lieutenant Massie, would you call me 'shipmate' and not 'Your Highness'? After all, we're in the same company," Prince Lander said, pointing to the black star patch on his shoulder.

"We are shipmates, sure. But you're also my prince. I'm afraid I can't pretend you're not. You must be a prince, and I must be your loyal servant."

"I suppose so," the young prince said, frowning.

"What's troubling you? Have you had those dreams again?"

"Of being carried off?" Lander sighed. "Yes. I'm always

afraid something bad will happen."

"I'm sorry to hear that, sir. The memory of Seddleton is still fresh," Massie said, peering into the distance with a scowl. "Now I'm growing afraid myself—afraid of this poor visibility. I can't see well enough in this growing fog."

"I can still see *Burnley's* mast there, two—no, three!—points off the starboard bow. She still has her sails set," Lander said. "She should hail if there's danger, should she not?"

"Aye, but Captain Grimble doesn't always hail us with great haste. Please pass the word for Captain Walters. Say that I beg he will take in sail. Say we cannot see well enough to scout."

"Aye, sir!" Lander said, and he scurried off.

Massie kept at his vigil as fog swept over the ship. He could see almost nothing now, and he turned back to peer through the gathering mist on deck. The ship was not yet slowing.

"On deck there!" he shouted at a passing sailor. "Hayes! Go and wake the king."

"The king?" Hayes asked.

"Aye, the king," Massie said. He swerved through coiled ropes and sailors at their stations. "Captain Walters?" he called. The deck was dense with fog. There was no response. "Commander Tagg!" No answer.

He found the bell rope and rang it hard. "All hands, take in sail! Heave to and drop anchor. Where's the officer of the watch? Find Captain Walters and Commander Tagg!"

370

He heard calls and answers, the sounds of sailors stumbling through the fog.

King Whitson appeared on deck in his nightshirt, rubbing at his eyes. Just then a rending crack sounded and the ship grounded to a halt, spilling all hands forward. Pained groans and harried cries accompanied the grinding churn of wood pressing against rock.

"Boathooks!" Whitson called above the clamor. He rose slowly, with a wince, from the deck. "Deploy boathooks and get us off that rock! Master Owen, take a lamp and check the hold. I have no doubt we are sprung. Start the pumps."

"Aye, sir!"

"Hamp!" Whitson shouted to a hurrying sailor.

"Aye, Your Majesty?"

"Please go below and beg the queen to come on deck."

"Aye, sir!"

"Carry on, bucks!" the king shouted above the buzzing din on deck. "We must save our ship! Remember what precious cargo we carry."

"It's too late, Your Majesty!" Massie shouted, panting as he ran up. "I've been over the side. *Vanguard* is wrecked. It's only a matter of time—"

Before he could finish explaining, the ship lurched and began sinking rapidly.

"Where is *Burnley*?" Whitson asked. "Can anyone see her sails?"

"There's no sign of her, sir," Massie said. "And they don't answer hails."

"They never warned us, neither," Prince Lander said, joining his father.

"Launch all boats," Whitson called. "Start the mothers and children over first, then every doe. Massie, you go. Lead them to shore."

"Aye, sir," Massie said, then hurried through the press of active sailors. "Make a lane! All boats overboard!"

Hamp reappeared, looking nervous.

"What is it, Hamp?" the king asked.

"It's the queen, Your Majesty," he said, swallowing hard. "Queen Lillie is gone."

"Gone?" Whitson asked. "Gone where?"

"By Flint's own sword," Lander said, eyes wide and terrified. "She's carried off."

from *The Wreck and Rise of Whitson Mariner*

Chapter One

A MISSION

Picket Longtreader moved through the fog, uncertain which way to turn. He was careful to be quiet. The enemy might be lurking just beyond the bank of mist ahead.

He hoped they were.

Picket could only faintly make out the swish and tap of his companion's deft steps. Smalls, the prince, was with him. And Picket was with the prince, heart and soul.

The fear was there, familiar and clear. Picket inhaled, acknowledging its presence while at the same time assigning it a place of service. It would have to sharpen his mind. Fear would not, could not, be his master. Not today. There was too much at stake.

His parents needed him. His brother, Jacks, needed him. Picket hoped this was his chance to free some, or all, of them. If any were still alive. He swallowed hard and hurried on.

After another minute, he sensed that the prince had stopped moving. He felt a touch through the fog. Smalls appeared beside him, out of the mist, a worried look on his face. He bent close to Picket's ear and whispered, "This is a perfect place to keep slaves for their mine: deep in this valley, near the river, in the foothills of the High Bleaks. But we should have heard them long ago. I haven't heard one shout or the rattle of a single chain. Have you?"

"Nothing," Picket answered. He was worried that Smalls would want to stop, to return to the main force a mile back, where Lord Victor Blackstar and Captain Helmer waited with a regiment of soldiers capable of liberating the slaves they'd been assured were here. "I want to go on."

"I'm not sure that makes a lot of tactical sense," Smalls said.

Picket knew he was right. Especially with the prince himself present. But Smalls had insisted on personally accompanying his friend on this mission. He said that honor demanded it. Now that they were here, Picket didn't want to turn back.

"It's my family," Picket said, a catch in his voice. He thought of Heather, his sister and closest friend. He remembered the hopeful look on her face when she said goodbye to him a few days before. "Heather's counting on us." They *had* to be here.

Smalls nodded reluctantly. "We can't do this alone, Picket," he said. "We observe. We report back. We're only scouting. Do you understand?"

"Yes, Your Highness," Picket said, bowing his head quickly.

They moved forward, Smalls rubbing at his eyes. Picket considered for a moment the weight that must press on

his friend. Smalls had been revealed as Jupiter's heir, had triumphed in a strategic battle, and now served as the open leader of the cause and an object of hope to rabbits across Natalia. Saving the prince, as Picket had done so heroically at Jupiter's Crossing, had been easy compared to the task before Smalls now.

A resistance to unite. An impossible foe to conquer. A kingdom to win.

The Lords of Prey were great birds, an ancient alliance of raptors that had haunted the rabbits of Natalia since Whitson Mariner first touched land with his wandering community. From their home in the High Bleaks, they had frequently attacked rabbits throughout the Great Wood, and beyond. Whitson's heirs all fought them, but only King Jupiter had truly driven them back.

Jupiter's heroic victories had ushered in an era of flourishing unlike any in history. But that golden age ended when he was betrayed by Garten Longtreader, Picket and Heather's uncle, and delivered over to Morbin Blackhawk. King Jupiter was killed and the kingdom was lost. Morbin and his Lords of Prey, allied with wicked wolves under the command of Redeye Garlackson, burned and fouled vast swaths of the Great Wood.

Some rabbits gave in to the new order, but many more went into hiding or joined the secret citadels, an uneasy alliance against Morbin's forces. King Jupiter's heir, revealed to be Heather and Picket's friend Smalls, achieved a crucial victory at Jupiter's Crossing. But the task remained enormous and the cause fragile. Visions of the Mended Wood sometimes felt like a hopeless, happy dream, destined to be dashed to ashes in an awful waking moment.

The fog hung thick and the ground fell away as Picket and Smalls descended from the foothills into the rocky valley below. They could now hear running water. Picket saw white fog before and above him, dark stone beneath his feet. Apart from a whispering wind, the faint water flow, and their footsteps, it was quiet. Too quiet.

Picket was just about to suggest that they head back and report when he heard a faint thrashing borne along on the wind. He couldn't tell where it came from. Picket expected Smalls to stop, but the prince moved forward, quickening his pace. Picket followed.

Smalls reached for his sword, and Picket drew his own. He hadn't used it in earnest since he flew over Jupiter's Crossing and put an end to Redeye Garlackson. He was ready to use it again, if he had to, to free his family from their cruel captors.

The fog began to clear, and Picket caught a glimpse of what they had been hearing. A river. More shapes were coming into view, but Smalls pointed urgently to the back of a small wooden hovel. They dove behind it as the fog thinned.

Smalls motioned for Picket to wait while he peered around the corner of the beat-up shed. The prince looked long and hard while Picket leaned against the brittle wall, his sword at the ready. Smalls finally turned back, a puzzled expression on his face. He shook his head. There was nothing moving. He nodded to the other corner of the shed.

Picket slid into position and slowly edged an eye beyond the wooden wall. Hopeful only moments before, he now watched as curtains of mist rose and fell in the strengthening wind and the scene was revealed. He saw a soot-stained hillside cave, apparently an abandoned mine. He saw the river, a rotting dock propped on its rocky bank, and a large collection of hovels like the one they hid behind. Nothing else. No one else. The mining camp, a riverside collection of dingy broken-down sheds, appeared deserted.

He frowned, and Smalls sighed. Picket felt his excitement and battle dread drain away, turned to bitter disappointment. He felt hollow, suddenly weak and cold. He hated the idea of returning to Heather with nothing and seeing her face when he told her he had failed to bring their family back. His muttering moan was lost in the wind.

Then another sound came, loud, urgent, and angry, arresting his reverie and sending a wild surge of panic through his body. Smalls cried out as Picket spun around and looked up.

Three massive birds of prey swooped down on them, talons flashing, hideous shrieks pouring from their razor beaks.

Chapter Two

THE CHASE

Picket froze for a moment, but Smalls never hesitated. He broke through the fragile wall of the hovel, dragging Picket inside just as the foremost bird struck, slicing past in a terrifying flight. The two other raptors landed behind and tore into the shed with their talons. But Smalls and Picket were already barreling out the front door and running for their lives along the stony bank.

"Stay sharp!" Smalls shouted. Picket scanned the shoreline as his feet pounded the ground, his vision bouncing in the wild panic of their flight. No boats. No signs of life. Nothing but this endless row of broken-down sheds. They raced past the mine site, choosing not to enter and risk being trapped.

Picket glanced back, fearful of the frenzied shrieks and beating wings that grew louder and louder. The birds were airborne again, bearing down on the two fleeing rabbits. Picket felt as vulnerable as he ever had. Terror filled him, and he ran harder, catching up with Smalls, whose wide eyes darted all around as he sped on.

They weaved between buildings to elude the pursuit. Most were small hovels like those they had first encountered, but occasionally they hurried past a larger, longer, sturdier building. They ran hard, a thin sliver of hope pushing them on. Backward glances told Picket their weaving escape was buying precious time but wouldn't save them. One of the birds had gone aloft, calling out to the others, who pursued them along the ground, flying expertly between the sheds, gaining on the rabbits every second.

"They're on us!" Picket said.

"Follow me!" Smalls shouted. Instead of dodging around the next building in their path—one of the large, longer ones—Smalls plowed into it, once again breaking through the wooden wall. Picket followed, crashing through behind Smalls, and the two rabbits rolled onto the wide floor among shards of wood. The nearest bird beat his wings in a halt outside and clawed at them through the broken wall. The hole wasn't large enough for the bird to enter, but Picket felt a vicious slash across his back as he rolled into the first of many wooden support columns. He turned and drew his sword, and both rabbits slashed wildly at the flashing talons.

The rest of the wall was shredded in seconds by the three attacking raptors, and soon their enemies were inside. What had seemed a large room became a death trap as the massive birds filled it, breaking everything in pursuit of the two rabbits. Picket's ears rang with their horrible shrieks, their frenzied advance making strategy impossible.

Picket jumped back, staggered up, ran, and stumbled backward. Several columns lined the middle of the building, and the birds smashed through them as they came. Picket swung wildly with his sword, never knowing what he might be striking. He ended up on his back near the far wall, pain and wild rage a fire in his mind as he watched a raptor coil and strike, tearing through a third column in his race to finish Picket off forever.

Picket found his feet and dove backward, through the far door, rolling onto the hard stone as the building collapsed on the attacking birds, sending a plume of dust and debris into the air and momentarily obscuring the enemy.

Picket searched frantically for Smalls. When he saw him only a few feet from the wreckage, he hurried toward him. The strong young rabbit had come through somehow. Picket gasped with relief. Smalls struggled to stand and picked up his sword, his weary arm dragging the tip along the stones. Picket reached for his own sword, but it wasn't there. He turned to face the rubble alongside the prince.

The dust cloud settled, and the only sounds were the gasping breaths of the two battered rabbits. They inhaled, bending, trying to recover and make sense of their escape. An eerie silence filled the valley. Finally, Picket smiled.

"Your Highness, that was—" he began. But he was cut short when the ground shook, the rubble rumbled, and a bird's head appeared through the debris. With a terrific leap the raptor broke free of the ruined building, scattering tattered sections of the wreckage. Shaking his wide wings, he rose above the rabbits with a horrifying screech.

Picket's eyes widened, and a cry died in his throat. Terrified, he glanced at Smalls. Smalls set his feet, raised his sword, and gave a defiant shout.

The story continues in
The Green Ember Book II: Ember Falls

(Available at SDSmith.net/store, Amazon, and wherever fine books are sold.)

Get a Free Audiobook and Keep up with author S. D. Smith

Sign up for S. D. Smith's newsletter and receive a free audiobook!

www.sdsmith.net/updates

If you loved the book, please give it a review online now. Positive reviews help so much. Thank you.